RETURN TO PEMBERLEY

FENELLA J MILLER

Boldwood

First published in 2009 as *Mr Bingley and Miss Bennet*. This edition published in Great Britain in 2024 by Boldwood Books Ltd.

Cover Design by Colin Thomas

Cover Photography: Colin Thomas and Alamy

A CIP catalogue record for this book is available from the British Library.

Paperback ISBN 978-1-83603-436-0

Large Print ISBN 978-1-83603-435-3

Hardback ISBN 978-1-83603-434-6

Ebook ISBN 978-1-83603-437-7

Kindle ISBN 978-1-83603-438-4

Audio CD ISBN 978-1-83603-429-2

MP3 CD ISBN 978-1-83603-430-8

Digital audio download ISBN 978-1-83603-431-5

Boldwood Books Ltd
23 Bowerdean Street
London SW6 3TN
www.boldwoodbooks.com

1

'Darcy, what do you think of my new home?' Mr Bingley enquired anxiously as he ushered his guests into the entrance hall where the staff were lined up for inspection.

His friend looked around and nodded. 'It will do, Bingley. It is exactly as you described it. The situation is ideal, not too far from Town, and what I have seen of the grounds they have been well maintained. This entrance hall is spacious; no doubt the other rooms equally so.'

His sister Caroline immediately fluttered to Darcy's side. 'Mr Darcy, how right you are to say so. It is nothing compared to Pemberley of course; there is nothing so beautiful as your estate in Derbyshire. Hertfordshire is nothing compared to that. However, I am sure we shall all be very comfortable here, Charles. As long as we have each other, we shall not be starved of acceptable company.'

The housekeeper stepped forward and curtsied politely. 'Shall I show your guests to their rooms, sir? There will be a cold collation served in the small dining room at noon. Cook thought you might wish for something after your journey.'

He nodded and smiled amiably. 'Thank you, Nicholls, I am sure you have everything as it should be. Caroline, Louisa, if you care to view your apartments, Darcy, Hurst and I shall stroll around the grounds until you return.'

'Bingley, I am a trifle fatigued after the journey. I think I shall find somewhere to put my feet up for a while.'

'Hurst, you are a lazy devil. Come, Darcy, surely you are not tired? Nothing so trifling as a carriage ride from Town will put you out, I am sure.'

Darcy laughed. 'Show me the interior first, my friend. If the ladies are to return in half an hour that shall not be time enough to view the grounds.'

Bingley led him through the drawing room, the smaller parlour, the breakfast room and the dining room before arriving at the billiard room. 'Shall we play a frame or two whilst we wait, Darcy?'

'It would be better to leave it until after we have eaten. We would scarce have got into the game before we would have to leave it.' He strolled across to the long windows that opened onto the terrace. 'I cannot tell you, Bingley, what a relief it is to be out of town. Although it is empty of society I still feel myself pursued every time I appear in public. Do you not find every matchmaking matron on your tail, hoping to entice you to offer for their daughter?'

'I do agree. It is what I most dislike about being there. Here in the country people are more natural, are prepared to walk from place to place regardless of the weather.' He joined his friend to gaze out onto the well-manicured park. 'The deer and sheep that keep the grass looking so smart are leased to me, along with the house. I have already made myself known to the principal families in the neighbourhood. I shall introduce you at the ball tomorrow.'

Mr Darcy yawned. 'No doubt we shall both be fawned upon; I am certain that news of our circumstances will have been much discussed. Sometimes I am tempted to offer for the first eligible young woman and be done with it. Pemberley needs a hostess and Georgiana would benefit from a sensible female in her life.'

'Is your sister still at Pemberley with her companion?'

Mr Darcy nodded. 'She is almost an adult and I believe I must make different arrangements for her soon.'

'Bring her here for a visit sometime. My sisters dote on her.' He frowned as he considered Darcy's last remark about marrying for convenience. 'I shall not marry for practical reasons; I intend to marry for love.'

The sound of the ladies in the distance cut short their conversation. 'I am intending to enjoy myself here, and I know that both my sisters are looking forward to dressing in their finest and impressing the locals. Come, Darcy, let us join Caroline and Louisa. This afternoon we shall ride around the park and you must give me your opinion of the farms. I might consider purchasing Netherfield if you think it suitable.'

* * *

The evening of the ball duly arrived and, as always, Mr Bennet refused to accompany his wife and five daughters. Jane stood obediently in front of the mirror, waiting for her maid to finish adjusting her gown. 'I own that I am pleased with this dress; the neck is not too low and so I shall not have the bother of taking a shawl.'

'The turquoise beads sewn around the hem and neckline are perfect. I have never seen you look in better countenance. I am sure there shall be none more beautiful attending the ball this evening,' Jane's sister Elizabeth said.

Jane reached out to replace a strand of dark hair that had escaped from her sister's elegant arrangement. 'Your damask-rose silk is equally attractive, Lizzy. I believe we have both made an extra effort to impress. It is a blessing our younger sisters are still obliged to wear white. I am sure that both Kitty and Lydia would be dressed in scarlet or emerald green if they were permitted.'

It was somewhat overcrowded in the carriage but they were used to that. It was already dark by the time they arrived and the pavement outside glowed orange in the light of the many flambeaux. The groom jumped down from the box and let down the steps and Mrs Bennet emerged first, the many egret feathers on her burgundy turban nodding in the breeze.

'Come along, girls, we do not wish to be tardy. There, Lady Lucas is ahead of us. Do hurry up, and make sure you do not mire the hems of your gowns on the path. I noticed it has been swept, but one cannot be too careful.'

Jane exchanged a smile with Elizabeth. Their mother said the same thing every time they attended. They followed dutifully up the stairs and into the assembly rooms; she could hear her three younger sisters chattering like sparrows behind her.

The band was tuning up ready to start playing the first reel. Already the place was abuzz with noise and the crystals on the chandeliers glittered in the candlelight. Jane looked around the crowded room and was relieved to see Lady Lucas had saved the usual spot for their mother and themselves close to the entrance, where anyone coming or going could be clearly seen.

'There are not nearly enough gentlemen here tonight. I fear I shall be obliged to sit out several of the dances as usual,' Elizabeth said.

'Things will be better when the regiment is established nearby. Do not despair, Lizzy. I am sure we shall both have sufficient opportunity to dance this evening.'

Jane threaded an arm through her sister's and they swept across the ballroom, not unaware of the many admiring looks they received from the gentlemen who *were* in attendance. Not wishing to crush their gowns, they gathered like gossamer butterflies in the space behind the matrons' chairs, talking animatedly to each other, but their eyes were on the door waiting to see the arrival of the party from Netherfield.

* * *

Charles found himself as eager to attend this local gathering as ever he had been when attending a smart occasion in society. He took more care with his appearance, and was ready and waiting in the drawing room long before the appointed hour. Darcy was there before him. He grinned. It was ever thus. His friend was always first at everything. 'I must say you look very fine, my friend. You shall have the ladies aflutter when you enter the assembly rooms this evening.'

Darcy raised an eyebrow. 'I have no interest in so doing. As you are well aware, Bingley, I prefer to be in the company of friends. I dislike dancing unless it is with someone that I know well, and I am sure that the whole evening will be tedious in the extreme.'

'You are a deal too finicky, Darcy. I am certain it will be a delightful evening. I have heard so much about the beauty of the Bennet girls, and I intend to dance with every one of them.'

'If I am particular, Bingley, then you are a deal too easily pleased. However, I shall not spoil your pleasure in the occasion.

Only, I beg you, do not insist that I mingle. You know I detest small talk – especially with parochials such as these.'

They travelled in two carriages: Charles, Darcy and Hurst in one; the ladies in another. Caroline and Louisa had no intention of having their new ball gowns creased. The carriage halted in front of the assembly rooms.

'My word, this is far larger than I anticipated. And it is already bustling. Gentlemen, I am determined to enjoy myself.' Charles glanced at his friend, who was looking bored. 'And even your disapproving face, Darcy, shall not spoil the evening for me.'

Darcy smiled, making him look less austere. He was a good fellow, and Charles valued his advice above anything.

They entered the noisy rooms and he and his party were immediately surrounded. He smiled and bowed, rather enjoying the attention he was engendering. He knew his friend, who was much handsomer than he – and far richer – was gaining a great deal of admiration from the assembled crowd. He wished Darcy would smile more, appear less forbidding and disagreeable, and was determined to make up for his friend's lack of humour by being more open himself.

He was soon acquainted with all the notable people in the room. He danced every dance and was angry when he heard that the ball was to close so early and talked of giving one himself at Netherfield. However, although he danced with most of the young, unattached females, he had eyes only for one. He had not been misled; all the Bennet girls were pretty, but Jane, the oldest, was a diamond of the first water. He led her out for the first of the two dances he was permitted to have with any one partner, and found her company to be as enchanting as her appearance.

'Miss Bennet, tell me, do you ride out around Longbourn?'

The young lady smiled as she dipped and curtsied in the

dance. 'Indeed I do, sir. I am the only one in my family, apart from my father, who likes to ride. My sisters prefer the carriage or their own two feet.'

As their hands met again he felt them tremble in his grip. She was an angel, so sweet and kind, and the loveliest girl he had seen in his whole life. He finished this dance and bowed low. 'I believe our second dance, Miss Bennet, follows immediately. I wish it was possible to lead you out for every dance, but I know it would be frowned upon.'

'I should not accept the offer of a third dance, Mr Bingley. But I look forward to dancing with you once more this evening as soon as the music starts again.'

She whisked away in a whirl of green taffeta and he glimpsed an enticing, well-turned ankle as she did so. He noticed that Elizabeth Bennet, almost as handsome as Jane, had been obliged by the scarcity of gentlemen to sit down for two dances. This would not do, when his friend was standing beside him. 'Darcy, I must have you dance. I hate to see you standing about by yourself in this stupid manner. You must dance.'

'I certainly shall not. You know how I detest it, unless I am well acquainted with my partner. At such an assembly as this, it would be insupportable. Your sisters are engaged, and there is not another woman in the room with whom it would not be a punishment for me to stand up with.'

'I would not be so fastidious as you are, for a kingdom! Upon my honour, I never met with so many pleasant girls in my life as I have this evening; there are several here who are uncommonly pretty.'

Darcy half-smiled at him. '*You* are about to dance again with the only handsome girl in the room.' He nodded towards the eldest Miss Bennet.

'Indeed! She is the most beautiful creature I ever beheld! But there is one of her sisters sitting down just behind you, and she is very pretty, and I dare say very agreeable. Let me ask my partner to introduce you.'

'You mean her?' Turning round he stared at Miss Bennet's sister, then catching her eye withdrew his own and said rather coldly. 'She is tolerable; but not handsome enough to tempt *me*; I am in no humour at present to give consequence to young ladies who have been slighted by other gentlemen. You had better return to your partner and enjoy her smiles. You are wasting your time with me.'

Charles watched him walk off, disappointed by his attitude. He wished Darcy would be less exacting in his standards, would put himself out to be more agreeable. He turned and went to claim his partner for the second time, pushing the unpleasant incident to the back of his mind.

'Miss Bennet, I have never had such a delightful evening in the country before this. And your sisters, so amiable and pleasing.'

'It is kind of you to say so, Mr Bingley. Miss Bingley and Mrs Hurst are charming; I believe that Miss Bingley is closer to you in age than Mrs Hurst?'

'Yes, she is indeed. I am most grateful to her for agreeing to be my hostess. My sister knows exactly how things should be done.' He saw her glance admiringly in Caroline's direction. 'Do you know, she has hired the extra servants that I require for my stay at Netherfield. She is so much better at dealing with the staff than I.'

They were separated by the dance but when they were rejoined Charles smiled at his partner. 'It is fortuitous that Caroline is still unmarried, I do not know what I should do without her. I should not be able to entertain, nor have my friends around me.'

'I am sure, sir, that she does everything with elegance. I do so marvel at her gown; it is the height of modernity. I have seen every lady present admiring it.'

'That is kind of you to say so. I shall be sure to pass on your compliments.' Charles dipped his head. 'It is her suggestion that I purchase an estate of my own, but I decided it would be more beneficial to rent initially.'

The music paused whilst the set regrouped for the second part of the dance. Charles kept her hand firmly through his arm. He was not going to allow any other gentleman to steal her away. 'Louisa has recently married Hurst and Caroline was her bridesmaid. Louisa is dependent on her judgement. She is very much attached to her sister; consequently, they are often with us.'

'Lizzy, Elizabeth, is my dearest friend and closest to me in age. She is kind and clever, but not a bluestocking like Mary. Kitty and Lydia are different again. There's no doubt you have noticed they are popular and high-spirited, but good girls and I love them dearly.'

He saw her glance to the group of military men who surrounded these younger Bennet girls. Lydia stretched up and whispered into a gentleman's ear, causing a ripple of dismay to pass along the row of seated matrons.

'Oh dear! She should not have done that.'

He laughed down at her rueful expression and she returned his smile. He liked the way she loved her sisters in spite of their foibles. Miss Bennet must be the most amiable girl in the room. The violins began to play and he whirled her away down the line, admiring her grace; she danced quite as well as anyone he partnered at society balls. He doubted there was anyone more elegant than his current partner.

'Miss Bennet, I had thought of giving a ball at Netherfield.

Do you think I shall have enough acquaintances to fill the room by then?'

'More than enough, Mr Bingley. I suspect that everyone here would consider themselves most favoured if they were to receive an invitation to such an event.'

'But would you? Would you come if I invited you?'

She blushed and in her confusion trod on the hem of her gown and he was obliged to lead her to one side for a moment. 'I do beg your pardon, Mr Bingley, for being so clumsy. There, I have been lucky, I have not torn the silk.'

'Shall we rejoin the set, Miss Bennet? I have no wish to miss a moment longer of the dance.'

The dance ended far too soon and he was obliged to relinquish his partner and seek the next.

He was satisfied with the evening, had enjoyed every moment he had spent with the delightful Miss Bennet. It was Darcy's loss if he chose to remain aloof from the company.

When eventually the evening ended and they returned to their carriages, he was pleased with the outcome of his first venture into local society. He was determined to further his acquaintance with Miss Bennet and was hopeful that an invitation to dine at Longbourn would arrive the following day. Indeed, he would send his sisters to pay a morning call on the Bennets to ensure that this was forthcoming.

2

It was after midnight when the Bennet family returned to their carriage. The distance to the village of Longbourn was short, but no one of any consequence would consider walking to an assembly. Jane sat in the corner, Mrs Bennet next and Elizabeth in the other. Kitty, Lydia and Mary occupied the seat opposite.

It was a sad squash. The rattle of the wheels over the cobbles as they pulled away was accompanied by a continuous stream of chatter from the three youngest Bennet girls and their mother. Jane and Elizabeth were happy to sit quietly, each lost in her own thoughts.

Jane recalled every moment she had spent in the company of Mr Bingley and the way he had smiled down at her. She felt her cheeks flush as she recalled how particular he had been in his attentions. He had not danced twice with any other young lady. The younger girls had danced every dance, not being as particular in their requirements as Elizabeth and she, and Mrs Bennet had not seemed to object.

They descended from the carriage in high spirits, to find that Mr Bennet was still up. If he was not exactly eager to hear how the evening had progressed, he was at least willing to sit and listen with a degree of attention.

'Oh! My dear Mr Bennet,' her mother trilled as she rushed into the drawing room. 'We have had a most delightful evening, a most excellent ball. I wish you had been there. Jane was so admired, nothing could be like it. Everybody said how well she looked; and Mr Bingley thought her quite beautiful, and danced with her twice. Only think of *that,* my dear: he actually danced with her twice; and she was the only creature in the room that he asked a second time. First of all, he asked Miss Lucas. I was beside myself that he stood up with her; but, however, he did not admire her at all; indeed, nobody can, you know; and he saw our Jane as she was going down the dance. So, he enquired who she was, and got introduced, and danced with her next. He also danced with Miss King, with Maria Lucas, and the fifth with Jane again, and the six with Lizzy, and then the *Boulanger...*'

'If he had any compassion for me,' her husband said impatiently, 'he would not have danced half so much! For God's sake, say no more of his partners. Oh! That he had a sprained his ankle in the first dance!'

'Oh, dear,' continued Mrs Bennet, 'I am quite delighted with him. Mr Bingley is so excessively handsome. His sisters are charming women; I never in my life saw anything more elegant than their dresses. I dare say the lace upon Mrs Hurst's gown—'

Here she was interrupted again as Mr Bennet protested against any further descriptions of finery. As he refused to listen to anything more about clothes, she regaled him in great detail about the rudeness of Mr Darcy and how everyone had thought him proud and far too high in the instep.

When Jane and Elizabeth were alone in their bedchamber, Jane – who had been cautious in her praise of Mr Bingley before – expressed to her sister how very much she admired him.

'He is just what a young man ought to be: sensible, good-humoured, lively; and I never saw such happy manners! So much ease, and with such perfect good breeding. Did you not think so, Lizzy?'

'He is also handsome, which a young man ought likewise to be, if he possibly can. His character is thereby complete.'

'I was very much flattered by his asking me to dance a second time. I did not expect such a compliment.'

'Did not you? *I* did for you. But that is the one great difference between us. Compliments always take *you* by surprise, and *me* never. What could be more natural than his asking you again? He could not help seeing you were about five times as pretty as every other woman in the room. No thanks to his gallantry there. Well, he certainly is very agreeable, and I give you leave to like him as much you wish. You have liked many a stupider person.'

Jane leant forward to squeeze her sister's hand. 'You are dear, Lizzy. And so funny. I do wish you had had a better time yourself.'

'I did enjoy myself, Jane. But you are a great deal too apt, you know, to like people in general. You never see fault in anybody. All the world is good and agreeable in your eyes. I never heard you speak ill of a human being in my life.'

'I would wish not to be hasty in censoring anyone; but I always speak what I think.'

'I know you do; it is *that* which makes me wonder. With *your* good sense, to be so honestly blind to the follies and nonsense of others! Affectation of candour is common enough; one meets it everywhere. But to be candid without ostentation or design – to take the good of everybody's character and make it still better, and never say anything of the bad – belongs to you alone.' Elizabeth turned so that Jane could begin to undo the buttons at the rear of her gown. That done, Jane carefully slid the dress over her sister's shoulders and held it so that Elizabeth could step out of it without damaging the delicate material.

'Thank you, Jane. Now, let me do the same for you.'

Being tidy girls they didn't drop their ball gowns upon the floor but carefully took them into the closet to hang them up. Although they shared a maidservant, Sarah, who would have done the task for them in the morning, they had no wish to make extra work.

'I am not at all fatigued. Shall we go down and make ourselves a drink of milk? I believe I heard our parents retiring a short while ago.'

Jane thought this an excellent notion. 'Yes, I am far too excited to sleep at the moment. My head is buzzing with the delights of the evening. I have never met *anyone* like Mr Bingley.'

Her sister sniffed. 'And you like this man's sisters too, do you? Their manners are not equal to his, you know.'

'They certainly were not – at least not at first. However, they are very pleasing women when you converse with them privately. Miss Bingley is to live with her brother and keep his house; and I am much mistaken if we shall not find a very charming neighbour in her.'

'I am not so sure, Jane. They were certainly not deficient in good humour when they were pleased, nor in the power of being agreeable when they chose to, but I believe they are both proud and conceited. We must enquire further about them and also Mr Bingley and his disdainful friend. I am certain that both Mrs Long and Lady Lucas will know everything there is to know about the Netherfield party.'

Indeed that was the case, and when Charlotte and Maria Lucas arrived with their mother the following morning to discuss the details of the ball, Jane was able to ask them, without appearing too bold, for the information she desired.

'Oh yes, Jane, we know everything about the Bingleys,' Charlotte told her eagerly. 'His sisters were educated in one of the private seminaries in Town, and they have a fortune of £20,000 each. They are used to associating with people of the highest rank. They must, indeed, find us poor company after that.'

Jane shook her head. 'I am certain they do not; after all, why should they choose to come and live amongst us if they thought that?' She didn't like to enquire directly about Mr Bingley, but Elizabeth was not so inhibited.

'What about Mr Bingley? What have you discovered about him?'

This time it was Maria who replied. 'Well, Lizzy, it seems that Mr Bingley inherited property to the amount of nearly £100,000 from his father, which will bring him five thousand a year from his investments. His father intended to purchase an estate but did not live to do it. Mr Bingley cannot make up his mind where he wishes to settle, and he is, as it were, trying out Netherfield to see if this is where he wishes to live. It is possible, of course, as he has such a favourable lease, according to my papa, that he will not bother to purchase, but merely rent.'

Jane waited for her sister to enquire about the tall, handsome man who had snubbed her so rudely, but she remained silent, her eyes sparkling with humour. 'Charlotte, what about the married sister: Mrs Hurst? Mr Hurst did not have a great deal to say for himself. I do not believe he danced more than twice the whole evening.'

'Neither did he, Jane. I believe that he is not especially wealthy, and therefore is quite happy to be a house guest with his brother-in-law at every opportunity.'

Jane strolled across to the window of the upstairs sitting

room she shared with her sister. The autumn mist had cleared, the trees glorious in their golden raiment. She sighed. 'It is a lovely day; I am so happy to be here, surrounded by my friends, and with so much to anticipate in the future.' She could not help but think about Mr Bingley when she spoke those words.

She turned and a speaking look passed between her and Elizabeth. 'Well, Lizzy, if you shall not ask about him, then I shall do it for you. I am certain that you wish to know more about Mr Darcy and why Mr Bingley has such an objectionable friend.'

Maria clapped her hands. 'I am so glad you have mentioned him. I heard my mother talking to Mrs Long last night. I have ever so much to tell you about *that* gentleman.'

'He must be as rich as Croesus; no man could feel himself to be superior to everyone else unless he was,' Elizabeth said dryly.

'He is indeed, Lizzy. He has a huge estate in Derbyshire, called Pemberley. I do not know how many thousands of acres, but I expect it is several. I believe he has £10,000 a year, and there was mention of a younger sister, but I do not know her name. It would seem he has been friends with Mr Bingley for a considerable time and Mr Bingley relies on Mr Darcy's judgement and opinion in everything.'

There was the sound of footsteps approaching the door and the four girls looked up, their conversation interrupted. The door burst open and Lydia stepped in.

'Mama demands that you girls come down. She says it is impolite of you to be closeted up here alone. You must come and join in the conversation directly.'

Jane held her hand out to her sister and pulled her to her feet. 'Come along, Lizzy; it will not be so bad. Cook has made sweet pastries and she promised we should have them this morning.'

Downstairs the two older matrons could be heard conversing volubly about the previous night's entertainment.

'Charlotte, we were just talking of you. *You* began the evening well. You were Mr Bingley's first choice.'

'Yes, but he seemed to like his second better.'

Mrs Bennet simpered. 'Oh! You mean Jane, I suppose, because he danced with her twice. Be sure that *did* seem as if he admired her; indeed, I rather believe he *did*. I did hear something about it, but I hardly know what, something about Mr Robinson.'

Lady Lucas intervened. 'Perhaps you mean what I overheard between him and Mrs Robinson; did not I mention it to you? Mrs Robinson asked him how he liked our Meryton assemblies, and whether he did not think they were a great many pretty women in the room, and *which* he thought the prettiest? And his answer immediately to the last question. "*Oh! The eldest Miss Bennet, beyond a doubt; there cannot be two opinions on that.*"'

Jane felt herself blush. She wished everyone's attention was not centred upon her. Being pretty was hardly something to be proud of. It was God-given. Having a kind disposition was, in her opinion, far more important.

'Upon my word!' Mrs Bennet exclaimed. 'Well, that was very decided, indeed. That does seem as if... but, however, it may well come to nothing, you know.'

Jane lowered her eyes and wished the conversation would move on to other matters.

'My overhearings were more to the purpose,' said Charlotte. 'Mr Darcy is not so well worth listening to as his friends, is he? Poor Eliza! To be only just *tolerable*.'

Mrs Bennet interrupted with further instances of how disagreeable and top-lofty Mr Darcy was. Jane felt her mother was being overly strict in her censorship.

'Are you quite sure, ma'am? Is not there possibly a little mistake? I certainly saw Mr Darcy speaking to Mrs Long, and you said that he didn't speak to her at all.'

'Aye, because she asked him how he liked Netherfield, and he had no choice but to answer; but she said he sounded very angry at being spoken to at all.'

'Miss Bingley told me that he never speaks much, unless among his intimate acquaintance. With *them* he is remarkably agreeable.'

'I do not believe a word of it, my dear Jane. If he had been so very agreeable he would have talked to Mrs Long, now, would not he? But I can guess how it was; everybody says that he is eaten up with pride, and I dare say he had heard somehow that Mrs Long does not keep a carriage, and had come to the ball in a hack chaise.'

Charlotte smiled sympathetically at Elizabeth. 'I do not mind his not talking to Mrs Long, but I do wish he had danced with Eliza.'

'Another time, Lizzy,' Mrs Bennet said. 'I would not dance with *him*, if I were you.'

Elizabeth was openly laughing and Jane was relieved to see that she took the whole incident in such good spirit. She would have been mortified at being so slighted.

'I believe, ma'am, I may safely promise you never to dance with him under *any* circumstances.'

Charlotte helped herself to a second pastry. 'His pride does not offend *me* so much as pride often does, because in his case there is an excuse for it. One cannot wonder that so very fine a young man, with family fortune, everything in his favour, should think highly of himself. If I may so express it, I believe he has a *right* to be proud.'

Elizabeth chuckled. 'That is very true. And I could easily forgive *his* pride, if he had not mortified *mine*.'

Jane noticed that Mary was gathering herself to enter the conversation. 'Pride is a very common failing, I believe. By all that I have ever read, I am convinced that it is very common indeed, that human nature is particularly prone to it, but that only a few of us who do not cherish—'

'That is all very well, Mary, and I am sure you are perfectly correct, but I believe we have heard quite enough on the subject of Mr Darcy and his pride,' Elizabeth interrupted.

Jane waited for Mary to flounce off in high dudgeon but the moment was averted by one of the younger Lucas boys jumping up from the carpet where he had been playing spillikins with his brother. 'If I was as rich as Mr Darcy, I should not care how proud I was. I should keep a pack of foxhounds, and drink a bottle of claret every day.'

'Then you would drink a great deal more than you ought, and if I were there to see you I should take away your bottle directly,' Mrs Bennet said.

This friendly argument between her mother and the child continued throughout the remainder of the visit, and Jane felt no need to intervene. When the Lucas party departed she was glad to have a moment to herself.

'I'm going to change into my habit and take a ride around the park. I feel the need to clear my head. Is that acceptable, ma'am?'

Mrs Bennet beamed her approval. 'Of course, Jane, my love; it is very possible you might meet Mr Bingley doing the same.'

She returned from her ride, having met no one of interest, to find her mother and Elizabeth preparing to play a morning call at Netherfield.

'Oh there you are, Jane. We have been waiting for you this

age. How are we to go anywhere without the horse to pull our carriage?'

'I apologise, ma'am. I had no idea I had been away so long. It will not take me above fifteen minutes to change into something suitable and join you in the hall. By that time the groom should have been able to put Sinbad between the traces.'

Upstairs her maid was waiting, clean water in a jug, and a muslin gown, of the prettiest green dimity, hanging on the rail ready for her to step into.

She donned her stockings and the necessary undergarments, slipped into her dress, had her hair adjusted and was downstairs within her allotted time, with only the last two buttons on her spencer to fasten.

'There you are. You have made excellent time, my dear. Mary is about to practise on the pianoforte, and Kitty and Lydia have walked into Meryton to see Mrs Philips. So it will not be uncomfortable in the carriage with only the three of us.'

Jane exchanged smiles with her sister. 'That gown, Lizzy, with the stripes in dark pink, is a great favourite of mine. And your bonnet, now it has the cherries on the brim, is a perfect complement.'

There was no need to make conversation on the three-mile journey to Netherfield, their mother filled every space of the carriage with her chatter. Jane had no time to worry about her second meeting with Mr Bingley, for they with there before she had time to collect her thoughts.

As their carriage trundled up the long drive, the Lucas carriage passed them travelling in the opposite direction. Mrs Bennet craned out of the window and waved. 'There, I knew we should have left sooner. Lady Lucas will already have asked them to dine. And I so wanted them to come to Longbourn first.'

Jane patted her mother's arm. 'I am certain they will have

your invitation in mind; after all Mr Bingley spoke of it to me when we were in the second set last night.'

Her mother looked sharply at her. 'Why didn't you think to mention it until now, Jane? Did he say when would be convenient for him?'

Jane shook her head. 'No, ma'am, I said we would no doubt be calling to pay our respects and it could be arranged then.'

'Capital news; then I shall invite him for the day after tomorrow. That is a reasonable time, don't you think, Lizzy? I shall not ask anyone else apart from Mr Bingley and his party. It would be too many, and Mr Bennet does not like to entertain.'

'It is a shame, ma'am, but we have to ask the Netherfield party in its entirety.'

'Lizzy, I am sure that Mr Darcy will be on his best behaviour,' Jane said. 'He can hardly behave in any other way if he is under our roof. I think that Mr Bingley's sisters are not nearly so supercilious as you imagine. I am hoping that you will come to like them as much as I do.'

They were received cordially by Miss Bingley and her sister Mrs Hurst. Of the gentlemen there were no sign. It was not the done thing to enquire too closely after their whereabouts. However, the dinner date was arranged and they returned in the carriage twenty minutes later well satisfied with the visit.

'I hope you shall be a little more forthcoming, Lizzy, when they come to dine with us the day after tomorrow.'

'I find I do not like them, ma'am. However, as Jane is partial to all the Bingleys, I promise I shall make every effort to be charming and witty and non-judgemental when they come.' She looked across at Jane and shuddered dramatically. 'Let us pray, Jane, that Mary does not wish to entertain us.'

3

'Our guests shall be arriving imminently, girls. You will remember to behave prettily?'

'Mama, you do not have to tell *us* how to behave,' Elizabeth said. 'It is the younger members of the family who need your correction.'

Jane did not wish an argument to develop. She was so looking forward to seeing Mr Bingley again. 'Lizzy, I shall attend to that. I shall go at once and speak to Kitty and Lydia, remind them to be on their best behaviour.'

As she hurried back upstairs she could hear a vehicle arriving. The Netherfield party had arrived. The clock struck the hour; they were exactly on time. She abandoned the thought of going anywhere apart from to the drawing room in order to be waiting when they were announced.

Miss Bingley and her sister were dressed in the first stare of fashion. She felt almost dowdy by comparison; but then Mr Bingley caught her eye and she forgot everything else. After the necessary greetings had been exchanged, she found herself seated with Caroline.

'Miss Bingley, I do so admire your gown. Damask silk is so becoming, and the beading around the hem is exquisite.'

'Thank you, Miss Bennet. I was saying to Louisa how well you and your sister look considering your gowns were made by a local seamstress.'

Mr Darcy was standing looking bored at the far side of the room and immediately her gaze turned in his direction. Miss Bingley jumped to her feet. 'Pray excuse me. I must go and speak to Mr Darcy.'

Her place was immediately taken by Mr Bingley himself and she thought how kind it was of her friend to leave the space beside her vacant so that her brother could sit down.

'Miss Bennet, what a delightful ensemble you have on this evening. Green is the perfect colour for you.'

'That is kind of you to say so, sir. How are you settling in at Netherfield? Do you enjoy country pursuits?'

'I do. I find London a sad and busy place. It is one event after another and a fellow never has a moment to himself.'

'I, too, prefer the countryside. When I visit my relatives in Gracechurch Street I always enjoy my stay, but I am always relieved to return to Longbourn.'

She was so immersed in her conversation that she failed to hear the dinner gong. It was not until Lydia appeared at the door that she realised they were alone in the drawing room.

'Mama said you are to come at once, Jane. We cannot be seated until Mr Bingley has come in.'

For the second time Jane's cheeks coloured. How remiss of her to have kept the party waiting. He offered her his arm and smiled down at her sympathetically. He was so understanding, in tune with her every thought. As the meal progressed, she barely noticed what she ate. He was seated beside her and they conversed quietly together whenever they had a moment.

When he eventually took his leave, he smiled at her in a most individual way and promised to call very soon. She could hardly credit how much she liked him when she had only met him twice. He must be the most pleasing gentleman she had ever met, but she would not allow herself to think too fondly of him; after all, they were barely acquainted.

* * *

Two weeks after Mr Bingley and his party dined at Longbourn, they were all gathered at the home of Sir William Lucas for an evening of varied entertainment. Also present were Mrs Long and her two nieces, plus Colonel Forster and several junior officers. This was much to the delight of Kitty and Lydia Bennet.

'Miss Bennet, Louisa and I are so glad to see you this evening,' Miss Bingley said. 'Without your company we should have no one of any interest to converse with.'

Jane was flattered that Miss Bingley should wish to seek her out. 'These social events at Lucas Lodge are always lively affairs. I seldom have time for conversation of any sort.'

'I wish to speak to you, Miss Bennet, as I have just received some new music from London and thought you might like to borrow it. Charles tells me you are an accomplished player on the pianoforte.'

'I do not know how he can say that; he has not heard me play.' Jane smiled. 'However, I should dearly love to see what you have been sent. Thank you so much for offering to share it with me.'

'Pray, excuse me, Miss Bennet, but I have promised to keep Mr Darcy company. He does so dislike being with people he is not acquainted with.'

She walked off, the epitome of elegance. Jane was not alone

for many moments before Bingley joined her. 'Miss Bennet, is this not a delightful party? I love to see a group of friends enjoying themselves. I noticed that my sister spent a considerable time with you. She holds you in high esteem.'

'I am sure she does not, sir. However, I much admire her style and elegance. She has a wardrobe of the most beautiful gowns. Her modiste has excelled herself tonight.'

He glanced across at his sister and then looked down at her. 'I agree, Miss Bennet, Caroline's gown is very fine, but not half so pretty as yours.'

Jane spent a great deal of time with Bingley that evening and by the time the Longbourn party were gathering to leave, she was even more convinced that there was no one in the world quite like him. She believed herself, for some reason, to be a firm favourite with his sisters. The more frequently they were together, the more it served to increase her partiality.

As she and her sister were preparing to go out to a card party, Elizabeth told her what everybody was saying. 'Jane, I have to tell you what everyone is saying about you and Bingley. That it is generally evident whenever you meet that he admires you and is quite open in his preference for your company.'

'I do hope so, Lizzy, for I am already decidedly partial to him. I enjoy every moment we spend together. We have so much in common.' She adjusted the string of beads threaded through her hair. 'But I can assure you, I am not making too much of his attention. He is cordial to all the young women he meets.'

The sound of footsteps running past the door reminded her it was time to depart. She was reluctant to talk about what his precise attentions might mean. It was far too soon to believe his affections might be engaged.

Tonight Mr Bennet had accompanied them. There was nothing he liked better than a game of cards in convivial company. Without any contrivance on her part, she found herself at a table partnered by Bingley.

'I am glad we do not play for high stakes, Miss Bennet. I almost lost my inheritance playing with card sharps.'

'How shocking! You do not look like a gambler, Mr Bingley.'

'I did not know such a person could be identified just by looking at them.' He grinned and she returned his smile. 'Darcy came to my rescue; it was when we met. He has been my friend ever since. Without his sound advice, I should have come to grief on more than one occasion.'

Jane paid little attention to her cards and apart from learning that they both preferred to play *vingt-un* rather than *commerce* discovered little more about his abilities in this pastime. During the supper break, they were seated together at a small table and able to speak more privately.

'I noticed that Mr Darcy did not join in the card games. Does he not like to play?'

He shook his head. 'He dislikes frivolity of any sort, much prefers to spend his time in serious conversation on subjects that I find tedious.'

'It is strange, sir, that you apparently have so little in common with your closest friend.'

'I consider that is why we get on so well. Do they not say that opposites attract?'

Jane thought about that comment when she was in bed that night, her sister already asleep beside her. Had he been trying to warn her that because they were so similar in outlook he did not find her attractive?

* * *

Caroline Bingley swept into the drawing room and waited, tapping her foot until Charles looked up from his newspaper. 'Miss Bennet is coming to visit this morning. She is to walk over. Perhaps you and Hurst could go out and meet her?'

Hurst ignored the question and continued to stare morosely out of the window. Charles was delighted. The more time he spent in Jane Bennet's company, the happier he was.

'I shall go at once, but surely she is not coming on her own?'

'I expect Elizabeth Bennet shall accompany her; she usually does. I have promised she can be returned in our carriage. To walk in both directions would be the outside of enough, even when the weather is so mild today.'

Darcy appeared in the vestibule. 'I believe the exercise will do me good. I shall come with you, Bingley.'

Charles was glad to have his friend's company, but surprised. He had shown no partiality for walking long distances since they had arrived at Netherfield. Charles smiled; perhaps there was a special reason that Darcy wished to walk across the fields with him. Maybe he was not the only one interested in a Bennet sister.

They walked companionably, having no need to be forever talking when together. It was Darcy, from his superior height, who spotted the girls.

'I see them, Bingley. I must say it is refreshing to see young ladies prepared to take exercise in this way.'

The two young women arrived, slightly breathless, at the stile. He thought that they both appeared invigorated by their walk. He stepped in front of Darcy and offered his hand to Jane.

'Miss Bennet, I cannot tell you how delighted I am to see you both this morning. Allow me to assist you. It would be a tragedy indeed to tear your pretty gown.' She smiled sweetly and held out her hand, allowing him to lead her a few yards down the path. Her sister answered for both.

'We are honoured indeed, sirs, to be escorted the remainder of the journey. Did you think that we might become lost?'

'No, Miss Elizabeth, that is the last thing I would expect of you.' Darcy moved over to offer his hand but she hopped nimbly across the wooden structure before he could reach her side.

Caroline and Louisa were waiting to greet them as they returned. 'I do hope you are not too fatigued. It is so kind of you to come all this way on foot.' His sisters exchanged knowing glances and he frowned. Instantly Caroline's expression changed.

'Please, do come inside. The maid shall conduct you both to a chamber where you can refresh yourselves.'

He watched Jane run lightly up the stairs beside Elizabeth, hoping to catch a glimpse of ankle. A tap on his arm reminded him he was not alone and should not make his admiration so plain.

'Bingley, shall we repair to the billiard room and leave the ladies to their conversation?' Darcy said.

'I think not. I prefer to stay. But you and Hurst must suit yourselves. I am certain we can survive without your company.'

He could hear his friend chuckling as he strode away towards the rear of the house. He must have been mistaken. Darcy had been speaking the truth: he had only accompanied him for the exercise and not to spend time with Elizabeth Bennet.

'Come along, Charles, do not dither about out here,' Caroline urged. 'I have ordered refreshments to be served in the drawing room and then I am hoping to persuade Miss Bennet to accompany me in some duets.'

When Jane and Caroline were playing together, he went to sit beside Elizabeth Bennet. 'Your sister plays beautifully. It is a pleasure to listen to her. Shall you entertain us this morning?'

'I do not sight-read as well as Jane. I should make a sad mull of it. Like you, I am content to sit and listen.' He felt her attention wander and looked across the room to see that Darcy had joined them.

His friend flicked aside his coat tails and settled down to listen with obvious enjoyment. He was sorry when the sonata ended but pleased he could now converse with Jane. He stood up. 'Excellent! I have never enjoyed a duet so much. Miss Bennet, there is something I particularly wished to show you. Do you have a moment to walk in the garden with me?'

'I should like to see your garden, Mr Bingley,' Elizabeth Bennet said, 'if you would allow me to join you?'

'Miss Elizabeth, I shall be delighted to have the two prettiest ladies in Hertfordshire to walk with.'

All at once the entire party were fussing and flapping and putting on bonnets and shawls, and he knew he was not to have a moment alone with Jane before she left. Caroline took Jane's arm, leaving him to walk with her sister. He could not but help hear Caroline extolling the virtues of Georgiana's proficiency in music and that no one else was quite as good as Darcy's sister.

They were admiring the horses when Caroline complained she had mired her hem in something quite unmentionable, and both she and Louisa retired clucking like offended hens. At last, he could walk with Jane; Darcy must entertain Elizabeth.

When the stable clock struck two he was disappointed. 'I am sorry that you have to return, but I believe that we are to meet again at Lucas Lodge very soon.'

'We are, sir. I am looking forward to it. Excuse me, we must go in and bid farewell to your sisters and thank them for their invitation.'

He bowed and she curtsied, and then taking her sister's arm she vanished through the archway, leaving him bereft.

* * *

Although Jane had met Bingley and his sisters at two morning calls, as well as three evening engagements, she wished to have the opportunity to further the friendship. So it was with eagerness that she arrived at the house of Sir William and Lady Lucas knowing the Netherfield party would also be there.

Halfway through the evening Jane was conversing with Elizabeth and Charlotte Lucas in an anteroom before returning to the ballroom.

'Lizzy, I have noticed that Mr Darcy is favouring you with searching glances,' Jane said. 'I am certain that he is revising his opinion. I do wish you would reconsider your feelings towards him.'

Elizabeth looked shocked. 'I do hope you are mistaken, Jane. That man is the very last person I would wish to have regarding me with anything other than dislike. I certainly have not changed *my* opinion of *him*. I have watched him on occasion, and he has not improved with better acquaintance, I can assure you. Do you know, he was listening to my conversation with Colonel Forster a while ago. I can hardly call that good manners.'

'It is because he has developed an interest in you, Lizzy. Did I not say so just now?' Jane saw her mother beckoning to her and promptly excused herself. Whilst she was conversing with her mother she watched Charlotte lead her sister to the pianoforte.

'Mama, Charlotte has persuaded Lizzy to play for us. I do

hope Lady Lucas's guests shall listen and do not talk whilst she sings.'

Elizabeth acquitted herself well. Her performance was pleasing, though by no means capital. After a song or two, and before she could reply to the entreaties of several that she should sing again, she was eagerly succeeded by her sister Mary.

Mary, being the only plain one in the family, worked hard at improving her knowledge and accomplishments, and was always impatient to display them to others. Jane could sense that Mary's audience were not well pleased. They had much preferred Elizabeth's easy and unaffected manner.

However, Mary, at the end of an especially long concerto, was persuaded by Lydia and Kitty to play some Scotch and Irish airs in order that there could be dancing at one end of the room. Immediately Mr Bingley approached her.

'Miss Bennet, I do hope you will join me in a reel?'

Jane smiled. 'I should be delighted, sir – you know how much I enjoy dancing.' She looked across the room where she could see Mr Darcy standing beside Sir William. 'I do wish that your friend, Mr Darcy, felt more inclined to mix. Does he not enjoy these occasions?'

Mr Bingley stared at his friend. 'He does not like to dance. Well... only if he knows his partner. He much prefers to converse, but it is no matter to me. As long as I can dance with you, Miss Bennet, I shall be a happy man.'

Whilst they were waiting for the set to form Jane saw her sister walking behind Mr Darcy and Sir William. Her host immediately turned and was obviously suggesting that Mr Darcy dance with her. To her astonishment Mr Darcy smiled at Elizabeth and bowed, obviously inviting her to join the set. She was not surprised when he was refused.

However, instead of being angry at the rejection, Mr Darcy

seemed amused and she was quite certain he was watching Elizabeth with admiration. Mr Bingley took her hand and she forgot everything apart from the joy of dancing with the young man who was so dear to her heart.

When they paused to allow another couple to join in, she glanced across the room to see that Miss Bingley had joined Mr Darcy. They were both looking across at Elizabeth, who was talking animatedly to Charlotte. It was quite obvious that, whatever Miss Bingley was saying, Mr Darcy's attention was not on her words but on Elizabeth.

Jane could not wait to discuss what she had seen with her sister. No sooner were they private in their own apartment than she brought the matter up.

'Lizzy, was I mistaken or did you refuse to dance with Mr Darcy this evening?'

'I had no idea you were studying my movements so closely. Do not you remember that I said I would never dance with him?'

'Mr Darcy did not appear in any way put out by your refusal; indeed, I believe you have enhanced your reputation by turning him down.'

'I should think it was a novel experience for him. No doubt his huge fortune makes sure he is always received with raptures by any unattached young lady he might ask to partner him.'

'It must be so difficult for Mr Darcy to be always fawned upon, never knowing if he is being appreciated for his own worth or for his estate in Derbyshire.'

'Jane, I should not waste your sympathy on that man. He positively revels in the experience; after all, does not Miss Bingley do it all the time, and he makes no effort to stop her from so doing?'

'You must not say such things, Lizzy. I am sure that Miss Bingley is merely being polite to a close family friend.' Her sister's laughter filled the room and she was forced to smile herself.

'And you, Jane? Did you enjoy your evening?'

'You know that I did; when I was not in the company of Mr Bingley, I was with his sisters. I do wish that you could like the more, Lizzy. They are so well educated, and I have learnt a great deal from them in a short acquaintance.' Her sister snorted inelegantly. 'They have travelled a great deal, you know, and they mix in the very best society and have many amusing stories to share. I am sure that you would enjoy their company if you could just try a little harder to like them.'

Elizabeth yawned and blew out the candle on the small table at her side of the bed. 'I cannot like his sisters, but I do find myself drawn to Bingley. It is a great pity his friend is so proud and disagreeable. I cannot see why Bingley tolerates that man.'

'I believe that Mr Darcy can be quite charming when he is with people he knows well. I believe that his diffidence is caused by shyness, and not by being proud. Anyway, it was altogether a most enjoyable party and I cannot wait until the next one.'

'I expect that we shall be overrun with military gentlemen wherever we go, now the regiment is established at Meryton for the winter. Although I have no inclination to be entertained by them, I must own they add colour with their scarlet regimentals, to any occasion.'

'I agree. It will be pleasant not to have to sit out quite so much when we attend the assembly in Meryton. I believe it will be the liveliest winter we have known for a long time in this neighbourhood.' Jane blew out her own candle and settled down, but it was some time before she fell asleep as her thoughts were so full of Bingley.

* * *

Several days later Jane was in the drawing room with the rest of her family, and her younger sisters could talk of nothing else but the officers. Mr Philips had met most of them and was in a position to introduce his nieces when they appeared every day at his house. They had no further interest in Mr Bingley, or the Netherfield party; all they wished to talk about were the captains they had met.

After listening all morning to their effusions on the subject, Mr Bennet coolly observed, 'From all that I can collect by your manner of talking, you must be two of the silliest girls in the country. I have suspected it some time, but I am now convinced.'

Kitty was disconcerted and made no answer, however Lydia, with perfect indifference, continued to express her admiration of Captain Carter and her hope of seeing him in the course of the day, as he was going the next morning to London.

'I am astonished, my dear,' said Mrs Bennet, 'that you should be so ready to think your own children silly. If I wish to think slightingly of anybody's children, it should not be of my own, however.'

'If my children are silly, I must hope to be always sensible of it.'

'Yes... but as it happens, they are all of them very clever.'

'This is the only point, I flatter myself, on which we do not agree. I had hoped that our sentiments coincided in every detail, but I must so far differ from you to think our two youngest daughters uncommonly foolish.'

Jane listened to this exchange and wished that instead of talking about Kitty and Lydia's silliness, her father might consider doing something about it. It was with some relief the exchange was interrupted by the entrance of the footmen with a note for her. Quickly she opened it.

'Well, Jane, who is it from? What is it about? What does he say? Well, Jane, make haste and tell us; make haste, my love.'

'It is from Miss Bingley, ma'am. I shall read it to you.'

My dear friend,

If you are not so compassionate as to dine today with Louisa and me, we shall be in danger of hating each other the rest of our lives, for a whole day's tête-à-tête between two women can never end without a quarrel. Come as soon as you can on the receipt of this. My brother and the gentlemen are to dine with the officers.

Yours ever, Caroline Bingley

Jane could hardly believe she had been so favoured. It was no matter that Mr Bingley was away dining elsewhere; she would enjoy the company of his sisters.

'Can I have the carriage?'

'No, my dear, you had better go on horseback because it seems likely to rain; and then you must stay all night.'

'That would be an excellent scheme,' Elizabeth said, 'if you are sure that they would not offer to send her home.'

'Oh! Lizzy, the gentlemen will have Mr Bingley's chaise to go to Meryton; and the Hursts have no horses for their carriage,' Mrs Bennet replied.

Jane did not wish to go even such a short distance on horseback when the weather was likely to deteriorate. Then she would be obliged to stay overnight and might not be a welcome guest. 'I should much rather go in the coach.'

In spite of her entreaties, Mr Bennet was not to be moved; the carriage horses were needed on the farm and if she wished to visit Netherfield she would have to go on horseback. As her family waved her off she felt the first few spots of rain and was tempted to return. The heavens opened when she was no more than halfway there, and by the time she arrived at Netherfield she was drenched to her skin and heartily regretting her decision to come.

Miss Bingley and Mrs Hurst were amazed to see her. 'My dear Miss Bennet, we had no idea you should be obliged to ride. Come in at once and we shall find you something dry to wear.'

'Miss Bingley, you are too kind. Mr Bennet could not spare the carriage horses and as you had been so precise in your wish that I come and join you this evening I did not like to disappoint.' She stood in a growing puddle in their hall and was glad that Mr Bingley was not there to see her in such disarray.

'I shall take you at once to a guest chamber,' Miss Bingley cried. 'I believe that you are of a similar size to me and my gowns should fit you best.'

Jane dripped her way up the stairs and along the spacious corridor to the room that was to be hers. 'Thank you, Miss Bingley, I must apologise for being such a trial.'

'Think nothing of it, Miss Bennet. Louisa and I are delighted to have you here.'

A maidservant was waiting to assist her and Jane was happy to remove her sodden garments and be enveloped in a large bath towel. She was warm and dry and sitting by the fire in a borrowed robe when Miss Bingley hurried in, followed by a second girl carrying an armful of gowns.

'Here we are, Miss Bennet. I shall leave you to make your choice. Betty shall bring you down when you are ready and I have ordered tea to be served in the small drawing room.'

Jane selected the plainest of the gowns. It was of fine wool in a pretty shade of blue. She thought the high neck and long sleeves would be warmest and she was feeling decidedly chilly. She sneezed several times whilst she was dressing and was obliged to ask for a clean handkerchief as her own was too wet and of no use at all.

Downstairs the ladies greeted her warmly, and now she was warm and dry she no longer felt regret at making the journey in such inclement weather.

'It will not be possible for you to return this evening. Do you wish me to send a footman to Longbourn to inform your parents?'

Jane shook her head. It was far too wet to expect anyone, even a servant, to venture out on horseback. 'Thank you, Miss Bingley, but that will not be necessary. I am certain that my parents will understand it is impossible for me to return tonight. I must apologise again...'

'Please do not, my dear Miss Bennet. The weather is no fault of yours, after all. Now, shall I pour you some tea?'

The evening passed pleasantly enough. The dinner was elegant, but Jane found her appetite had deserted her and she could do no more than push the food around her plate. Her throat was sore and she had recourse to use a handkerchief on many occasions.

'I am feeling a trifle unwell, pray excuse me. I think it would be wise for me to retire.'

'Of course, I believe that you might have caught a chill.' Miss Bingley pulled the bell strap and when a footman appeared she sent him to fetch Betty to escort Jane to her chamber.

Jane bid Mrs Hurst and Miss Bingley goodnight, glad that the gentlemen had not returned from their dinner engagement to see her distress.

* * *

Mr Bingley hurried through the rain leaving his friends to follow as they would. A footman was waiting to open the front door and he walked in shaking the rain from his beaver hat. 'Here, take my coat – it is decidedly wet.' He turned as Darcy arrived in the hall. 'That was a splendid evening, was it not? Shall we go and join the ladies?'

As he headed for the drawing room he heard Darcy suggest to Hurst that they repair to the billiard room for a brandy. He smiled – did his friend find Caroline's exacting attentions too much?

'Good evening, ladies. Have you had a pleasant evening?'

Caroline looked up as he walked in. 'Charles, we have such bad news for you. Miss Bennet rode over to join us for dinner and was caught in the storm. She was unable to return due to the inclement weather.'

He was at a loss to know why this should be bad news; he was delighted to think of Miss Bennet staying under his roof. She must have gone upstairs and would be returning at any moment. There was nothing he would like more than the opportunity to further his acquaintance with her. He was about to say so when she continued.

'She had to retire early as she felt unwell. We are both most concerned; but we are hoping it is no more than a head cold.'

'I shall go at once and speak to Mrs Nicholls. I wish she had not ridden; if I had not gone out she could have used our carriage.'

'Charles, if you gentlemen had remained in, we should not have felt it necessary to invite Miss Bennet in the first place.'

With these words ringing in his ears he hurried to the housekeeper's room and was relieved to find she was still at her desk preparing the menus for the following day. 'Nicholls, I am most concerned to hear that Miss Bennet is unwell. I wish to make sure that you are taking proper care of her. Does she have an abigail to attend her?'

The housekeeper, who had stood up politely on his entrance, nodded. 'Yes, sir, that has been taken care of. I also went up myself with a soothing drink. She has a pitcher of fresh lemonade at her bedside and I have instructed the girl to sleep in the dressing room on the truckle bed so that she can hear the bell and attend to Miss Bennet immediately.'

'Excellent. It would appear that you have done everything necessary. I shall speak to you first thing to ascertain how Miss Bennet is.'

He left Nicholls, satisfied that everything had been done as he would have wished. He did not want to join Darcy and Hurst in the billiard room, but neither did he want to sit and chat to Caroline and Louisa. He would go to the library; he would be private there.

The sconces were still alight and it was the work of a moment to kindle a candlestick and take it with him. There was no fire lit, but it was not unduly chilly. He sank into an armchair and tried to make sense of his thoughts.

He had only known Jane Bennet for a few weeks, but already he knew himself to like her above all others he had ever met. The moment he had seen her standing with her sister at the first Meryton assembly, he had been drawn to her. He smiled; she was by far the loveliest woman in the room, and if he was honest that is what had attracted him initially.

Her nut-brown hair, perfect oval face and sparkling eyes had enchanted him; but it was her sweet smile, her gentleness and ease of conversation that had held him at her side. He had learnt since that, like him, she preferred to be outdoors and on horse-back rather than on foot. He closed his eyes and let his mind drift back to the various conversations they had shared.

She was not especially witty, unlike her sister Miss Elizabeth, but had a lively sense of humour and was ready to share a jest as long as it was not at anyone else's expense. He recalled having told her about a young lady of his acquaintance who had an unfortunate encounter with a flock of geese.

She had laughed at his description but had then said how she hoped the young lady had not been too frightened by the experience. What other woman would have such a kind heart? Caroline and Louisa certainly did not; they were always quick to criticise and laugh at another's misfortune. But then, one could not choose one's relatives, only one's friends.

The sound of laughter coming from the drawing room told him that Darcy and Hurst had changed their minds. He supposed he had better join them; it would look decidedly odd if he was the only member of the party missing.

'Oh, there you are, Charles. We were about to send out Mr Darcy as a search party. I have sent for coffee and a supper tray. You must come and join us.'

He took his drink and sat facing the pianoforte whilst Caroline took her seat and began to play a sonata for their entertainment. She played well, but he had heard it so many times before he could nod and smile at the appropriate places and she would not know he was not giving her his full attention.

When he had heard that Miss Bennet was unwell, this had made him realise he was becoming seriously attached to her. She was everything a young lady should be. She had a natural reserve of character that he could not fail to admire. He might wish that Mrs Bennet and her younger sisters were the same. But were her unfortunate relatives a barrier to him pursuing Miss Bennet seriously?

He had imagined himself in love before, and was certain that other young ladies had imagined themselves in love with him, but this was different. His lips twitched as he remembered a particular young lady whose designing mother had pounced on him on his first appearing in society. This poor girl had been pretty enough, if one liked a Dresden miss, but she was unable to utter a word without dissolving into giggles and simpering at him from behind her fan. He did not believe he'd had a sensible conversation with her all evening.

Miss Bennet was to that young lady as chalk is to cheese; he could talk to *her* all night on any subject without feeling he was being pursued. In fact, despite the obvious drawbacks to her background, he was forced to admit that he was beginning to feel that his sentiments were serious. He hid a yawn behind his hand. Anyway, whatever Caroline and Louisa liked to believe, he was well aware that their fortune came from trade. The Bingley background bore no comparison to Darcy's. For him it would be a downward step indeed to ally himself with a family such as the Bennets.

4

Mr Bingley was so early downstairs that he was obliged to step over maidservants, sacking tied around their waists, scrubbing the vestibule floor. He picked his way between them, too concerned with the health of his guest to bid his usual cheery good morning. As on the previous evening, he found his housekeeper in her room.

'Nicholls, have you heard from Miss Bennet's room?'

'I have just sent up. The girl will be down directly with the information, sir. I shall come to you at once – where will I find you?'

'I shall be in the library. Have coffee sent to me as soon as it is made. Also I should like flowers picked from the hothouse, and any fruit available from the orangery; these must be prettily arranged and sent up with my compliments.'

He paced the library, waiting for the sound of footsteps bringing him the news he hoped would be good. He had been waiting so long he decided to go to the breakfast parlour and see if his sisters were down. He met Caroline in the passageway and they walked together, discussing the health of their guest. He was drinking coffee when the housekeeper eventually bustled in.

'I apologise for keeping you waiting, Mr Bingley, but Miss Bennet had finally fallen asleep just as the message arrived. Betty, the girl who is looking after Miss Bennet, thought it best to let her sleep.'

'But she is awake now? How is she? Tell me at once; we have been most anxiously waiting for news.'

'Miss Bennet is decidedly poorly. She has a high fever, a headache and a sore throat.'

Mr Bingley turned to his sister. 'Caroline, you must go up at once and see how she is. She must not think of going home. Give her my best wishes for a speedy recovery.'

Jane woke for a second time and she knew herself to be too ill to ride home. She could hear Betty conversing quietly in the dressing room with the girl who had brought up the tray.

'Betty, I fear that I am in decidedly poor health. I have a fever and headache as well as a sore throat. Please inform Miss Bingley that I shall require a message to be sent to Longbourn asking for the carriage to be sent for me.'

Scarcely fifteen minutes had gone by before Miss Bingley appeared in person. 'My dear Miss Bennet, we shall not hear of you returning until you are fully recovered. My brother is most concerned that you are unwell and blames himself for having taken the carriage and obliging you to ride to Netherfield.'

It was too painful to talk but Jane managed to whisper her thanks and ask for pen and paper in order to write a note to her sister.

My dearest Lizzy,

I find myself very unwell this morning, which, I suppose, is to be imputed to my getting wet through yesterday. My kind friends will not hear of my returning home until I am better. They insist also on my seeing Mr Jones, the apothecary, therefore do not be alarmed if you should hear of his having been to see me. Excepting a sore throat and headache there is not much the matter with me.

Yours, etc.

The note written, there was nothing else she could do apart from sip the soothing tisane that the housekeeper had sent up. She settled back amongst the pillows, the comforter pulled up to her chin, and listened to the rain falling outside and the crackle of the fire in the grate.

* * *

Charles was in the breakfast parlour with Mr Darcy and his sisters when a footman announced an unexpected visitor. To his astonishment Elizabeth Bennet stood there, her face glowing with good health, having obviously walked the three miles from Longbourn to Netherfield.

He jumped to his feet and heard Mr Darcy doing the same. 'Miss Elizabeth, good morning. I am delighted to see you here. It was my intention to send the carriage for you later this morning. I had no idea that you should walk when the weather is so unpleasant.'

'I enjoyed the walk, thank you, Mr Bingley. How is my sister? I could not rest until I had come to enquire for myself.'

'We are most concerned; she has spent a restless night and

has a high fever.' He turned to his sister Caroline, who was exchanging glances with Louisa. 'Caroline, Miss Elizabeth wishes to be with Miss Bennet immediately. Surely you could show her upstairs yourself?'

He remained on his feet until Caroline had escorted their visitor from the room. 'Darcy, I am most impressed by this determination to come and nurse her sister; I hope that Mr Jones, the apothecary, shall not be late in coming this morning. I shall not be at ease until he has examined Miss Bennet.'

Mr Darcy resumed his seat and picked up his discarded cutlery. 'Bingley, I am certain that Miss Bennet has contracted a cold, nothing more alarming than that. It seems to me a trifle excessive to walk three miles in the mud rather than wait to come in a carriage. Come now, my friend, finish your meal and allow Caroline and Louisa to take care of the patient and her sister.'

'It shows that Elizabeth Bennet is a loving sister. I cannot see either Caroline or Louisa doing the same.' He saw his friend smile slightly at the image of either of these elegant young ladies appearing as she had.

'I would like to think that someone would walk to my bedside if I was unwell,' Bingley went on. 'And anyway, you must admit that Miss Elizabeth looked well in spite of her long walk.'

He noticed Darcy's expression change and detected a look of appreciation in his eye and knew his friend was recalling the image.

'Miss Elizabeth's eyes are the finest I've seen.'

He was surprised at his friend's interest. He did not believe he'd ever heard him use such glowing terms about a woman. Was his friend not so impervious as he had first thought?

What sort of young lady would eventually capture Darcy's

heart? That she would have to be from a good family, have lineage as respectable as his own, would be essential. But what if he fell in love with a woman who was unsuitable? Would he let his head rule his heart? This would instantly rule out Miss Bennet's sister. He smiled slightly at the notion of Darcy becoming so enamoured he forgot his ancient lineage and followed his heart. His speculations were interrupted as Caroline appeared at the head of the stairs with the news he was waiting for.

* * *

Jane dozed fitfully as she reclined on the daybed, a warm cover draped across her aching body. She was woken by the sound of voices approaching her sitting room. Overjoyed she pushed herself upright, looking expectantly at the door.

'Miss Bennet, see who is here to visit you. Miss Elizabeth has walked across the fields, by herself, in horrible weather in order to be at your side.'

'Lizzy, I am so glad.' She could manage nothing more, for she felt too unwell and hoped that her smile was enough to show how pleased she was to see her sister.

'My dear Jane, did you think that I should leave you languishing here alone?' She glanced up at Miss Bingley before continuing. 'Three miles is nothing to me; neither are dirty stockings and a mired skirt. Unfortunately the carriage was not available this morning so I had no alternative but to walk.'

Miss Bingley smiled. 'I shall leave you to catch up, Miss Elizabeth. Please do not hesitate to ring and ask for anything that you might require to alleviate your patient's condition.'

'Thank you, you have been too kind.'

Miss Bingley left them together. Immediately Elizabeth tossed her cloak and bonnet to one side and swiftly unlaced her stout walking boots. 'If I leave these by the fire, Jane, no doubt they shall be dried out by the time I wish to put them on this afternoon.'

Jane did not feel herself equal to conversation and after Miss Bingley had left them together found she could attempt little beside expressions of gratitude for the extraordinary kindness she was receiving. Elizabeth silently attended her.

When a basket of hothouse fruit and a huge vase of flowers arrived with a note from Mr Bingley wishing her a speedy recovery and sending his warmest regards, she was most gratified.

'Where shall I put the arrangement, Jane?'

She gestured towards a side table. 'Place them there, Lizzy, then I shall be able to look at them all day. How kind of Mr Bingley to think of me and to go to so much trouble.'

Later on, Miss Bingley and Mrs Hurst joined them upstairs. 'The apothecary is due to come this morning, dear Miss Bennet. Is there anything at all that we can do to make you feel more comfortable?'

Jane smiled weakly and shook her head. 'You are too good, Miss Bingley.' Even those few words were painful to her raw throat. She was offered soothing drinks, cool pillows to rest on and, at Elizabeth's suggestion, a bowl of tepid water was fetched and her face bathed in it.

Eventually they left her to rest and the three ladies gathered at the far side of the room; Jane watched them from half-closed eyes. She was pleased to observe that her sister seemed in a fair way to becoming firm friends with both Miss Bingley and Mrs Hurst.

She felt cosseted and loved, but far too ill to enquire after Mr Bingley. It was enough to know that he was thinking of her as she was of him. When the apothecary came in and examined her he told her that she had contracted a violent cold.

'Miss Bennet, I would advise you to return to bed and stay there until you are feeling more the thing. I shall prescribe you some draughts to ease the headache and lower your fever.'

Jane was happy to do so; she felt far worse than she had when she had awoken. As she dozed she could hear the soft murmuring of voices and knew that her sister had not quit her side for a moment, and that both Miss Bingley and Mrs Hurst had remained close by as well.

'Jane, it is three o'clock. I shall have to go. It will be dark soon. I do not like to leave you when you are so unwell. Miss Bingley has offered me the use of their chaise.'

Jane felt her eyes filled with tears. 'Oh, Lizzy, please do not go. I feel so much more comfortable with you here.'

There was the rustle of skirts and Miss Bingley appeared at the bedside. 'Miss Elizabeth, it is obvious that Miss Bennet would be happier with you here. Please, will you not stay at Netherfield for the present?'

'I am most obliged, Miss Bingley. Thank you, I should feel more sanguine here with Jane whilst she is so poorly. Could I presume upon your kindness and ask you to send a servant to Longbourn to collect clothes for Jane and me? I shall pen a note to my family so that they are not unduly alarmed.'

'I shall have the carriage sent for. You shall find writing materials in the escritoire in the sitting room.' Miss Bingley leant down and smoothed out the rumpled sheets. 'You must not concern yourself, my dear Miss Bennet. Mr Bingley is most anxious that you should be made comfortable and says that you must not consider returning home until you are fully recovered.'

* * *

Mr Bingley was reluctant to leave Netherfield until the apothecary had declared that Miss Bennet, although very poorly, was in no danger. He had been imagining the worst, for a sore throat – if neglected – could lead to a putrid sore throat, and such a condition could prove fatal. But she had, as Darcy had supposed, contracted only a feverish cold. He wished that he could go up and see for himself how she did.

The day seemed interminable and he could settle at nothing. Reports from the sick room were not encouraging. He could not bear to think that Miss Bennet was suffering and he unable to alleviate it. He went to see Nicholls to ensure that everything that could be done for the patient was in hand. 'Did the flowers and fruit go up as I instructed? Did my note go as well?'

'Yes, sir, they did. I can assure you that everything is in place to ensure that Miss Bennet is comfortable at Netherfield.'

All day Darcy remained at his side, offering encouragement and distraction in equal measures.

Mr Bingley sent a second note up and, on receiving word that Miss Bennet was resting, he allowed himself to be enticed into a game of billiards with his friend and Hurst.

'It is getting dark, Bingley. You had better send for the carriage. Miss Elizabeth cannot be expected to walk home.'

'Good heavens! I shall do so at once – thank you for reminding me.' He met Caroline in the hall.

'I was just coming to find you, Charles. Miss Bennet wishes her sister to stay and I have come down to send the carriage to Longbourn to fetch what belongings they might need.'

'Is the patient worse?'

'No, but she is no better for sure.' She rang the bell and the butler appeared and she gave her instructions. 'Now, Charles, do not look so worried. I am certain that our guest shall be recovered in a day or two.'

Mr Bingley returned to the billiard room and explained the new arrangements to the other gentlemen. He could not tell from Darcy's expression whether he was pleased or not by the news that Elizabeth was to remain at Netherfield with them.

At half past six, Louisa sent for their guest to join them for dinner. When she entered he bowed and took her hand. 'Miss Elizabeth, how is your sister doing? I am hoping to hear good news this evening.'

'She is much the same, Mr Bingley. It is most generous of you to accommodate us in this way, and I thank you for it. My sister is rarely ill, you know. That is why it was such a cause of alarm to me to hear she had succumbed so quickly.'

'I cannot tell you how excessively I dislike being ill myself. It is indeed shocking to have such a bad cold,' Caroline said, but then turned her attention back to Mr Darcy.

As soon as the last cover was removed Elizabeth excused herself and returned upstairs. The rest of the party removed themselves to the drawing room. Immediately Caroline spoke out against their unexpected guest.

'I do declare, Miss Elizabeth is nothing like her sister. Do not you think, Mr Darcy, that her manner is very bad indeed, a mixture of pride and impertinence? She has no conversation, no style, no taste and little beauty.'

'I agree, Caroline,' Louisa said. 'She has nothing, in short, to recommend her, but being an excellent walker. I shall never forget her appearance this morning. She really looked almost wild.'

'She did indeed, Louisa. I could hardly keep my countenance. Very nonsensical to come at all! Why must she be scampering about the country because her sister has a cold? Hair so untidy, so blowsy!'

'Yes, and her petticoat; I hope you saw her petticoat, six inches deep in mud, I am absolutely certain; and the hem which had been let down to hide it not doing its office.'

Mr Bingley had heard quite enough of this. 'Your picture may be very exact, Louisa, but this was all lost upon me. I thought that Miss Elizabeth Bennet looked remarkably well when she came into the room this morning. Her dirty petticoat quite escaped my notice.'

'But you observed, Mr Darcy, I am sure,' Caroline said, turning to his friend. 'I am inclined to think that you would not wish to see your sister make such an exhibition.'

'I certainly would not.'

'To walk three miles, or four miles, or five miles, or whatever it is, above one's ankles in dirt and alone, quite alone! What could she mean by it? It seems to me to show an abominable sort of conceited independence, and a certain indifference to decorum.'

'What it shows, in my opinion, is a degree of affection for her sister that is very pleasing,' Mr Bingley said to his sister.

'I am afraid, Mr Darcy,' Caroline continued in a half whisper, 'this adventure has rather affected your admiration of her fine eyes.'

'Not at all,' he replied, 'they were brightened by the exercise.'

His friend was taking a very close interest in Elizabeth's appearance. This was not the first time he had admired her eyes. Could the impossible be happening? Was Darcy becoming attached to her?

Darcy nodded at him, as if to reinforce this point and to tell him that he did not join in this general criticism.

'I have excessive regard for Jane. She is really a very sweet girl. I do wish with all my heart to see her well settled. With such a father and mother, and such low connections, I am afraid there is no chance of it.'

'I have heard you say that her uncle is an attorney in Meryton.'

'Yes, and they have another, who resides somewhere near Cheapside. I think that is capital!' added Caroline, and both his sisters laughed.

He jumped to his feet. He was heartily sick of this conversation. Miss Bennet was everything she should be, and it was hardly her fault her family did not live up to the exacting expectations of his sisters. 'If they had uncles enough to fill all Cheapside it would not make them one jot less agreeable.'

'It must very materially lessen their chance of marrying men of any consideration in the world,' Darcy commented, his face serious.

Having heard enough on the subject for one evening, Mr Bingley moved away from the group to stand alone at the far end of the room, lost in thought. He had not considered, until that moment, more than that he found Miss Bennet a delightful companion, that she occupied his every waking moment. It was not until Darcy had said out loud that he did not believe her to be a suitable match, that he had considered the future.

His friend's opinion gave him pause for thought. He trusted Darcy's judgement in everything, but in affairs of the heart he believed *he* had the more experience. It was not until Miss Bennet had become so unwell that he had understood how much she had come to mean to him.

He stared unseeing at a hideous portrait hanging to one side of the fireplace. What was it about her that made his pulse beat faster? In his mind's eye he saw her smiling up at him. Her eyes were a curious mix of green and brown, and she often had a few shining curls escaping at the nape her neck. Her lips were usually parted, revealing two rows of even teeth. He shuddered as he remembered when, several years ago, he had fancied himself in love with the squire's daughter.

She had lovely golden hair, big blue eyes and a perfect figure; but what he had liked especially about her was the fact that she did not talk overmuch, but listened intently to everything he had to say without interruption. It was not until he had been in her company several times that she laughed out loud, a lovely sound, and he turned in delight. To his horror he had seen that she had a mouthful of ruined teeth – it was small wonder the poor girl had been told to keep her mouth closed. He sat in the window seat and gazed down the room at his friend, who was now reading a newspaper.

He could well imagine Darcy's reaction if he were to tell him he intended to offer for Jane. (Although she must still be Miss Bennet when he addressed her, in his heart she was already *his Jane.*)

Darcy would raise his eyebrows and say, 'I do not believe you have considered this as you should. Think about her background; do you really wish to be associated with such a woman as her mother?'

Or perhaps he would say something more conciliatory, but still as damning. 'My dear Bingley, Miss Bennet is a beautiful woman, is everything you could possibly wish for in a wife.'

He would leap to his feet in excitement waiting to be given his friend's blessing and then Darcy would continue: 'However, she is not the woman for you. Her relations are intolerable and, after all, you have not known each other more than a few weeks, hardly time for Miss Bennet to make a lasting attachment.'

Indeed, now that he thought of it, although she was always delightful company, and smiled warmly at him when they danced, she was not the sort of young woman to make a show of her feelings. He would have to go on his own instincts and believe that she held him in high esteem. Perhaps he was imagining there was more to their relationship than there actually was. He knew *his* heart to be engaged, but perhaps Miss Bennet did not feel the same way?

Well, not yet, anyway. But they had the whole winter before them. That was ample time to get to know each other, and he thanked God for the whim that had brought him down to Hertfordshire.

It was quite late when Elizabeth rejoined them. 'How is Miss Bennet? Is she resting comfortably?'

'Yes, thank you for enquiring, Mr Bingley. She is finally asleep.'

'I am sure you have pleasure in being with your sister, and I hope it will soon be increased by seeing her quite well.' Charles wished his sisters would not speak so severely about Elizabeth. He thought she was most agreeable.

'Thank you, Mr Bingley, it is gratifying to know that you hold my sister in such high regard.'

He watched her walk towards the table upon which there were a few books. Perhaps there were not enough for her to find something that she liked? 'Miss Elizabeth, I shall go at once to fetch you something else if you cannot find anything to read on the table. I have a library, but I wish my collection were larger for your benefit and my own credit; but, idle fellow that I am, although I have not many, I have more than *I* ever looked into.'

'It is kind of you to offer, Mr Bingley, but I shall find something that will suit me perfectly from what is available in here.'

'I should like to choose a book for your sister to read when she is feeling well enough. What sort of thing does she like?'

Elizabeth picked up the books on the table, examining the

spines. 'She prefers a novel. She has recently read a book called *The Mysterious Protector*. It was in the circulating library. We both enjoyed that novel. She also enjoys books on the flora and fauna of different countries.'

'I have a far wider choice in the library. Let us go there immediately and select something together that you may take up to her.'

'I am astonished,' his sister Caroline called, 'that our father should leave so small a collection of books. You have such a delightful library at Pemberley, Mr Darcy!'

Mr Darcy looked up from the newspaper he was perusing. 'It ought to be good. It has been the work of many generations.'

'And then you have added so much to it yourself – you are always buying books.'

'I cannot comprehend the neglect of a family library in such times as these.'

'I am sure that there is nothing that can add to the beauty of that noble place. Charles, when you build your house, I wish it may be half as delightful as Pemberley.'

He laughed at his sister's comment. With all his fortune he knew he could never build anything to rival Darcy's estate.

'I would really advise you to make your purchase in that neighbourhood, and take Pemberley as your model. There is not a finer county in England than Derbyshire,' Caroline cried.

He grinned at his friend. 'I will buy Pemberley itself if Darcy will sell it.'

'We are going to the library; I wish to choose something for Miss Bennet to read when she is feeling a little better.'

Darcy put down his newspaper. 'Then I shall come with you. There is nothing worth reading in here, and I have finished with this.'

'Are neither of you going to join us in a hand of cards?' Mr Hurst enquired as they walked past the card table.

As it was perfectly clear that they were not going to do so, Charles did not bother to answer. Two footmen hurried ahead of them in order to light candles in the library. He frowned. Why had Darcy chosen to accompany them? He was already monopolising Elizabeth and their scholarly talk on the merits of books he had never heard of would not help him choose something suitable for her sister.

Then, to his consternation he heard the trill of his sister's voice. 'Please, allow me to accompany you. There is nothing I like better than to spend an hour or so in the library.' This was the outside of enough! 'Caroline, the last time you opened a book it was full of fashion plates. I do not believe you have ever read an entire novel in your life.'

His sister stopped in the passageway and her eyes narrowed. 'If you would prefer that I did not come, you only had to tell me so, Charles. There was no need to be offensive.' She turned and stalked back into the drawing room, leaving him feeling decidedly uncomfortable.

'Never mind, Bingley. I shall go back and smooth her ruffled feathers. I can select a book for myself tomorrow,' Darcy said.

'Mr Bingley, this is a delightful room. I am certain we shall find exactly what Jane likes best.'

Twenty minutes' searching produced a gothic novel and two beautifully illustrated books on the wildlife of Scotland. 'Thank you so much for your assistance in this matter. I do so wish Miss Bennet to be comfortable whilst she is here. I feel responsible for her illness.'

The young woman, whom he was beginning to like very well, smiled warmly. 'Good grief! There is absolutely no need to blame yourself. Important as you are in the neighbourhood, I do not believe you have power over the weather, Mr Bingley.'

He chuckled at her wit. Her sister did not have such a facility with words, but he did not consider it necessary to be erudite in order to be interesting. Being able to converse on commonplaces was far more important in his opinion.

'I shall not come back into the drawing room, sir. I have been away too long from my sister. I must go up and see how she is.'

He watched her run lightly up the wide oak staircase and thought how pretty she was; not as lovely as her sister, of course, but with her ready wit and fearless disposition she would make someone an excellent wife. He was smiling as he returned to the drawing room and Darcy caught his eye, raising an eyebrow in characteristic fashion.

He grinned and walked across to join him, speaking quietly so that they would not be overheard. 'I have been enjoying a pleasant interlude in the library with Miss Elizabeth. She has taken up the books I selected, but shall return with news on how the patient does.' He waited for his friend to comment but was to be disappointed on that score. 'No doubt there is an extensive library at Longbourn and she has learnt to love reading from being there.'

'Very possibly; however, she would do better to listen more and voice her opinions far less.'

'By that, I must assume that she did not defer to you?'

'No, she did not.'

Bingley was not sure from this conversation whether his friend was attracted or repelled by Elizabeth's outspokenness.

He joined the card game, but was interrupted when Elizabeth returned to say Jane was far worse and that she could not leave her alone.

'I shall send for Mr Jones at once. It does not matter how late the hour; I shall not rest easy until I know that Miss Bennet is in no danger.'

'I do not think that a local apothecary shall do in this case, Charles. Rather send to London for an eminent physician tomorrow.'

'Oh no, Mr Bingley, Miss Bingley, that is too kind but quite unnecessary. Mr Jones will do very well, and could be sent for in the morning, if my sister is not decidedly better.'

Charles no longer had any pleasure in the evening. He felt miserable at the thought that the young lady, who had become dear to him, was tossing and turning in discomfort upstairs whilst they were enjoying themselves below. His sisters agreed that it was a wretched affair, but soon repaired to the pianoforte to sing duets. He would go to find the housekeeper and give her directions that every possible attention must be paid to the patient and her sister.

He left the drawing room in search of Nicholls. During the time he had spent in the library he had learnt a deal about Jane's preferences. He would order her the food she liked. That was the least he could do in the circumstances.

After knocking on the housekeeper's door, he waited until it was opened to him. 'I was about to come and speak to you, sir. Miss Bennet has taken a turn for the worse. I have sent up cool water to bathe her temples and a tisane to help reduce the fever.'

'Excellent; however, I wish you to note down a list of Miss Bennet's favourite foods. She likes scrambled eggs, but not soft-boiled; she prefers tea to coffee and hot chocolate not at all. Her preferences are sweet rolls and fresh butter and honey, and sometimes she enjoys a muffin toasted at the fire.'

'I shall ensure that she gets tea on her tray in future, and as soon as she is able to eat I shall make sure she has the things you mentioned.'

'Good. As to other meals, a nourishing fresh vegetable soup is a great favourite of hers. As soon as she is well enough I wish her to be given breast of chicken with lemon sauce and potatoes mashed with butter and cream.' He rubbed his chin; had he recalled everything he had been told? Yes. The housekeeper would not wish to know that she did not sketch but played the piano, although he had been pleased to glean these details for himself.

5

'Jane, I am going to write a note to Longbourn and ask our mother to visit, and then she can decide if you are well enough to leave.'

'I am so sorry to be a nuisance, Lizzy, such a lot of trouble. I am feeling hot, but a little better than I did last night.' Jane wished that her family were not obliged to come to Netherfield. Miss Bingley and Mrs Hurst were everything that was kind, but she knew they found Mrs Bennet and her younger sisters rather too lively.

'I shall get dressed this morning. I have no wish to receive visitors lying in my bed as I did yesterday.'

'I shall allow you to put on your robe and sit in front of the fire in the parlour, but dressed you shall not get.'

When Jane was settled Betty brought in a tray upon which was a small portion of scrambled eggs, a single sweet roll, a pat of butter and small dish of honey. The chambermaid followed with the tray of tea.

'Lizzy! Look at this! It is all my favourites; how could the cook know what I liked?'

'Because Mr Bingley asked me last night. Which reminds me, he also selected three books for you to read when you are feeling better.'

She handed them to Jane who saw at once they were exactly what she enjoyed. 'How kind of him to think of me in this way. I hate being a trouble to him.'

'*He* is not at all put out by us being here; in fact you must stop worrying immediately about putting him out in any way. He would not have spent so long selecting your books and organising your breakfast if he did not wish you to be here.'

'I am glad that he cannot come up and see me as I am. Is my nose very red? I am sure that I look a sorry sight. I cannot imagine what Miss Bingley and Mrs Hurst must think of me. They are so elegant. Do not you think so, Lizzy?'

'I shall not tell you my opinion of those two ladies – for you already know it – although I am forced to admit they dress to advantage. However, I must admit that Miss Bingley has appeared to be showing you the correct amount of solicitude. I cannot fault her there.'

Everything on the tray looked so appetising. 'I believe that I shall try this breakfast after all.' After eating, Jane felt a little stronger. She blew her nose and sniffed loudly. 'Do you remember, Lizzy, your first assembly at Meryton?'

Her sister smiled. 'I do indeed. I had my regulation white muslin gown and talked of nothing else for weeks. Then on the morning of the dance I came out in a rash. It was all you could do to persuade me to accompany you.'

'I can recall you spending the entire evening hiding behind your fan whilst I enjoyed the dancing. It all seems so long ago, and now our sisters are following in our footsteps.'

Elizabeth removed the remains of the breakfast tray and joined her sister in a second cup of tea. 'I could wish that Kitty and Lydia *were* more like us. They have little reserve and although we had our come-out early, I do not believe we have ever behaved as they do.'

'What about that young man we met when we were staying in London who fancied himself in love with me and wrote me poetry?'

'Yes, it was execrable. What I remember is that we were walking into Meryton and I was reciting parts to you when the very gentleman we were laughing at popped unexpectedly out of the general stores.'

'I was never so embarrassed in my life. In my shock I stepped sideways and was up to my ankles in a puddle and covered *you* in muddy water.'

Her sister laughed out loud at the memory. 'It was no more than we deserved. He was a pleasant gentleman; I wonder what happened to him?'

'And what about the young man who was staying in Meryton two summers ago? He was madly in love with you – he was forever calling at the house. I believe that our mother thought you had made a match of it.'

'The man was a simpleton – he could scarcely string a coherent sentence together.' She smiled at Jane. 'But I must admit he was prodigiously handsome and according to Aunt Philips had a fortune of three thousand pounds a year!'

'Not enough to tempt you, Lizzy.'

'Absolutely not; only love would make me contemplate giving up my independence to any man.'

Jane felt her throat protesting at all the talking and laughing she had been doing. 'I agree. I shall never marry either, unless I am in love – nothing else matters in my opinion.'

She felt too fatigued to continue and closed her eyes, allowing herself to daydream about marrying a man she loved.

She was almost certain that she had found him already; she would talk to her sister about it when she felt a little better.

* * *

Charles was waiting anxiously for news of the patient. 'How is Miss Bennet this morning, Nicholls?'

The housekeeper smiled happily. 'The young lady has eaten breakfast and much enjoyed it, sir. I believe she is feeling a lot better.'

'I am relieved to hear you say so; I was most concerned when I saw that a note had been sent to Longbourn.'

He strolled back to the breakfast room where Darcy and his sisters were gathered; Hurst rarely appeared before noon. 'Good morning; Miss Bennet is feeling much better, but I have still sent for the apothecary. I do not intend taking chances in this matter.'

'I saw a note addressed to Mrs Bennet waiting to be delivered when I came down earlier,' Caroline said. 'Are we to expect a visit from that delightful lady?'

Darcy looked up. 'Well, Bingley? Are we to have that pleasure?'

'Do not look so appalled, my friend; you may make yourself scarce. I am sure that Mrs Bennet will be coming to see her daughter, and shall not stay after.'

He had not long left the breakfast room when Mrs Bennet, accompanied by her two youngest daughters, was announced. Immediately Mr Bingley went out into the hall to greet them. He nodded and smiled and allowed her babble to pass over his head. While Caroline was giving up-to-date information about the patient, he had leisure to examine Jane's mother.

Underneath the plumpness of her cheeks he could detect a physical resemblance to her eldest; it was impossible to see the colour of Mrs Bennet's hair as it was hidden under a spectacular turban of purple silk, extensively decorated with matching feathers. However, the colour of her eyes was exactly the same mix of green and brown as those that he admired so much.

Mrs Bennet suddenly turned back and addressed him directly. 'Mr Bingley, Mr Bennet and I wish to thank you for taking care of our eldest girls; I am sure that Jane is getting the best possible consideration at Netherfield and that without your attention she would be far worse than she is already.'

'It is my pleasure, madam, and I am certain that both the patient and Miss Elizabeth shall be delighted that you have come so promptly to visit.'

He wandered into the drawing room to find his friend hiding behind a newspaper. 'It is quite safe to emerge, Darcy. They have gone upstairs for the moment. However, when they come down I shall expect you to do the pretty and not leave me on my own. I hope having both her mother and her two younger sisters visiting will not cause Miss Bennet to have a relapse.'

'It would certainly send me into a decline. I believe I can feel the need to go out for a long walk around the park coming upon me.'

Laughing, Bingley threw himself into an adjacent chair. 'Don't you dare abandon me; just having you glowering in the background should be enough to curtail the visit.'

A little later Jane was woken by the unmistakable sound of her mother, Lydia and Kitty approaching her rooms. They had obviously responded to the note with alacrity. She barely had time to push herself upright before that the door was flung open and her mother rushed in.

'My dear Jane, we have been beside ourselves with worry for you. I am most relieved to find you a little better. I do not believe that your illness is alarming, but on the other hand the longer you remain here the better it will be.' Her mother smiled archly and Jane knew immediately what she was inferring.

'I should like to come home at once, ma'am. I am causing nothing but a nuisance at Netherfield.'

But her mother would hear none of it. 'My dear, you shall not budge from here until you are quite well. Mr Bingley is all anxious attention; you must stay here as long as possible.' She looked across at Elizabeth. 'I suppose that you could come back with us, Lizzy, now that Jane is a little better. Then Miss Bingley would have to sit with her and that would be no bad thing.'

'If Jane is to stay here, ma'am, then so shall I. Shall we wait until the apothecary visits and go by his advice?'

Jane hoped this gentleman would advise her immediate return to Longbourn, but he did the opposite and also advised against removal. Resigned to staying, at least for another night or two, she vaguely listened to the chattering about this and that. Thankfully Miss Bingley appeared and invited her mother and sisters to come down to the parlour. Jane hoped that they would not stay too long. It was the outside of enough having both Elizabeth and herself to contend with, without anyone else.

* * *

Mr Bingley was poised to greet his visitors as they arrived in the drawing room. 'Mrs Bennet, I hope you have not found Miss Bennet worse than you expected?'

'I have, sir. She is a great deal too unwell to be moved. Mr Jones said we must not think of moving her. We must trespass a little longer on your kindness.'

'Miss Bennet removed! It must not be thought of. My sister, I am sure, will not hear of her removal.'

Of course Caroline agreed with him. Mrs Bennet then explained to them in great detail the excellence of Jane's character. He agreed with her on every point. She ended her monologue by asking how long *he* intended to stay at Netherfield, as she knew that he had a short lease.

'Whatever I do is done in a hurry, and therefore if I should tire of Netherfield, I should probably be off in five minutes. At present, however, I consider myself as quite settled.'

Elizabeth smiled encouragingly at him. 'That is exactly what I should suppose of you, Mr Bingley.'

'You begin to comprehend me, do you?'

'Yes; I understand you perfectly.'

'I wish I might take this as a compliment; but to be so easily seen through I am afraid is pitiful.'

'No, as it happens. It does not necessarily follow that the deep, intricate character is more or less estimable than someone who is less complicated.'

'I did not know before that you are a study of character. It must be an amusing study.' He noticed that Darcy was taking a close interest in their conversation.

Elizabeth replied at once. 'Yes, but intricate characters are the most amusing. They have *that* advantage.'

Mr Darcy joined in. 'The country does not generally supply you with many subjects for such a study. In a country neighbourhood you move in a very confined and unvarying society.'

Elizabeth was having none of this. 'But people themselves alter so much that there is something new to be observed in one forever.'

Mrs Bennet felt moved to speak, and Mr Bingley watched Darcy look at her in disdain and then turn silently away.

The lady turned to him. 'I cannot see that London has any great advantage over the country for my part, except the shops and public places. The countryside is still pleasanter, is it not, Mr Bingley?'

He nodded vigorously. 'When I am in the country, I never wish to leave it; in Town it is pretty much the same. They have each their advantages and I can be equally happy in either.'

Mrs Bennet scowled at his friend. 'Aye, that is because you have the right disposition. But *that* gentleman seemed to think the country was nothing at all.'

'Indeed, ma'am, you are mistaken,' Elizabeth said, blushing for her mother. 'You mistook Mr Darcy. He only meant that they are not such a variety of people to be met within the country as in Town, which you must acknowledge to be true.'

'Certainly, my dear, nobody said there were. As for not meeting with many people in this neighbourhood, I think there are few neighbourhoods larger. I know we dine with four-and-twenty families.'

Charles was obliged to turn away in order to keep his countenance. His sister Caroline was less delicate, and directed her eyes towards Mr Darcy with a very expressive smile. Elizabeth deftly changed the subject by asking her mother if Charlotte Lucas had been at Longbourn since her coming away.

He glanced at the mantel clock. Surely Mrs Bennet and her daughters had already stayed the requisite time? He was relieved that Caroline had not offered them refreshments, for then they would be here forever. Although he was inordinately fond of Jane, Mrs Bennet was not the sort of person one usually associated with. She had far more too much to say, and most of it was either offensive or nonsensical.

One thing mentioned was the fact that when Jane had been fifteen years old and staying in London there had been a young man so in love with her he had written her poetry. Perhaps he should endeavour to compose some verses himself in honour of her beautiful face and sweet smile. He looked up to see Darcy smile at Elizabeth in a particular way and wondered again about his friend's interest. But what did she think of him? He watched her closely but could see no signs of partiality. Rather, she seemed to like provoking Darcy. Surely a novel experience for his friend!

Then Mrs Bennet began repeating her thanks to him for his kindness to her daughter.

'It is my pleasure, madam. It is no more than you would do for myself or my sister if we had been so struck down when visiting Longbourn. You must not consider it at all.' Charles stared pointedly at Caroline and she added her remarks.

'Miss Bennet and Miss Elizabeth are welcome here as long as necessary, Mrs Bennet. We are pleased to have them with us, and you may have no fears they will not be well looked after at Netherfield.'

As they were leaving, the youngest Bennet girl, Lydia, approached him. She had easy manners and an air of assurance that belied her age.

'Mr Bingley, do you remember that at Meryton you promised you would hold a ball here? It would be the most shameful thing in the world if you do not keep your promise.'

He did recall speaking about it at the first assembly – the one at which he had met Jane. If he held a ball at Netherfield, he would be able to spend an entire evening in her company and there was nothing he would like better.

'I am perfectly ready, I assure you, to keep my engagement; when your sister is recovered, you shall, if you please, name the day of the ball. We would not wish to be dancing while she is ill.'

Lydia declared herself satisfied. 'Oh! Yes, it would be much better to wait until Jane is well; by that time most likely Captain Carter shall be at Meryton again. When you have given your ball, I shall insist on them giving one also. I shall tell Colonel Forster it will be quite a shame if he does not.'

It was with a general sense of relief that Mrs Bennet and her daughters departed. With an embarrassed smile in his direction Elizabeth returned to her sister, and he did not blame her in the slightest. Instantly Caroline and Louisa began to censure Mrs Bennet and her daughters, including Elizabeth.

He was pleased to notice that Darcy, however prevailed upon to join in the criticisms, remained aloof from it all. 'Darcy, shall we escape from the house for an hour or two? I need to clear my head and an energetic gallop around the countryside will do it admirably.'

During the ride he had the opportunity to mull over the visit by the Bennets. How could such a vulgar woman have produced such a paragon as Jane? He wondered how *she* had such impeccable manners when her younger sisters were little better than hoydens. His horse stumbled because of his inattention. He lost his stirrups and almost his seat.

Darcy laughed as he regained his balance and took control of his mount. 'You are wool-gathering, Bingley. And from the expression on your face you are thinking of Miss Bennet.'

'I was, Darcy. I was considering how the older girls are so different from their mother and the younger ones; I wonder where they learnt how to behave?'

'Perhaps it is from their father. Remember, before you become too attached, what sort of family Miss Bennet comes from. Would you wish to tie yourself permanently to them?'

'And what of you? Have you not an admiration for Elizabeth?'

'I cannot think what you mean.'

'No? You are not attracted to her?'

'Perhaps. Yes, I admit it, I am. I have never seen such fine eyes before. And she is very spirited. But it would never do. Her family are abominable.'

'I will not have you include Jane in that condemnation. She is everything a man could wish for in a partner.'

'That's as may be; but Mrs Bennet is the most vulgar woman I have ever met, and apart from Elizabeth Bennet her sisters are little better than common flirts.'

Darcy kicked his horse into a canter and Bingley had little time to dwell on the subject until they were walking through the wood, giving the beasts time to cool down. If he offered for Jane he could take her away from her garrulous mother and feckless sisters, give her the kind of environment she deserved. He sighed. Love was a difficult journey fraught with dangers for the unwary traveller; he would talk some more with his friend on the subject later that evening.

Once changed and presentable he sent immediate enquiries to the sick room and was relieved to hear that Miss Bennet was a little better. Of his sisters he saw little, believing that they spent most of the day with the invalid, and it wasn't until the evening that Elizabeth joined their party in the drawing room.

* * *

'Miss Bennet, we shall leave you to rest this afternoon. You are looking pale after so many visitors.'

'Thank you for sitting with me this morning, Miss Bingley, Mrs Hurst. I have enjoyed your company; but you are correct, I do feel a trifle fatigued.'

Her sister escorted them to the door and then closed it with a decided snap. 'I do not see why they wish to spend the entire morning with us. I believe that I know as much about their wardrobes and their acquaintances in Town as they do!'

Jane smiled. 'You must not make fun of them; they have shown me nothing but kindness. I cannot understand why they should wish to make me an intimate, but I do deeply appreciate the honour.'

'Well, *you* did not hear them talking with Mr Darcy last night. You cannot imagine what he said about an accomplished woman.' Elizabeth straightened, linked her hands behind her back and stared haughtily down her nose. Jane instantly knew whom she was mimicking. '"The word is applied to many a woman who deserves it no otherwise than by netting a purse, or covering a screen. But I am very far from agreeing with you in your estimation of ladies in general. I cannot boast of knowing more than half a dozen, in the whole range of my acquaintances, that are really accomplished."'

Jane giggled. 'You have caught him to perfection, Lizzy. Poor man, I cannot see why you have taken him in such dislike.'

'He is the most pompous man I have ever had the misfortune to meet. If he expects a woman to be perfect then it is no wonder he is still unmarried. I doubt there is a woman good enough for him.'

'Please, Lizzy, can you not try to like him just a little? He is a good friend of Bingley's and you are well aware that I am halfway to falling in love with *him*.'

'Halfway? My dear Jane, you are already head over ears! But I like Mr Bingley – you have my full permission to love him as much as you wish. Hopefully you will not have to live with Mr Darcy if you marry his friend.'

'I do love him – you are right to say so. He is everything I have ever wanted in a partner. However, do not talk as though the matter is settled between us. At the moment we are good friends, but he has made no mention of the future and it is not my place to speak of it if he does not.' Jane knew that whatever happened she would not embarrass him by revealing how much she loved him until *he* was ready to declare himself.

'Lizzy, it is time that you repaired to your own room and changed for dinner. Promise me you will behave?'

'I shall promise to be polite to everyone for your sake, dearest sister.' And with a smile and kiss, she ran out laughing.

6

Tonight the card table did not appear. Darcy had told him he intended to write a letter to his sister, Georgiana. Caroline was watching the progress of this missive, constantly interrupting him by asking him to add messages to his sister from her.

Charles turned to his brother-in-law. 'Well, Hurst, shall we have a hand of piquet? Everyone else is happily occupied. Miss Elizabeth has her needlework, and Darcy his letter to write.'

It was hard to concentrate on the game with the constant chatter between Caroline and the laconic answers from Darcy. Eventually he was moved to intervene, as Caroline was giving the poor fellow no chance to complete his note.

Conversation flowed back and forth and he was pleased to notice that Darcy and Elizabeth appeared to be getting a great deal of pleasure from it. They discussed whether it was a good thing to be influenced by a friend or to be of firm character and to make up one's own mind.

'By all means,' he interrupted, 'hear all the particulars, not forgetting their comparative merits; decide which will have more weight. I assure you that were Darcy not such a great tall fellow, in comparison with myself, I should not take half so much notice of his opinion. I declare I do not know a more awful object than Darcy, on occasions, and in certain places – at his own house especially, and of a Sunday evening when he has nothing to do.'

His friend smiled, but Charles could see that he was rather offended. He noticed that Elizabeth hid her own amusement, perhaps not wishing to add to Darcy's discomfiture. Caroline told him he was talking nonsense.

'I see your design, Bingley,' Darcy eventually said. 'You dislike an argument, and wish to silence this one.'

'Perhaps I do. Arguments are too much like disputes. If you and Miss Bennet will defer yours until I am out of the room, I should be very thankful; then you may say whatever you like about me.'

'What you ask,' said Elizabeth, 'is no sacrifice on my side. Mr Darcy had much better finish his letter.'

His friend took her advice and returned to his writing, leaving him to consider whether in fact he did allow himself to be too influenced by others. When the letter was completed, Caroline moved at once to the pianoforte and began to play. From his position on the sidelines, he watched Darcy staring at Elizabeth. Then to his astonishment when Caroline began to play a lively Scotch air, his friend got to his feet and walked over and addressed their guest.

'Do not you feel a great inclination, Miss Bennet, to seize such an opportunity of dancing a reel?'

She smiled but made no answer, and so Darcy repeated the question obviously surprised at her silence. 'I asked if you would care to join me in a reel?'

'Oh! I heard you before; but I could not immediately determine what to say in reply. You wanted me, I know, to say yes, that you might have the pleasure of despising my taste. However, I always delight in overthrowing those kind of schemes, and cheating a person of their premeditated contempt. I have therefore made up my own mind to tell you that I do not want to dance at all, and now despise me if you wish.' Elizabeth smiled sweetly at Darcy and Charles could see that he was disarmed by it and smiled down at her with equal charm.

'Indeed, Miss Bennet, I should not dare.'

The two fell into a softly murmured conversation, which he could not overhear; he could see his sister looking daggers and knew her to be jealous. Caroline had set her cap at Darcy years ago, but so far his friend had been no more than polite. He thought the interest was all on her side. How much of this was because his friend was a handsome and desirable husband, or because he was rich, he did not care to speculate.

Darcy would be much better off with someone like Elizabeth; she was the first woman with the courage to stand up to him and maybe this had piqued his interest. She seemed to be always teasing him, and it only seemed to make Darcy more determined to be in her company. Bingley thought of all the women who had thrown themselves at Darcy over the years.

There had been Clarissa something or other. She had been everything his friend wanted for a wife – from a good family, pretty and quite definitely not opinionated. He grinned. The poor girl had been so terrified of Darcy she barely opened her mouth in his presence.

Then the most recent was the daughter of an earl, Lady Marianne Carruthers. This young lady was incomparable, reasonably intelligent and with a pedigree better than Darcy's. Lady Marianne had been as determined as her mother to capture him. Bingley smiled at the memory. Poor Darcy had been reduced to peering around doors before entering the room in case either of the ladies were waiting for him. In the end he had retreated in the middle of the season to Pemberley where he was safe.

The girl had eventually been married to a duke twice her age. It was no wonder she had been desperate to make his friend the alternative. Some had even pretended not to be interested in the hope that that would catch his attention, but they had been easy to see through. Whereas with Elizabeth it was genuine. Whether Darcy would still be intrigued by her if he did manage to win her respect Charles did not know. However, it would be fascinating to find out.

He suspected that Caroline would not find it interesting. In fact he was certain that she would do everything in her power to turn his friend against Jane's sister. He frowned. He wished everyone to be happy and comfortable, but he feared there were some stormy times ahead.

Jane was hoping that Elizabeth would call in and speak to her before she retired. She was feeling a little better and more than ready to be entertained before she went to sleep. A little after eleven o'clock the door opened softly.

'Are you awake, Jane? Shall I come in and tell you how the evening went?'

'Oh, yes, come in, Lizzy. Tell me, in what way did Mr Darcy displease you this evening?'

Once settled comfortably beside her on the bed, Elizabeth began to tell her about her evening. 'Miss Bingley invited me to play but I refused. I shall not perform and have her pour scorn on my efforts.'

'And Mr Bingley, what did he say for himself this evening? Did he enquire after me?'

'Of course he did, you goose. He was most insistent that I take his good wishes up with me. So far I believe you have had three books, three notes, a fruit bowl and a flower arrangement; I do not think he could do more if he tried.'

'He has been very kind, but he could do so much better than me. I have no fortune, and my family connections leave a lot to be desired.'

'In Mr Darcy's opinion perhaps, but I am certain Bingley would not let something like that stand between him and the woman he loved. Do you know, Mr Darcy asked me to dance with him.'

Jane was astounded. 'I thought he never danced! I take it from your smile that you refused.'

'Indeed I did. I vowed never to dance with him after he was so insufferably rude to me at the Meryton assembly a few weeks ago.'

'It is odd, do not you think, that he asked you in the first place? I wonder if he is developing a fondness for you? What other reason could there be?'

Her sister scrambled from the bed. 'What fustian you speak sometimes, my dear sister. I am certain he only asked me in order to find fault with the way I danced.'

'Surely not? He is everything that is polite. I cannot believe he would be so ungentlemanly.'

'Well, you have not spent as much time in his company as I have recently. He finds country people of little interest and believes London society is superior in every way. As for the idea that he would lower himself to develop a *tendre* for a provincial like myself, it is quite absurd! Have you forgotten Mr Darcy is the owner of Pemberley and in receipt of £10,000 a year?'

'Oh, Lizzy, do be serious.'

'I am being serious. Mr Darcy has not the slightest interest in me, I can assure you. Now, you must go to sleep and I shall see you in the morning.'

Dutifully Jane lay down, but *she* was not so sure. Lizzy and Darcy? Was it possible that both she and her sister were about to be involved with the gentlemen at Netherfield?

Jane felt so much better the following evening that after she had eaten the supper that had been sent up, she allowed Elizabeth to help her dress. 'I own, Lizzy, that it will be pleasant to be in company again after being shut up here so long.'

'Jane, you have not been short of visitors, surely?'

She felt her cheeks colour. Her sister's sharp intelligence had understood at once that she was referring to Mr Bingley. He had not come himself to see her – that would not have done – but every day he had sent messages of encouragement. Now that she was feeling better she could not wait to see him and thank him in person for his kind enquiries.

In the drawing room both Miss Bingley and Mrs Hurst greeted her with many profusions of pleasure and made themselves so agreeable that Jane felt her sister had been sorely mistaken in her opinion of them. But, when the gentlemen entered, she could not help but see that Miss Bingley's eyes were instantly turned towards Mr Darcy. Hers were drawn to Mr Bingley who rushed to her side.

'My dear Miss Bennet, I am so glad to see you down here with us. How are you feeling? Here, allow me to adjust your cushions.'

Laughing, Jane waved him away. 'I am very comfortable, thank you, Mr Bingley. I have been well looked after. And I must thank you personally, for the messages, fruit and flowers and books that you have sent to my bedchamber these past days.'

'It was entirely my pleasure, Miss Bennet. I do believe that fire is not sufficiently powerful to keep you warm.'

She watched as he piled logs onto it and when he suggested that she moved to the far side of the fireplace, so that she was further from the door, she agreed. This meant sitting on a *chaise longue*; immediately he placed himself beside her, and they were able to talk privately together.

'I am so pleased to be here after so long upstairs. I must apologise for being a sore trial and adding extra work to your household.'

'Enough! I shall have no more talk of apologising or of being a nuisance. You could stay here all year and I should not be dissatisfied.'

Jane felt her cheeks colour under his scrutiny. Was she reading more into his remarks than he meant? Surely if he said such a thing it must mean he returned her affections in some measure. She decided to answer flippantly, not to take his words too seriously. 'You might not be, sir, but I can assure you my family would have something to say on the matter. I should be sorely missed.'

'Indeed you would. What I should have said, my dear Miss Bennet, is that I should never tire of your company.' He smiled at her and she felt herself dazzled by his charm and affability. 'Did you know that Miss Lydia reminded me that I had promised to hold a ball here, Miss Bennet? I said I could not possibly do so until you were well enough to attend. Should you like me to hold a ball at Netherfield? I would like to know your opinion on the subject?'

'I should like that above anything, Mr Bingley. When shall you hold this ball do you think?'

He was not able to make a reply as Miss Bingley, hearing the mention of a ball, turned suddenly towards him and said. 'Fie, Charles, are you really seriously considering holding a dance at Netherfield? I would remind you, before you do so, to consult the wishes of the present party; I am much mistaken if there are not some among us to whom it will be rather a punishment than a pleasure.'

'If you mean Darcy, he may go to bed if he chooses before it begins. But as for the ball, I have been telling Miss Bennet it is quite a settled thing. And once Nicholls has made white soup enough, I shall send around my cards.'

He turned back to her with a grin. 'Darcy does not like to dance; he prefers to talk. Now, Miss Bennet, you must tell me what it is that you most like to do with your time.'

'I like to ride. Unfortunately, no one else in my house enjoys the pastime, so I take my rides alone.'

'You shall do so no longer. In future we shall go out together. I am sure that no one could object to us riding if we take a groom with us.'

'I should enjoy that greatly; however, I cannot make definite plans as I never know when a riding horse shall be available to me.'

'In which case, I shall provide your mount myself.'

Jane spent a delightful evening discussing the pleasures of the countryside as opposed to Town until Mr Bingley was called away to turn the music for his sister. This gave her the leisure to observe *her* sister. Elizabeth and Mr Darcy were engaged in a lively exchange and she did not understand the half of it, she much preferred to talk of commonplaces or even to sit in silence, if Mr Bingley was beside her.

The pianoforte was opened and conversation ceased. When she and Elizabeth retired after the tea tray had been circulated, she knew herself to be almost recovered.

'We must return to Longbourn, Lizzy. We shall outstay our welcome here.'

'I agree. We shall send a note asking for the carriage to come and collect us tomorrow.'

However, the message was returned from home that the carriage was not available until the following Tuesday, which would have meant, Jane realised, her spending an entire week at Netherfield. Elizabeth did not require much urging to ask Mr Bingley if they could possibly use his carriage and return to Longbourn immediately.

Miss Bingley remonstrated. 'My dear Miss Bennet, could you not be persuaded upon to stay? We shall be bereft of company when you have gone, and surely your parents could spare you both for just *one* more night?'

Jane looked helplessly at her sister who shrugged in resignation. 'If you insist, Miss Bingley, then we can do nothing but agree.'

When she met with Mr Bingley in the drawing room later and told him that she intended to leave the following morning he was dismayed. 'My dear Miss Bennet, you are hardly recovered yet. I know that you believe that you are, but you are still too pale. It would be much better if you stayed several days longer.'

'I shall do no such thing, Mr Bingley, but thank you kindly for requesting it. It is time that I returned. My sister and I have presumed on your generosity for far too long already.'

Jane knew that she was right. Her every inclination was to agree; there was nothing she could like better than to stay indefinitely at Netherfield in the company of a young man she had come to love. However, she knew where her duties lay. She would not stay a moment longer than the following morning.

On Sunday, after morning service, they said their goodbyes. Miss Bingley embraced her most tenderly, and promised to come and visit her at Longbourn. When they entered the carriage Elizabeth appeared in the liveliest of spirits.

As the vehicle pulled away she settled back on the squabs and smiled at her sister. 'I am sorry to be going home in some ways, Lizzy, but I believe we had begun to outstay our welcome. I do not know why you and Mr Darcy seemed so set on arguing.'

'We were not arguing, my dear, merely exchanging opinions in a lively way. I, for one, am happy to be returning. I do not feel comfortable anywhere else but Longbourn.'

The coach trundled up the drive and Jane was expecting to be greeted with delight by her mother. In this she was to be disappointed, as her mother thought they should have stayed longer. Mr Bennet, who was usually very laconic in his expressions of pleasure, appeared really glad to see them both.

'I am so glad to be home, Papa. I am still not quite recovered, but it would have been wrong to have stayed at Netherfield once I was almost well.'

'I am happy to have both of you back here. The place has been the poorer for your absence.'

'Come and sit down in the drawing room, Jane, and tell me everything that Mr Bingley said to you. I am certain that his feelings are engaged. His attentions are so special whenever he is next to you.'

Jane glanced despairingly at her sister. She had no wish to be interrogated on this subject; she was not going to build up her hopes or encourage her mother's aspirations to have a rich son-in-law.

'Jane, you do not look at all well. I believe the carriage ride has caused you to start a megrim.'

'It has, Lizzy. I had much better go to my bed and lie down for a few hours.'

Not allowing her mother to argue, she was willingly bundled

upstairs and into the bedchamber she shared with her sister. 'Do I have to actually retire to bed, Lizzy? I should much rather remain as I am.'

'I shall close the shutters and the door; that should be sufficient to keep out unwelcome visitors.'

Jane removed her slippers and pelisse and settled comfortably on the bed whilst the shutters were closed. 'I am sorry to leave you to our mother's questioning, but...'

'I understand exactly; I am quite capable of resisting the most strenuous of interrogations. I promise she will not hear anything *you* would not like from me.'

Left alone in the gloom Jane closed her eyes and let her mind drift back over the private conversations she had had with Mr Bingley. She sensed that his friend, Mr Darcy, did not approve of their intimacy. She prayed that this formidable gentleman would not influence Mr Bingley against her. She smiled; at least she knew that both Miss Bingley and Mrs Hurst would take her side. They had shown themselves to be good friends to her. Had they not given her a pretty scarf as a parting gift?

She knew that *she* loved him, and she was almost sure that he returned her affection, but until he made it clear she must keep her feelings to herself. There was nothing she disliked more than a young lady who wore her heart on her sleeve. If her mother had the slightest inkling that she might become Mrs Bingley, the news would be all over the village and into Meryton in no time.

This would not happen. Until Charles... she believed she could call him that to herself now... until Charles made an offer, or at least spoke of having a future with her, she would insist that she was merely a friend of his sisters and nothing more. It would be easier that way.

7

Jane went down for breakfast, secure in the knowledge that her sister had answered all her mother's questions about their visit to Netherfield. She took her place at the table, about which the rest of her family were gathered, glad that no one remarked on how little she had put on her own plate.

Mr Bennet rested his arms upon the table and gazed at his wife. 'I hope, my dear, that you ordered a good dinner today, because I have every expectation there shall be an addition to our family party.'

'Who do you mean, my dear? I know of nobody that is coming, I am sure, unless Charlotte Lucas should happen to call in, and I hope my dinner is good enough for *her*. I do not believe she often sees such a thing at her own house.'

'The person of whom I speak is a gentleman and a stranger.'

Mrs Bennet's eyes sparkled. 'A gentleman and a stranger! It is Mr Bingley I am sure. Well, Jane, you never dropped a word of this – you sly thing! Well, I am sure I shall be extremely glad to see Mr Bingley. But, good Lord! How unlucky! There is not a bit of fish to be got today. Lydia, my love, ring the bell. I must speak to Hill this moment.'

Jane put down her knife and fork, leaving her coddled egg and slice of ham untouched. She knew it was not to be Mr Bingley, for he would have mentioned it when they were talking last night. She waited, as eager as the others, to know to whom her father was referring.

'It is not Mr Bingley. It is a person I never saw in the whole course of my life.' Eventually her father explained that he had received a letter a fortnight before from his cousin, one Mr Collins, who would inherit Longbourn after his death. Jane knew, as did they all, that Longbourn was entailed, but this was the first time she had heard mention of the man himself.

Both she and her sister had attempted to explain to their mother the nature of an entail. However, it was a subject upon which Mrs Bennet was beyond the reach of reason; she continued to rail bitterly against the cruelty of settling the estate away from a family of five daughters, in favour of a man whom nobody cared anything about.

Her father then proceeded to read out a very long letter from Mr Collins, who it seemed was a clergyman who had just moved to a living under the patronage of someone called Lady Catherine de Bourgh. Jane was relieved when the letter came to an end.

'At four o'clock, therefore, we expect this peacemaking gentleman to arrive,' Mr Bennet said. 'He seems to be a most conscientious and polite young man, upon my word; and I doubt not will prove a valuable acquaintance, especially if Lady Catherine should be so indulgent as to let him come to us again.

'There is some sense in what he says about the girls, however; and if he's disposed to make many amends, I shall not be the person to discourage him.'

Jane had heard this part of the letter without understanding exactly what Mr Collins had meant. 'It is difficult to guess in what way he can mean to make us the atonement he thinks our due, but the wish is certainly to his credit.'

Elizabeth was disgusted by the manner in which Mr Collins deferred to Lady Catherine. 'He must not do, I think. I cannot make him out. There is something very pompous about his style; what can he mean by apologising for being mixed up in the entail? We cannot suppose he would help it, if he could. Do you expect him to be a sensible man, sir?'

'No, my dear; I think not,' her father replied. 'Upon my word I find him quite the reverse. There is instability and self-importance discernible in his letter, which promises well. I am impatient to see him.'

Later on that day she and Elizabeth escaped the chaos of preparation for this unexpected and unwanted visitor by taking a walk in the park. 'Lizzy, why do you think that Mr Collins has come at this time? Papa is still in the prime of his life. I do hope he is not coming in the expectation of moving into Longbourn at any time soon.'

'Of course he is not, but I have no idea why he is coming today. We must wait until he arrives and then no doubt he will tell us at great length and in interminable detail. I am as eager as Papa to see if he is as ridiculous as his letter.'

At four o'clock Mr Collins duly arrived at their door. Jane was introduced after her mother, and Mr Collins seemed to take a singular interest in her, which she found decidedly uncomfortable. He was a tall, heavy-looking young man of five-and-twenty. His manner was grave and stately and his speech very formal.

He had not been sitting long with the family before he began to praise Mrs Bennet for having so fine a family of daughters.

Jane exchanged a glance with her sister who raised an eyebrow and hid her smile behind her hand.

During dinner her father scarcely spoke at all, but when the servants were withdrawn he turned to their guest.

'Mr Collins, it would seem from your letter that you are very fortunate in your patroness, Lady Catherine De Bourgh.' He could not have chosen a better subject. Mr Collins was eloquent in her praise. In fact by the time he had finished his discourse, Jane felt she knew as much about his patroness as he did.

Lady Catherine had a sickly daughter, her estate was called Rosings, and a great deal more that she had already forgotten. When it was time for tea, her father seemed glad to take his guest into the drawing room again. After the tray was removed he invited Mr Collins to read aloud to the ladies. Their guest immediately said that he never read novels, much to the disgust of Kitty and Lydia. Other books were produced and after some deliberation he chose Fordyce's sermons. She saw her younger sisters' horror as he opened the volume and before he had, with monotonous solemnity, read even three pages, Lydia interrupted him.

'You know, my Uncle Philips talks of turning away one of his men. My aunt told me so herself on Saturday. I shall walk into Meryton tomorrow to hear more about it, and ask when Mr Denny comes back from Town.'

Jane was scandalised by her younger sister's incivility. 'Lydia, hold your tongue. Have you no manners at all?'

Lydia seemed almost surprised by Jane's reprimand. However, Mr Collins was very offended, and laid aside his book with a heavy sigh. Then followed a homily about poor manners and everyone was much relieved when their guest agreed to play backgammon with their father. Even her mother apologised most civilly for Lydia's rude interruption and promised that it should not occur again, if he would resume his book. Jane was delighted that he preferred to play backgammon.

That evening, as she and Elizabeth were preparing to retire, Jane finally had time to discuss her sojourn at Netherfield. 'I am glad to be home, Lizzy, and I must say that I did enjoy being with Mr Bingley. Did you not think he is so good-natured, so affable, with all his staff? I do believe I never heard him say a cross word the whole time we were there.'

'Which is more than I can say for his friend. Mr Darcy had nothing good to say about anyone. He is so high in instep, I am surprised he can walk at all.'

'I cannot imagine two men so dissimilar; I wonder how they first came to be friends.'

'Perhaps Darcy is so proud he has made no friends and therefore when Mr Bingley came his way he snatched at the chance of having someone so affable to talk to.'

Jane smiled. 'Well, Mr Darcy cannot be all bad if Mr Bingley holds him in such high regard. And do you not think that both Miss Bingley and Mrs Hurst are kind as well? Think how they looked after me when I was ill, and they are so experienced in the ways of the world. We could both learn a lot about society from being in their company.'

'What those two ladies could teach us is something I would rather not learn. I know that you like them both, but I think they are shallow. Their only good points are that they appear to enjoy your company and wish to be on intimate terms with you.'

* * *

The following day Jane and Elizabeth decided to accompany Lydia and Kitty into Meryton. Unfortunately Mr Collins was also to attend at the request of their father, who appeared most anxious to get rid of him and regain his library for himself. Jane had only agreed in the hope that she might meet Mr Bingley; she had no idea why Elizabeth came unless it was to accompany her.

They walked together, Kitty and Lydia in front, Mr Collins – with herself on one side and Elizabeth on the other – continuing to talk at great length of nothing in particular. All that was required of her was to answer civilly when he paused for breath.

Every time she heard the sound of a horse approaching, she looked up hoping it might be Charles. No sooner had they arrived at the High Street than she was dismayed to see both Lydia and Kitty were immediately staring ahead in their quest for officers. Nothing less than a very smart bonnet indeed, or a really new muslin in a shop window, could recall them. She looked in despair at her sister who raised her eyebrows and shook her head, nodding towards Mr Collins. It would not do to point out their sisters' immodesty when he was with them.

They had not been walking far when Jane saw a young man, a stranger to them, but with the most gentlemanlike appearance, walking with an officer on the other side of the way. This officer was the very Mr Denny, concerning whose return from London Lydia came to enquire, and he bowed to them as he passed.

'I wonder who that other officer is, Lizzy? No doubt, Kitty and Lydia will find out. We shall not be obliged to wait to be introduced by Mrs Philips.'

Mr Collins was slightly ahead of them, and they were able to confer privately for a moment. 'Look, Kitty and Lydia are already across the road,' Elizabeth said, 'and the gentlemen are turning back to speak to them. I must admit he is prodigiously handsome. He will be a definite asset to social occasions.'

Jane pursed her lips. 'I thought you had no time for military men, Lizzy?'

Elizabeth laughed at her sally. 'In the normal way, I do not.

But I am prepared to make exceptions for someone as pleasing as *that* gentleman.'

The girls led the two officers over and introductions were effected. Jane found the young man to be charming, and to have a happy readiness of conversation, but at the same time was perfectly correct and unassuming. She liked him immediately.

The sound of horses approaching made her look up and she felt her cheeks colour. This time it *was* Charles and Mr Darcy riding down the street. She glanced towards the new officer talking so animatedly with her sister. He was handsome, but no comparison to Charles, for he rode his horse as if born to it, and he looked so good-humoured, his eyes as blue as the sky.

She stepped away from the group, hoping that Mr Bingley would see her, and she smiled as he approached. Both gentlemen dismounted.

'Good morning, Miss Bennet, we were on our way to Longbourn to enquire how you did.'

'As you see, sir, I am fully recovered.' It was her intention to ask after the health of his sisters when she noticed Mr Darcy staring at Mr Wickham. Both men changed colour: one white, the other red. Mr Wickham after a few moments touched his hat, a salutation which Mr Darcy just deigned to return. What could be the meaning of it? It was impossible not to long to know.

She glanced up at Charles, but he appeared not to have noticed what had just occurred. 'I must bid you good day, ladies. I shall look forward to seeing you again, Miss Bennet.' Mr Darcy nodded and they regained their saddles and rode away. She heartily wished she had been walking only with her sister Elizabeth, and not surrounded by officers and Kitty and Lydia's chatter.

If that had been the case then Charles might well have

walked along with them. It seemed an age since she had spent any time alone with him. Perhaps she was making too much of his interest; perhaps she was imagining his attention. She couldn't bear to think of it; she must harden her resolve, must never let her family know that her feelings were engaged. For if he did not feel the same way and moved on, she would not have them distressed on her account.

As they walked home she and Elizabeth discussed what they had seen pass between the two gentlemen. Neither of them had any explanation as to why both had behaved so strangely.

It was not until after they had spent the evening at Mr and Mrs Philips's house, during which Mr Wickham had shown a decided partiality for Elizabeth, that she learnt the truth. The evening had passed pleasantly enough. Mr Collins had certainly enjoyed himself, but it was not the same for her unless Charles was present.

As soon as they were closeted alone in their bedchamber, Elizabeth said she had something astonishing to tell her about Mr Wickham and Mr Darcy.

'Please, Lizzy, I am far too fatigued to hear it now. Tell me about it tomorrow.'

It was not until later the following morning that she and Elizabeth could escape for a walk together. Immediately her sister began her tale.

'Jane, you will not believe what Mr Wickham told me last night. It would seem that he was the godson of Mr Darcy's father, and a very great favourite of his. The late Mr Darcy promised that Mr Wickham should have the best living when it became vacant; it was written in the will. However when the living was available and Mr Wickham was of age, it was given to someone else by Mr Darcy. It would seem, Jane, that the late Mr Darcy was one of the best men who ever drew breath and a true friend to Mr Wickham.'

Jane was horrified by the story. 'It is quite shocking. I cannot believe that Mr Darcy should go against his father's will in that way.'

Her sister became quite agitated on the subject. 'It would seem that Mr Wickham's father was the estate manager and devoted his entire life to the benefit of Pemberley. He was highly esteemed by the late Mr Darcy, a most intimate and confidential friend, according to Mr Wickham. He told me that if he had been less of a favourite, the present Mr Darcy might not have treated him so badly.'

'Lizzy, I am sure there must be some mistake. I cannot believe that Mr Bingley would hold Mr Darcy in such high regard if he was a man so unworthy of it. And yet I must agree with you – Mr Wickham gives every appearance of being amiable and of veracity. I cannot bear to think of his having endured such unkindness.'

It was too awful to contemplate, that a young man should have been so cast off by the closest friend of the man she loved. There could only be one explanation. 'They have both been deceived, I dare say, in some way or other, of which we can form no idea. It is just that people have perhaps misinterpreted them to each other. It is, in short, impossible for us to conjecture what causes or circumstances may have alienated them, without actual blame on either side.'

'Very true, indeed; and now, my dear Jane, what have you got to say on behalf of interested people who have probably been a consideration in the topic? Do you clear them too, or shall you be obliged to think ill of somebody?'

Jane forced a smile. 'Laugh as much as you choose, you will not laugh me out of my opinion. My dearest Lizzy, you must consider in what a disgraceful light this places Mr Darcy, to have treated his father's favourite in such a manner. One who his father had made a promise to provide for. It is impossible. No man of common humanity, no man with any value for his character, could be capable of it. Can his most intimate friend be so excessively deceived in him? Oh! No, I shall not believe it of him.'

'But I can much more easily believe Mr Bingley as being imposed upon, than that Mr Wickham should invent such a history himself. He gave me names, facts, everything mentioned without ceremony last night. If it be not so, let Mr Darcy contradict it. Besides, there was truth in his looks.'

'It is difficult indeed. It is distressing. One does not know what to think.'

'One knows exactly what to think,' Elizabeth said firmly.

Jane could think with certainty of only one. Charles, if he had been imposed on, would have much to suffer when the affair became public. She wished with all her heart that it would turn out to be a sham, that both Mr Wickham and Mr Darcy could somehow be exonerated of bad behaviour.

The carriage arrived as they emerged from the shrubbery. It was Charles and his sisters arriving for a morning call. She was relieved that Mr Darcy, on this occasion, had not accompanied them. 'Lizzy, is my nose red? Have I smuts on my face?'

'No, you look lovely as usual. You must not fret; I am certain that if you appeared dressed in black bombazine from head to toe he would still find you perfect.'

Smiling, Jane hurried forward to greet the guests; she could see Charles appeared as pleased to see her as she was to see him. He did not release her hand until Miss Bingley coughed pointedly.

'Miss Bennet, we have come specially to invite you to my ball.

It is to be held at Netherfield next Tuesday night. I did not wish to send you a card, but invite you in person.'

'That is kind of you, Mr Bingley. I know we are all looking forward to the event with eager anticipation.' She turned to welcome Miss Bingley and Mrs Hurst.

'Miss Bennet, it seems an age since we have met you. What have you been doing with yourself whilst we have been separated so long?'

'We have a guest with us. He is a cousin of Mr Bennet's, a Mr Collins. It has meant that I have been obliged to remain at home to assist my parents in entertaining him.'

'I expect that he shall wish to come to the ball next week as well. An extra gentleman is always welcome. Is he not, Louisa?' Miss Bingley asked.

Jane led the ladies inside where her mother was waiting in the drawing room. She had no time to talk to Charles in private, but whenever she glanced up from her conversation with his sisters it was to see his eyes resting upon her. They had not been with them more than ten minutes when Miss Bingley, followed immediately by her sister, jumped from her seat.

'Oh, Caroline, Louisa, are we to leave so soon?' Charles shrugged in resignation and smiled at her. 'I have had no time to talk to Miss Bennet.'

Without answering the ladies swept from the room, and he had little choice but to follow. Jane watched him go, knowing that it was the noise that had driven Miss Bingley and Mrs Hurst away. They were ladies of superior delicacy. No doubt they found too much inconsequential chatter unsettled their nerves.

That evening the conversation was all about the forthcoming ball. Jane knew it should be a happy evening for her in the society of her two friends and their brother. She had seldom been so contented, had so much to look forward to. She pushed the unpleasantness about Mr Wickham and Mr Darcy to the back of her mind; she would not discuss it further, even when her sister brought the matter up. It was nothing to do with them – it was best left alone.

She was content with her daydreams about the moment when Charles would go down on one knee and declare his love for her. Every time they met she loved him more and was finding it increasingly difficult to hide her partiality. The ball at Netherfield would give him the perfect opportunity to make his feelings clear.

8

Preparation for the ball had thrown his entire household into chaos, and Charles wished to escape from the bustle and confusion. He found Darcy and Hurst hiding in the billiard room. His friend grinned as he came skulking in.

'Ah ha! I had a wager with Hurst that you would join us very soon. Such matters are best left to the ladies.'

'You are quite right, Darcy. You did warn me to absent myself. I cannot imagine what possessed me to agree to holding the ball at Netherfield. I have never seen such a fuss and botheration. God knows why the banisters have to be polished?'

Darcy laughed out loud. 'God knows, indeed, my friend. It would seem that your guests shall find you wanting if there is a single finger mark upon the banisters, so polished they must be.'

Hurst shook his head, not following the conversation at all. 'This is a mystery to me; the ball is being held in the ballroom, not upstairs.'

Charles exchanged smiles with his friend. 'The ladies shall go upstairs, Hurst. They must have a chamber in which to withdraw, in order to arrange themselves and attend to any minor repairs that may arise. There also has to be, so Caroline informed me, a room for their maids to wait.'

'And the white soup? Has Nicholls made sufficient do you think, Bingley?'

'Devil take the white soup, I say. They shall have lobster patties, and whatever else cook fancies. I have no further interest in the subject.'

He stomped across to a convenient armchair and slumped down, stretching out his legs and closing his eyes. He had been looking forward to the evening, believing it would be an occasion when he could spend several hours in the company of Miss Bennet, whilst his sisters would be otherwise occupied, and his friend not watching his every move with disapproval. If Jane gave him the slightest indication that she loved him, he would make her an offer.

However, if he had known it would take so much effort on everyone's part, he would have suggested a dinner party instead. He felt Darcy looming over him and reluctantly opened one eye. 'Go away, Darcy, I have no wish to converse with you. *You* have not been obliged to oversee table decorations, to inspect silverware, and admire floral arrangements.'

Darcy chuckled. 'I should hope not. And in future, my friend, I should think you would have the sense to stay well away. Why else did you ask your sister to be your hostess, if it was not to arrange such things for you?'

He sat up, his good humour immediately restored. 'Are you intending to enjoy yourself tonight, Darcy?'

'I always intend to enjoy myself, Bingley; unfortunately circumstances, more often than not, conspire against this happening.'

'Well, I intend to devote the entire evening to entertaining Miss Bennet. No, do not raise your eyebrows at me, Darcy. She is the most beautiful girl I have ever met, and her sweetness of disposition is matched by her happy nature. She is perfect in every way.'

Hurst, becoming bored with the conversation, grabbed a billiard cue and thumped it loudly on the boards. 'As long as I don't have to dance, I shall be a happy man. Now, gentlemen, are we going to play billiards or stand here gossiping all day?'

That afternoon when the ladies had retired to their rooms and Hurst was asleep in the billiard room, Charles suggested that he and Darcy walk around the grounds. There was something he needed to tell his friend and he could put it off no longer.

'Darcy, I have something to tell you and I believe that you shall not be best pleased.'

'Good God! What have you done? I shudder to think what it could be that is making you look so miserable.'

'I was obliged to invite George Wickham along with all the other officers. It would have been an obvious slight if I had not included him. I do not know why you have taken the fellow into such dislike, but I know you have.'

For a moment his friend did not answer. 'I cannot tell you why I hold Wickham in such contempt; let it suffice to say that I have every reason to distrust the man and know him to be dishonest. You must take my word on this, Bingley.'

'I must say Wickham seemed a pleasant enough fellow, but I shall avoid his company. Your word is good enough for me.'

'Thank you; it is a great pity that man is to come tonight. I shall not enjoy the ball knowing that he is under the same roof as I.'

Charles slapped his friend on the back. 'You had no intention of enjoying yourself before I told you this, Darcy. You are a famous curmudgeon. I think you have forgotten how to find pleasure in a simple event.'

* * *

At Longbourn one would have thought from the amount of fuss and excitement that the ball was to be held in this house. Tonight Mr Bennet was to accompany them, and Mr Collins also, which would mean a party of eight – and whichever way you looked at it, the carriage could not happily accommodate so many.

'Mr Bennet, I believe that you and Mr Collins shall have to ride tonight or our carriage must make two journeys. It is the outside of enough to expect us to crush our finery in the way that you propose.'

'I have no intention of riding, and I would not dream of asking a guest to do so either. Neither do I expect my horses to make the journey more than once. Mr Collins, myself and you, madam, shall sit in comfort on one side, and the girls manage the best they can on the other. Lydia and Kitty can sit on the laps of Jane and Lizzy; they have done so before, I am sure we can manage it tonight.'

He vanished into the sanctuary of his library before Mrs Bennet could continue to harangue him. 'Did you hear that, Jane? You are to have Kitty sitting on your lap tonight. I am sure that no other party shall be as embarrassed and overcrowded as we shall.'

'I think it would be better, Mama, if Lydia was to be seated, and Kitty and Mary on our laps. Lydia is by far the biggest of us all.' And there the matter was left.

Jane ran upstairs to her apartment knowing that Elizabeth

was already there making her preparations for the evening. As she entered her parlour, Lydia hurried out. 'It is so unfair that you have a maid to share, whilst Kitty, Mary and I must make do with one between us.'

'Lydia, as soon as we can, we shall send Sarah along to your chamber.'

Elizabeth was all but ready. 'Jane, wherever have you been? You have scarcely left yourself time to dress. The ball is starting in one and one half hours from now.'

'I know exactly when it starts, Lizzy. I have been counting the minutes off in my head since Mr Bingley came with his invitation four days ago.' She stepped on one side the better to admire her sister's ball gown. 'That dress is perfect on you, Lizzy. It could have been made by the finest modiste in town. We are so fortunate to have a seamstress locally who is able to copy the fashion plates for us in this way.'

'Yes, I rather think my choice of gold sarcenet over pale yellow silk is exactly right for me.' Her sister spun, allowing her matching gold slippers to peek out beneath her petticoats.

'It is a pity that you do not have a domino to match, but navy blue is perfectly acceptable with anything.'

Sarah, their shared maid, tipped out warm water into the basin so that she could begin her ablutions. She took special care. Everything about her appearance must be perfect this evening. Both Elizabeth and herself had washed their hair earlier in the day, and then been obliged to sit like mermaids in front of the fire waiting for it to dry.

The dress she was wearing was also new. They were all allowed one evening gown each year, and she was glad she had saved it for the ball at Netherfield. It was in her favourite colour, green, but this was not the usual shade she chose. It was eau-de-Nil, a very fashionable shade, and the low neck was finished with matching silk roses. The hem was decorated in similar fashion, and her evening slippers also had roses stuck upon them.

Her sleeves were short, and even with elbow-length gloves to keep her arms warm, Jane knew the matching wrap would be a useful addition to her ensemble. When the final pin was pushed into her hair she was ready to step into the gown.

Jane felt like a society belle and knew she had never looked better. Sarah draped the shawl around her shoulders and stepped back to admire her mistress.

'My, Miss Bennet, you look a treat. I reckon you'll be the prettiest at the ball.'

'Thank you, Sarah. Now, please go and assist my sisters in any way you can.' The girl smiled and vanished through the dressing-room door.

She slipped her reticule over her wrist, picked up her fan and was ready to leave.

'Come out, Jane. It is my turn to admire you in your new finery,' Elizabeth called from their sitting room. Jane had no need to ask what her sister felt – her expression told her everything.

Downstairs Mrs Bennet was waiting in the drawing room. Like them she did not choose to sit in case she creased her gown prematurely. She was smiling happily.

'You shall never guess, your father has been teasing us. We are to travel in two carriages tonight: Mr Collins, myself and Mr Bennet and Jane in one, and everyone else in the second. Mr Collins has kindly volunteered us the use of his chaise.'

'I am relieved to hear you say so, Mama. None of us wishes to be squashed this evening.'

'Indeed we do not, Jane. I must say that you look very fine, girls. Jane, I think that colour an excellent choice for you. I am certain that Mr Bingley will appreciate the effort you have taken.' She smiled coyly at Elizabeth and tapped her on the wrist with her fan. 'And you too, my love; I am sure there is at least *one* gentleman who will appreciate your beauty.'

Jane saw her sister frown and wondered to whom their mother could possibly be referring. She did not think that Mrs Bennet knew about Elizabeth's interest in Mr Wickham. Soon Mr Collins and Mr Bennet joined them, resplendent in their evening regalia. Lydia, Kitty and Mary arrived soon after in a flurry of white taffeta and giggles.

'Excellent, the carriages are outside. And, thank the Lord, it has not been raining in the past two hours.'

Jane knew her father was thinking of his horses, but the ladies of his party were relieved they would not get mud on their slippers. They travelled the short distance with more room, and less noise, than she was accustomed to inside the carriage.

'Look at that, the entire drive has been lit by flambeaux. Such extravagance! But then, Mr Bennet, think what *you* could do if you had £100,000 to spend as you pleased.'

He cleared his throat. 'Indeed, my dear Mrs Bennet, I think of nothing else, especially when the bills from the seamstress drop upon my desk.'

Their carriage pulled up behind the one containing Sir William and Lady Lucas, Miss Charlotte and Maria. Their coachman held the horses steady and a liveried footman ran forward to open the door and let down the steps. The first thing Jane noticed was that a carpet had been laid from the turning circle up to the front door. There was no danger of anyone's ball gown becoming soiled tonight.

Even Lydia and Kitty were subdued by the extravagance of the occasion. Mr Bennet, with Mrs Bennet on his arm, headed the party, followed by Mr Collins who had offered his arm to Elizabeth, and her sister had not been quick enough to refuse.

Jane knew it should have been she who followed her parents, but she was not bothered by such nonsense. She was just glad *she* did not have to listen to Mr Collins.

As they waited to go in, she turned to Lydia and Kitty. 'You must be on your best behaviour, girls. Do not flirt with the officers; behave yourselves. You especially, Lydia. In my opinion you are far too young to be out, and it is up to you to prove me wrong by behaving with decorum.'

Lydia ignored her words, but Kitty smiled. 'I promise I shall keep Lydia in check, Jane. I would not dream of upsetting you or Lizzy in any way.'

The spacious entrance hall was ablaze with candlelight. Handsome floral arrangements stood on either side of the door. Footmen offered to take the gentlemen's hats, gloves and outer garments; a row of smartly dressed maids waited to be of service to the ladies.

They were led upstairs to the very chamber that Jane had stayed in when she had been unwell. Set out on the tables was every requisite that they might need. The maid had accompanied them in order to help them remove their cloaks and check that their appearance was perfect. The room was remarkably quiet. Where were all the other ladies? She asked the girl and was told, to her surprise and Mrs Bennet's delight, that this room had been allocated to the Longbourn ladies alone.

Mrs Bennet was in high alt at the news. 'Only think of that, Jane; it is exactly as I thought. Mr Bingley holds you in such regard, he has everything done for your benefit.'

'Mama, I wish you would not speak so openly about such matters. There is no understanding between us. We are just good friends. If there was anything else, I should be the first to tell you.' Her mother smiled archly and swept out. Jane joined her sisters in the line waiting to be greeted by Charles and Caroline.

She dropped into a curtsy and he raised her from it, taking her hand to his lips. He murmured quietly, for her ears alone. 'I must remain here until all my guests arrive, Miss Bennet. But I intend to lead you out in the first and then devote all evening to your entertainment.'

Jane had no time to answer. She smiled in acknowledgement and nodded, but was then obliged to go into the ballroom and mingle with the other guests. She had not been in here before; there had been no need during her stay. It would have been presumptuous to ask Caroline to show her around the establishment when she was an *uninvited* guest.

Elizabeth touched her arm. 'It looks magnificent, does it not, Jane? No expense spared here; that is obvious. I had no notion that Netherfield had such a spacious ballroom as this. I believe it is almost as large as the assembly rooms at Meryton.'

Jane gazed round, her eyes shining. 'There is even a gallery for the orchestra, and there must be over one hundred gilt chairs arranged along the walls for those who do not wish to dance. Do you think they have an anteroom where the gentlemen can play cards?'

'I am sure that they do. That is why the place is so crowded; do you see, Jane, there are gentlemen here with their families that we never see at the assemblies, including our own dear father.'

Lydia and Kitty had already detached themselves from the Longbourn party and were weaving their way through the crowd towards the group of scarlet regimentals that could be seen at the far end of the room.

'Do you intend to dance much, Lizzy?'

'Did I not tell you? Unfortunately I am engaged for the first two dances with Mr Collins. I had hoped that Mr Wickham would be here but I cannot see him over there. Can you?'

Jane scanned the faces; she saw several that she knew but Mr Wickham was not amongst them. 'Lizzy, do not frown so. I am sure that he has not been excluded deliberately. After all, he is in the militia. Is he not answerable to others? He could have been called away to attend to matters for his regiment.'

She could see that her sister was not convinced by this feeble explanation, knew that she blamed Mr Darcy for Mr Wickham's absence. She would not think of that now. She had come to enjoy herself; but first she would talk to her friends. This would make the wait for Charles to come and claim her for the first dance seem less tedious.

Charles watched Jane and her sister vanish amongst the crowd. Jane looked ravishing tonight, and Elizabeth almost as beautiful. He wished that Darcy could take more pleasure in the evening; he had not liked to press his friend for further information about the rift between Wickham and himself. He vaguely recalled Colonel Fitzwilliam, who shared the guardianship of Darcy's sister, also mentioning that young man's name with loathing.

Wickham would be *persona non grata* at Netherfield in future. Whatever the reasons, he was disappointed that his friend would no longer feel inclined to mingle with the guests. He had hoped to see Darcy dancing with Jane's sister; whatever his friend said to the contrary, he knew that Caroline would not be so incensed against Elizabeth Bennet if she did not see her as a rival.

He was forced to return his attention to greeting the line of people and was puzzled, although relieved, to realise that Wickham had not been amongst those who had arrived. In a lull he turned to Caroline. 'I have not seen Mr Wickham tonight? Is he not coming?'

'Oh, I had forgot to mention it. He sent his regrets. It seems he has been called away to London on urgent business.'

That was excellent news; as soon as he was done, he would find Darcy and tell him the good tidings.

9

Mr Bingley stared with dismay at the row of guests still waiting to be greeted. He glanced towards the ballroom but could not see his Jane amongst the swirling crowd. The orchestra were already tuning up; no doubt they would play something or other until he was free to open the occasion with his chosen partner.

He had no idea that Caroline had invited so many to the event. He had left matters to her. The only party he had been intent on inviting had been those from Longbourn and the officers. He bowed and smiled and nodded for a further twenty minutes and then the queue had gone. He could still hear carriage wheels on the stones outside, but there was no one waiting for his attention.

'Caroline, I have done with standing here. Anyone who arrives after this must find their own way to the ballroom.'

'Charles, there are still at least ten more couples to come. It will look decidedly odd if you, as the host, are not at your station to greet them.'

He grinned, unrepentant. 'In which case, my dear Caroline,

you must make my excuses. The orchestra is ready to play and I am ready to dance.'

He heard her sniff of disapproval as he threaded his way through the throng and into the ballroom. He wished he was as tall as Darcy; then he could see over the heads of his guests and immediately locate his partner. Now, where would she stand? He remembered that the Longbourn party had gathered near the orchestra at the Meryton assembly he had attended. Perhaps that would be the best place to start his search.

Several hopeful matrons, no doubt with marriageable daughters, attempted to intercept him, but he was fixed in his determination to find his love. He emerged onto the dance floor, and stared down the long room. His smile widened when he saw his quarry.

He had always known that she was the most beautiful young woman he had ever met. Tonight his opinion was doubly confirmed. Jane stood next to Elizabeth, her head erect, her nut-brown hair piled up in a complicated arrangement. Her gown, of an unusual blue-green colour, moved around her figure like water in a pool.

Elizabeth saw him first and touched her sister's arm. Immediately Jane turned and the smile that lit her face made him clumsy, almost stopping him in his tracks. He recovered swiftly and strode towards her, bowing deeply.

'I believe this is my dance, Miss Bennet. Allow me to lead you out.'

She rested her gloved hand on his arm and he was the happiest man alive to have this lovely creature at his side. The conductor waved his baton and the opening chords echoed around the room.

* * *

Jane glided gracefully into the centre of the ballroom. She curtsied and he bowed and they waited for the other couples to make up the set. As soon as there were sufficient, the music began in earnest. Her feet had never felt so light, the music so enchanting. She scarcely saw the other dancers, her attention entirely on her partner.

'Mr Bingley, your sisters have surpassed themselves tonight. I had no idea that Netherfield was so grand. We could be in a fine house in London, not in deepest Hertfordshire.'

'Exactly so, my dear Miss Bennet. I believe that Hertfordshire has everything in it that a man could possibly desire. What reason do I have to return to Town?'

They were separated temporarily as they were obliged to dance around the other couples to meet again at the far end of the set.

'I believe that Miss Elizabeth is dancing with your cousin, Mr Collins.'

Jane glanced across at the adjacent set, concerned for her sister's discomfort. 'Oh dear! Yes, you are quite correct, Mr Bingley. That is indeed Mr Collins. He is a most willing gentleman, eager to please and not short of ready conversation.' She saw Mr Collins step on Elizabeth's toes for the second time in as many minutes. 'However, I do not believe that dancing is one of his strengths. But then he *is* a clergyman.'

He chuckled and she responded with a smile. 'Perhaps Miss Elizabeth will have more congenial partners later on. She is attracting a deal of attention from the gentlemen. I am not an expert on such things, but permit me to say that I think your ensemble tonight is delightful.'

Jane felt herself flush. 'Thank you, Mr Bingley. I was not sure of the colour; it is not in the usual way, you know. I am so glad that you approve.'

He whirled her around with such vigour as they danced down the centre of the set that she was too breathless to speak again for some time. At the end of the first reel they stood together waiting for those who wished to continue to rearrange themselves, and those who had had enough, to depart the floor.

'I do not intend to dance with anyone else tonight, Miss Bennet. I should like our second dance to be the supper dance. Would that be acceptable to you?'

Jane was not sure if she should remonstrate with him or if he expected her to agree to do the same. It would be marked by all the guests if Mr Bingley refused to dance with anyone but herself. She raised her eyes to stare earnestly at him.

'I am deeply honoured, sir, that you have decided I should be your only partner. However, you must dance with both your sisters and with at least one of mine or they will feel decidedly left out. Remember you are the host – it would not do to offend your guests.' For a moment she thought he would refuse but then he nodded amiably.

'You are correct, but do not think that I shall enjoy it for one minute. The only lady I wish to be with tonight is you.'

His eyes held hers and his hand tightened. Her heart beat so loud she was surprised he did not remark on it.

As the orchestra struck up the second set, Jane caught Elizabeth's eye and smiled sympathetically. It must be unpleasant to be obliged to dance twice with someone who stood on one's toes so frequently. Then she forgot her sister's woes in the pleasure of her own partner. Never had a fifteen minutes passed so quickly; of what they had conversed she had no idea. She, without a shadow of a doubt, knew herself to be the happiest woman in the room.

After the final curtsy and bow, Charles drew her arm through his and walked her out onto the terrace. Although it was

November the evening was surprisingly mild. The heat from the hundreds of candles and the press of people had made the ballroom unpleasantly warm.

'My dear Miss Bennet, do I need to send for your wrap? Shall you catch a chill out here?' His concern made Jane glow.

'No, Mr Bingley, it is a pleasure to be outside for a few moments. I am not the delicate flower that you imagine; it was most unusual of me to contract a cold so quickly after my drenching a few weeks ago. I am rarely ill, you know...' She stopped, appalled. Did he think she was recommending herself to him as a healthy specimen? But he took what she said without offence.

'Then that is something else that we have in common, Miss Bennet. I also have the constitution of an ox. I can even tumble headlong from my horse and not break a bone. I have frequently got wet through and never had so much as a sniffle from the experience.'

They strolled companionably up and down a few moments longer. They were not alone out there as several other couples were enjoying a respite from the dancing as well.

'Mr Bingley, I am afraid that I must go back inside. I believe that Mrs Bennet might become alarmed if she discovers that I am absent from the room.'

Instantly he was apologising for his thoughtlessness and inconsiderate behaviour. She stopped him with a laugh. 'You know how it is, Mr Bingley, my mother has five daughters and it is her dearest wish to see us all happily settled. The slightest sign of partiality on either our part, or a gentleman's, and she is ready to believe there is an offer coming.' Jane intended that Mr Bingley did not think *she* was pursuing him, whatever her mother might say.

'I know exactly what you mean, Miss Bennet. It would not do

to give the tabbies something to gossip over.' He escorted her back into the noise and light, and bowed low over her hand. 'I shall not leave you for long, Miss Bennet; I shall ask one of my sisters to dance and possibly one of yours as well, as you suggested, but then shall return to your side. I shall dance again with others later on.'

Jane saw Colonel Forster approaching to claim her for the next quadrille. 'I am dancing the next set with Colonel Forster and then I shall return to sit with our mother.'

'I shall come and find you there, my dear Miss Bennet. We can stroll around the ballroom, and make conversation together until it is time for our second dance. Then I shall have the great pleasure of leading you into supper.' He paused, a worried expression upon his face. 'You shall join me for supper, Miss Bennet, I hope?'

Jane nodded. 'I should be delighted, Mr Bingley, and look forward to spending more time with you later.'

Colonel Forster was an excellent dancer, as many of the military were, and a good friend of the family. They had completed almost the first set when he touched on the subject of Charles and herself. 'Mr Bingley appears very taken with you, Miss Bennet. He is a charming and amiable young man, and has a fortune of £100,000, I hear.'

Jane blushed painfully. This would not do. She did not wish him to be speculating on her behalf. Although *her* affections were engaged, and she had every hope that he reciprocated, nothing had been said by either of them that indicated a lasting attachment had been made. It would be better to stop this rumour before it reached her mother.

'Colonel Forster, Mr Bingley and I have much in common, but it is his sisters that I am friends with, you know. He is a kind gentleman, and pays me attention for his sisters' sake, but there is nothing more to it, I do assure you.'

He looked at her narrowly, then nodded. 'If you say so, my dear, but you do make a handsome couple.'

For the remainder of the dance the conversation was on general things: the excellence of the orchestra, the lavishness of the decorations, the excessive number of guests, and the delights of the supper to come.

As Jane was threading her way back to join Mrs Bennet, who was seated by Lady Lucas deep in conversation, she was startled to see her sister Elizabeth being led onto the floor by none other than Mr Darcy. She paused, standing a little behind one of the marble pillars, the better to observe without herself being seen. Charlotte appeared at her side.

'My word, Mr Darcy and Lizzy make a fine pair do they not?'

'Oh no, there is nothing like *that* between them. She holds him in dislike, is constantly telling me how proud and disagreeable he is. I am certain that he is only dancing with her because Mr Bingley asked him to.'

Her friend was claimed by Mr Collins and they walked off together leaving Jane alone to speculate on what had been said. Could Charlotte be correct? She watched the couple more closely, hoping to see something that would reveal how they felt about each other. She thought she detected admiration in his glance, but she might have been mistaken. They seemed to have little to say to each other initially and she wondered why he had asked her if that was the case, and why Elizabeth had accepted.

Then she saw the conversation commence. Before long it had become quite animated. She smiled. It would be better if Elizabeth let go her dislike of Mr Darcy. She stiffened as she watched his expression change. She knew what had taken place.

Elizabeth had asked him about Wickham, and he had taken offence at it. But it was not until later that evening that she learnt more.

* * *

Charles had seen his friend dancing in the adjacent set and noticed that they had not parted amicably. He waylaid Darcy and drew him to one side. 'So, Darcy, you danced with Miss Elizabeth?'

'How observant of you; Bingley. I can assure you I merely did so in order to be polite.'

'I noticed you were arguing again; has she been teasing you?'

'Teasing? No, she is impertinent; I have no wish to discuss the matter.'

'Come now, Darcy. You must admit that she is braver than any of the other young ladies of your acquaintance. It must be a novel experience for you to have someone take you to task in that way. Normally they are fawning on your every word.'

Their conversation was disturbed by the arrival of Caroline. 'My dear Mr Darcy, are you not bored with the dancing? I am sure that, like me, you much prefer to converse with like-minded friends than skip about on the dance floor.'

Darcy replied politely and walked away. Charles could hear his sister talking as she followed him. He smiled, wondering if his friend would consider Caroline as a sycophantic admirer? Up till now he had been no more than courteous. The overtures had definitely come from her side. He would go and look for Jane – it would soon be time for the supper dance.

* * *

'Ah! There you are, Jane,' her mother said. 'Why are you not dancing? There are a dozen attractive gentlemen without partners. You only have to look in their direction and they shall be here immediately to ask you.'

Jane shook her head slightly. 'I have no wish to dance again, thank you, ma'am. I am engaged for the supper dance with Mr Bingley. I believe it is the one after this, and I do not wish to be overheated.'

'Indeed you do not, my dear. I see that he has not stood up so far with anyone apart from Miss Bingley, Charlotte and yourself. He has walked past several hopeful young ladies. I am sure that is a sign of his partiality to you.'

The music finished and Jane turned, eagerly scanning the crowd, waiting for Charles to arrive. She dreaded to think what her mother might say to embarrass them both, so moved away as soon as she saw him advancing in her direction.

His colour was hectic, his eyes alight with laughter. 'My word, that was a lively jig. I have scarcely got breath enough for our dance, Miss Bennet.'

'I shall be perfectly content to sit it out with you, Mr Bingley, if that is what you prefer.'

'Of course not – I am not such a weakling. Come, Miss Bennet, they shall start without us if we do not take our places right away.'

As the music faded the doors to the grand dining room were thrown back and he escorted her to a small table set aside from the others; she could only assume that he had planned it this way.

A footman immediately produced a glass of cool lemonade for her and champagne for him.

Two plates from the buffet table arrived moments later. She looked down in dismay at the amount of food piled on her plate.

'I shall never eat all this, Mr Bingley. It is delicious, no doubt, but I have not such a prodigious appetite.'

He grinned. 'No matter. Leave what you do not wish to eat, Miss Bennet. I told him to put on one of everything. I had no notion Caroline had ordered such a variety.' He poked through the mound on his own plate. 'Good grief! I believe there is a slice of apple tart and a portion of junket or some such underneath the savouries.'

Jane's hands flew to her mouth. 'Oh dear! What shall we do? I am partial to lobster patties, but not when they are served with apple pie.'

He looked truly perplexed until he realised she was having difficulty containing her giggles. Immediately they were helpless with laughter. 'We cannot eat this. Shall I fetch you something else?'

'No, thank you, this lemonade is sufficient. I hope we will not hurt anyone's feelings if the plates are left untouched.'

He mopped his eyes. 'I cannot think what possessed the man to do this.' He stared more closely at the footman in question and then he turned to her, a look of bemusement on his face. 'You know, that footman, he is a groom. I believe that Caroline has dragged the poor fellow from the stables and decked him out in a borrowed livery for the evening. No wonder he had no idea what to serve us.'

Jane looked more closely at the footman, and underneath his periwig she could see his complexion was tanned. She could not see his hands as he was wearing white cotton gloves. 'Poor man, he must be finding it a sore trial feeding us after a stable full of horses.'

He turned to her and held out his hand. 'Miss Bennet, let us stroll about the house; the entrance hall is the quietist place at the moment.'

They left the mishmash of food and slipped away unnoticed; his guests were too busy devouring the delicacies that had been provided for them to be watching anything else.

'Mr Bingley, I heard very disturbing information about Mr Wickham and Mr Darcy. I could not believe what I was told and gave no credence to it. However, Mr Wickham does seem an honest gentleman, so I am in a quandary as I cannot understand why he should make up such a tale.'

'I am afraid I do not know the whole of the history and am quite ignorant of the circumstances which have principally offended Darcy; but I will vouch for my friend's good conduct and his probity and honour. I am perfectly convinced that Wickham has done some something to earn his opprobrium. I am sorry to say that this gentleman is not respectable. He must have been very imprudent and deserves to lose Mr Darcy's regard.'

'Have you met Mr Wickham before this, Mr Bingley?'

'No, I never saw him until the other morning at Meryton. I have no reason to question Mr Darcy. If he disregards the young man, then he must have done something dishonourable.'

Jane sighed. 'I hate to think ill of Wickham. He seems so amiable and Elizabeth seems quite taken with him. However, I am sure that you know more about the matter than I, and I do not intend to worry you with it any longer.'

'Darcy is like family to me, I hope you understand my loyalties must be to him even if I do not know the exact circumstances.'

'I do so agree; duty to one's family must be paramount in everybody's life. I should hate to disoblige my parents if it were possible to do otherwise.'

They continued their stroll about the circumference of the

ballroom. 'Have you made any plans for the Christmas festivities, Miss Bennet?'

'Yes, my aunt and uncle, Mr and Mrs Gardiner, come down to Longbourn for a week. We do not have a moment to ourselves, but I sincerely hope that you shall have time to call in and see us. Are you planning anything here, Mr Bingley?'

'After tonight I never wish to hold another function again. However, I expect that Caroline and Louisa will arrange some private parties. I shall let you know in good time so that you and your family may attend.'

They stayed together for a while longer and then Jane thought it best to return to the supper room before her absence was noticed. He went to claim Mrs Hurst for her dance and promised to return to her side as soon as it was done. She met Elizabeth in an anteroom.

'Jane, are you enjoying yourself? I have been watching you; I believe that you and Bingley seem perfectly matched.'

'I do hope so, Lizzy. He is everything I ever wanted in a gentleman. He is kind, amiable and I do believe he returns my regard. I shall not say too much on the subject, for he has not mentioned the future, but I believe I am not mistaken. And his sisters are my greatest friends; surely they must wish us to be connected?'

'I am sure that they do *not*, Jane. Bingley has monopolised you all evening; there are several young ladies smarting from his walking past without asking *them* to dance. Did you have time to ask him if he knew anything about this matter between Mr Darcy and Wickham?'

Jane told her what she had heard.

'I have not a doubt of Mr Bingley's sincerity,' said Elizabeth warmly, 'but you must excuse my not being convinced by assurances only. Bingley's defence of his friend was a very able one, I dare say, but since he is unacquainted with several parts of the story, and has learnt the rest from that friend himself, I shall venture still to think of both gentlemen as I did before.'

Jane was relieved when the subject returned to Charles and herself. She prayed that Elizabeth's confidence in his intention of making her an offer was not misplaced. He had not mentioned anything specific, but she was sure she had not imagined the attention he was paying her. Certainly her mother and Lady Lucas were convinced that she would soon be living as mistress of Netherfield.

Jane decided not to rejoin her mother but remain with her sister, Elizabeth, until Mr Bingley came to find her. She smiled warmly as he approached.

'Pray excuse me, sir, I must speak to an acquaintance. But first, may I compliment you on the success of your ball.' Elizabeth smiled and vanished into the crowd, leaving Charles much perplexed.

'My dear Miss Bennet, it has seemed an interminable time since I last spoke to you. Do you think I should have asked Miss Elizabeth to dance? She did not look especially pleased to see me.'

'No, sir, we had been discussing other matters and she was thinking of those things. Her expression was not in any way connected to your arrival.'

'In that case, we both have the approval of at least one sister. As we may not dance again, do you wish to sit down and play a hand of cards? Or you could introduce me to the people you know; I am all but a stranger in the area, am I not?'

Jane had no wish to waste a moment of their time on playing cards. They had not been perambulating around the place for many minutes when she observed that the orchestra were no longer playing.

'I believe that there is talk of singing, Miss Bennet. Do you wish to participate in this or shall we be observers?'

'I have no wish to perform in so public a place, thank you. But please, if there is any other young lady you wish to sing a duet with, I shall be pleased to listen.'

She noticed, with dismay, that Mary was first to take the piano stool. Her sister played a tune that she almost did not recognise and after a pause of half a minute began another. This time she sang and Jane wished that she had the courage to accompany her, for Mary's voice was not strong and her manner a trifle affected. There was nothing she could do, and fortunately her companion was unmoved by Mary's display. So she smiled at Mr Bingley and they resumed their conversation.

'At what time do you intend the last dance to be?'

'I have no idea, Miss Bennet. I have left all those matters to Caroline. I hope that you are not thinking of rushing away early?'

This was the last thing on her mind. 'No, Mr Bingley, I shall be happy for this evening to go on forever.'

Jane was given an extra fifteen minutes of private conversation with Charles, as for some reason their carriages were the last to appear. They departed without any fixed agreement between them as to when they should meet again, but Jane was content. She was almost certain that he returned her love, that his sisters approved of the connection and that it could only be a matter of time before he made her an offer.

On the return journey she volunteered to travel with her sisters and Elizabeth climbed in with Mr Collins and her parents. Even Lydia was quiet, apart from the odd comment to say how tired she was. She closed her eyes and could not help but smile at the thought of what might be the outcome of her next meeting with *him*.

No sooner were they private, their ball gowns hanging neatly in the closet, than the two sisters scrambled into bed, eager to discuss the events of the evening.

'Lizzy, I saw you dancing with Mr Darcy. Did you part on bad terms? I fear that you must have asked him about Wickham.'

'I did, and regretted it. He was most disagreeable and refused to tell me what I wished to know. I am sure it was his doing that Mr Wickham did not come to the ball. I was so looking forward to dancing with him. It quite spoilt the evening for me.'

'Charlotte thinks that he is interested in you…'

'Mr Wickham?'

'No, Mr Darcy. He only danced with Bingley's sisters and yourself. You might not have noticed how honoured you were, but others did.'

'That is nonsense, and you know it, Jane. But, I must admit he said nothing bad about Wickham, merely agreed that he was good at making friends but less so at keeping them. I cannot make him out at all. There are times when I find him an invigorating companion, but mostly his pride gets in the way of me liking him. Enough of me, I noticed that you and Bingley spent a deal of time together. And I was not the only one to remark on it, Sir William made a point of coming over and telling Darcy what a handsome couple you made.'

Jane felt a glow of happiness. 'I can tell you, Lizzy, that the more time I spend with him the better I love him. Although he did not say so in as many words, I am expecting him to visit in the next day or two. Can you imagine the transports of delight from our mother? Should you be pleased if I became Mrs Bingley?'

'You know I should, for I have already told you that I like him very well. I could not think of a better man to become my brother-in-law; however, I am not so sure about welcoming his sisters into the bosom of our family.'

Laughing, Jane leant over and blew out the remaining candle, leaving them in the soft glow of the fire. 'Imagine their delight at becoming part of *this* family? I think we should have the better of the arrangement.'

10

Jane dressed with careful attention the next morning, hoping Charles might come immediately. However, what took place after breakfast made further contemplation of the possibility of a match between herself and the man she loved take second place. She was occupied upstairs when she heard pandemonium erupt below. Her mother appeared to be very vexed about something. She moved towards the door, but heard hurrying footsteps approaching. Her sister came in, her face a little paler than was usual.

'Jane, it is as I feared. Mr Collins has just made an offer and I have refused him. However, he will not take my refusal seriously. Our mother is beside herself: she has run to seek support from the library and I expect to be summoned to answer for myself at any moment.'

Jane was not surprised by this revelation; although Elizabeth had not intimated she was aware of Mr Collins's intention, she knew her sister could not hold the man in high regard.

'Oh dear! Mama will be suffering from her nerves for days

after this. But you are right to refuse him, Lizzy. He is not the man for you.'

'I hope that I can convince our mother of that. I believe she was hoping I should marry him so that Longbourn shall stay in the family. This must be how Mr Collins intended to make recompense – by marrying one of us. Jane, you know my feelings on the subject of matrimony. I have little regard for it, but it would only be supportable if one's feelings were engaged. I could not contemplate a union of convenience.'

'And no more could I. I do hope Bingley does not come this morning when the house is in such an uproar.'

Sure enough, not long afterwards the summons came and Elizabeth was obliged to join their father in the library. 'I shall not change my mind, Jane. I know it would be helpful if the entail was circumvented in this way, but I refuse to marry Mr Collins; the man is a nincompoop.'

Jane was glad she had not been put in this situation; if Mr Collins had asked her what would she have said? She frowned. It did not bear thinking of; as she was officially as unattached as her sister, she might not have been so ready to refuse – not when accepting would please her mother. Elizabeth would not be so coerced, or feel obliged to do anything she thought was wrong.

'Jane, I cannot tell you how unhappy I am. Your ungrateful sister has refused to marry Mr Collins. It would be the answer to my prayers. I could die happy knowing that one of my daughters was living here in my stead. You must speak to her, convince her she must marry him for all our sakes.'

'I cannot do that, ma'am. Lizzy is adamant she will have none of him. Like me, she will not marry unless she loves her partner.'

Her mother threw up her hands in disgust. 'Love? What has that to do with the subject? One marries for the benefit of one's family and one's self; love may come afterwards if it wishes. No,

Lizzy must be made to see the advantages of this match. It is up to you to persuade her.'

'I have told you, it would do no good. You know once Lizzy has made up her mind she will not budge from it. Mr Collins must look elsewhere for his wife, I am sorry, but you must forget about a match within this family.'

Eventually, exhausted by the argument, Jane escaped to the garden. She glanced frequently towards the paddock, hoping to see Charles cantering across, but was disappointed. If only he would come this minute, her mother would go into raptures and Lizzy would be forgiven. When she returned to the house it was calm.

She had no doubt that her mother would not speak to Elizabeth for days to come. The atmosphere would be unpleasant, but she would remain apart from it all. This upset would not spoil *her* happiness. She was sorry that her sister should have to suffer in this way, but as long as neither Charles, nor his sister, were party to the argument she would be content to wait until it was her turn to receive an offer, one she would accept – unlike her sister and Mr Collins.

Charles had never enjoyed an evening so much. He knew his mind was made up. Tomorrow he would go and speak to Mr Bennet, ask if he could pay his addresses to Jane. He knew some of her relatives were not quite acceptable, but they could have no objection to his choice. She was everything a man could wish for in a partner.

The next morning he was surprised to find both Darcy and Caroline waiting to greet him in the breakfast parlour. 'It is a fine day in, but I did not expect to see either of you abroad so soon. I am going to break my fast and then ride at once to Longbourn.' He smiled at them and was shocked when they did not respond.

'It is as I feared, Miss Bingley. We have almost left the matter too late.'

'What matter? Why are you both looking so Friday-faced? Do you not intend to wish me joy?'

'Charles, you must sit down. We have serious matters to discuss. You must not be so precipitant in your desire to ask Miss Bennet to marry you. Have you considered to whom she is related? Her sisters are little better than flirts; and Mrs Bennet is the outside of enough. Surely you do not wish to have *her* for your mother?'

His joy in the day began to fade. 'I do not understand why you should say this, Caroline. Jane is a friend of yours. You have smiled on us both throughout these past few weeks. It is no matter to me that her sisters and mother are silly. It is Jane Bennet that I wish to marry. Why should *you* suddenly change your mind?'

It was Darcy who replied. 'My dear Bingley, are you sure that Miss Bennet reciprocates your feelings? It is obvious to all who know you well that your heart is engaged, but I do not believe that she feels the same way about you.'

'How can you say that? She has spent time with me and is always smiling and happy in my company. I am sure that she loves me.'

'I am certain that she does not; I agree that she enjoys your company, but I watched her closely throughout last night's event and at no time did I see her treat you with any more partiality and she did any other gentleman. I believe she has an open disposition, and it is her nature to be friendly with anyone who shows her kindness.'

Charles was beginning to have doubts. Darcy was a shrewd

fellow; if he had studied Jane Bennet and not seen what he thought was there, then maybe he had been mistaken in believing that she returned his affection.

'I know that she does not love me as much as I love her, but that will come. We have so much in common. I have never met a woman I liked half so much.'

'Charles, you have fallen in and out of love on several occasions these past few years. How do know that this is not another fleeting romance?'

He stared hard at his sister; she must be a fair-weather friend if she could disregard Jane in this way. No, his mind was made up. He would not let them persuade him not to chance his luck.

'I am determined to ask her. You shall not make me change my mind on this matter, my friend.'

'But would you wish her to accept you out of duty? Her mother is set on the match. Can you imagine the pressure that will be brought on the poor girl to agree, even if she is not in love with you?'

'Darcy, I have no wish to embarrass her by asking her to marry me if she has not been thinking of the future as I have.' He dropped into a chair, unable to believe that he could be wrong in his assumptions. 'However, I shall go over and speak to her myself, try and ascertain her feelings before I speak to Mr Bennet.'

'Why not leave it until you return from London? I know you have to go tomorrow; leave it until you return. This will give you time to consider your feelings.'

'I know how *I* feel – I love her and I intend to marry her, whatever you say. But I will compromise. A few days can make no difference either way. I shall go to Town. That way I will be back all the sooner.'

'I feel that I must warn you that everyone is expecting you to make an offer. Mrs Bennet was talking as if it was a certain thing. That odious woman made it perfectly clear to anyone who would listen last night that she expected Miss Bennet to be installed at Netherfield by the New Year.'

'In which case Jane would feel obliged to accept me whatever her own feelings on the subject, just to please her parents. I could not do that to her; I love her far too much to bring pressure on her to accept me. I shall let the rumours cool for a few days and then return to see how the land lies.'

He pushed himself upright, feeling he had aged ten years in the past ten minutes. He looked across at his sister, but saw nothing but sympathy in her expression. If it had just been she who was against the match he would have totally ignored it, but Darcy would not willingly misdirect him. He did not want his friends. What he wanted was Jane Bennet to love him as much as he loved her, and now he was committed to travelling to Town before he could speak to her.

* * *

When Charlotte Lucas came to visit later in the day she was asked for her opinion on the matter of Mr Collins and Elizabeth. Like Jane, she declined to comment on the subject. When Elizabeth passed quietly out of the room, Jane followed as did Kitty. She was surprised that Charlotte remained behind, but not that Lydia did. Her youngest sister would be determined to hear all she could on the matter.

Fortunately, this was to be the end of the discussion. All they had to endure over the next two days was the occasional peevish allusion from Mrs Bennet. As to the gentleman himself, he appeared neither embarrassed nor dejected, but made every effort to avoid Elizabeth. When they were obliged to meet, he was silent and resentful in her presence.

After breakfast Jane was pleased to accompany Elizabeth and her other sisters on a walk into Meryton. The primary purpose of this was to enquire if Mr Wickham had returned. He joined them as they were entering the town and attended them to their aunt's house, where his regret and vexation and his concern for everybody was well talked over.

Darcy had decided to travel back to Town with him, leaving the ladies in residence alone at Netherfield. As the carriage was approaching Meryton, Bingley saw Jane and decided to ask the driver to pull over so that he could make his farewells.

As he lowered the window to lean out he saw a group of officers surround her and watched her laughing and talking as if she had not a care in the world. Indeed, she looked as amiable and happy as when she spoke to him. He sunk back onto the squabs and the carriage bowled past the group.

Perhaps Darcy had been right all along – Jane was an open, affectionate girl and responded to all in the same way. He had read too much into it; he must think about what he should do next.

He would not give up so easily. He had enough love on his side for both of them.

Mr Wickham and another officer walked back with Jane and her sisters, but they were fully occupied by Kitty and Lydia, and she was able to talk privately with Elizabeth.

'Mr Wickham said, Jane, that it was better that he did not meet Mr Darcy, that to be in the same room, the same party with him, for so many hours together might be more than he could bear, and scenes might arise unpleasant to more than himself.'

Jane nodded sympathetically. 'That was good in him, Lizzy. You must know that I am still puzzled by the whole thing. Mr Bingley has assured me Mr Darcy is not the guilty party, but when I see Mr Wickham I cannot believe that he can be the villain of the piece.'

The gentlemen were invited in, but she could not concentrate on the conversation, was waiting, watching the drive, starting at every sound, hoping Charles would come to speak to her father that morning. He did not come, but not long after they returned to Longbourn a letter was delivered.

It was addressed to her. She opened it, reading the contents with dismay. She could not believe what was written there. Jane became aware that her sister was watching her closely. It would not do to reveal her disquiet now and distress the rest of the company. Pinning a false smile on her face, she pushed the letter into her pocket.

It was difficult to participate, but she believed no one, apart from Elizabeth, realised there was anything amiss. Somehow she remained composed until the officers took their leave. Once they had departed, Jane excused herself and, with a quick glance at her sister, left the room and ran upstairs. As soon as they were inside their own apartment she removed the letter.

'Lizzy, this is from Caroline Bingley; what it contains has surprised me a good deal. The whole party has left Netherfield by this time, and are on the way to Town without any intention of coming back again. You should hear what she says.'

Jane read an extract from the letter and Elizabeth was astonished.

'They are going to Grosvenor Street, where Mr Hurst has a house? They have all followed Mr Bingley to Town? It hardly seems possible, Jane.'

'There is more, Lizzy. Let me read it to you.

> *'I do not pretend to regret anything I shall leave in Hertfordshire except your society, my dearest friend; but we will hope, at some future period, to enjoy many returns of the delightful intercourse we have known, and in the meanwhile may lessen the pain of separation by very frequent and most unreserved correspondence. I depend on you for that.'*

Elizabeth was not convinced. 'The fact that Miss Bingley and her sister wish to remain in London is nothing to the gentlemen, Jane. I do not suppose that their absence from Netherfield will prevent Mr Bingley's being there. And although I know you will miss their society, as long as you have his, that is all that matters, surely?'

Jane was not so sanguine. 'But, Lizzy, Mr Bingley will not wish to be apart from his family at Christmas time. He must stay in London with them at least until the New Year.' She stared down at the letter, still not quite comprehending how things had come to such a pass. Had she imagined the closeness she and Charles had shared over the past few weeks?

'You must not fret about it, Jane. I am sure that Bingley will not be detained in London by his sisters. It is only a short drive after all.'

'Caroline is quite clear that none of the party will return to Hertfordshire this winter. I shall read that part to you.

> *'When my brother left us, he imagined that the business which took him to London might be concluded in three or*

four days; but as we are certain that cannot be so, and at the same time convinced that when Charles gets to Town he will be in no hurry to leave it again, we have determined to follow him there so that he may not be obliged to spend his vacant hours alone. I sincerely hope your Christmas in Hertfordshire may give you the gaiety this season generally brings, and that your beaus will be so numerous so as to not allow you to feel the loss of the three, of whom we shall deprive you.'

Jane looked at Elizabeth. 'It is evident by this that he comes back no more this winter.'

'No, Jane, it is only evident that Miss Bingley does not mean that he should.'

'Why would you think so? It must be his own doing. He is his own master, after all. But you still do not know all of it. I will read a passage which especially hurts me. I will have no reserves from you.

'Mr Darcy is impatient to see his sister, and to confess the truth, we are scarcely less eager to meet her again. We do not think Georgiana Darcy has her equal for beauty, elegance and accomplishment; and the affection she inspires between Louisa and myself is heightened into something still more interesting, in the hope that we dare to entertain of her being hereafter our sister. My brother admires Miss Darcy already, and he will have frequent opportunity now of seeing her on the most intimate footing; her relations all wish the connection as much as I. And a sister's partiality is not misleading me, I think, when I call Charles most capable of engaging any woman's heart. My dearest Jane, in indulging the hope of an event which will secure the happiness of so many, I am sure you will concur.'

Jane lowered the letter; her eyes filled. How could she have been so mistaken as to believe that he returned her regard? She swallowed and attempted to regain her composure.

'What think you of this sentence then, my dear Lizzy? Is it not clear enough? Does it not expressly declare that Caroline neither expects, nor wishes me to be her sister; that she is perfectly convinced of her brother's indifference, that she suspects the nature of my feelings to him? She means most kindly to put me on my guard. Can there be any other opinion on the subject?'

Elizabeth leant over and removed the letter from her slack fingers and read the contents for herself. This gave Jane time to recover, but she was aware that the letter did not please Elizabeth any more than it had done her.

'Oh, Jane, I think you are reading too much into this. I have a totally different opinion. Do you wish to hear it?'

Jane nodded. 'Most willingly.'

'You shall have it in few words. Miss Bingley sees that her brother is in love with you, but wants him to marry Miss Darcy. She follows him to Town in the hope of keeping him there, and then tries to persuade you that he does not care about you.'

Jane shook her head. Caroline Bingley was her friend; she could not be so devious.

'Indeed, Jane, you must believe me. No one who has ever seen you together can doubt his affection. Miss Bingley, I am sure, cannot. She is not such a simpleton. Could she have seen half as much love from Mr Darcy for herself, she should have ordered her wedding clothes already. But the case is this. We are not rich enough, or grand enough for them; she is the more anxious to get Miss Darcy for her brother from the notion that when there has been one intermarriage, she may have less trouble in achieving a second.

'But, my dearest Jane, you cannot seriously imagine that because Miss Bingley tells you her brother greatly admires Miss Darcy, you are the smallest degree less certain of *your* merit? When he took leave of you on Tuesday, I cannot believe it was within her power to persuade him that, instead of being in love with you, he is very much in love with her friend.'

'If I viewed Miss Bingley as you do, then your supposition might make me quite easy. But I know the foundation is unjust. Caroline is incapable of wilfully deceiving anyone; all I can hope in this case is that she is deceived herself.'

'That is right. You could not have started a more happy idea, since you are not to take comfort in mine. Believe her to be deceived by all means. You have now done your duty by her; I must fret no longer.' Elizabeth tossed the letter to one side and began to pace the room.

'Lizzy, my dear sister, can I be happy even supposing the best, accepting a man whose sisters and friends are all wishing him to marry elsewhere?'

'You must decide yourself, and if upon mature deliberation you find that the misery of disobliging his two sisters is more than equivalent to the happiness of being his wife, then by all means you must refuse him.'

Now Elizabeth was being nonsensical. Jane found herself faintly smiling. 'Lizzy! How can you talk so? You must know that though I should be exceedingly grieved at their disapprobation, I could not hesitate to accept him if he offered.'

'I did not think you would not; and that being the case, I cannot consider your situation without compassion. It shall all come out the way you wish, my dear Jane. You must not despair.'

'As Mr Bingley is not to return any more this winter, my choice will never be required. A thousand things may arise in six months.'

'Now *you* are being nonsensical, Jane. If Bingley cares for you as much as I believe he does, then it would take considerably more than six months for him to change his mind. Good heavens, Jane, he is a man of independent means. He has no need to listen to his sisters or to take their advice, he can follow his own wishes in this matter.'

Jane joined her and they walked to the window to stare out across the park in companionable silence. Could Elizabeth be correct? Would it make no difference if Charles was away from home for a few months? Perhaps she was dwelling too much on the matter.

She must remember how she had felt when in his company, how much he had said to her, how his eyes had looked into hers in such a way as to make their meaning clear. 'I am not sure, Lizzy. But maybe you are correct that Caroline is mistaken about Miss Darcy. I shall not despair of seeing Bingley here again. After all, as you say, it is only a short drive from London to Netherfield.'

'Of course it is, Jane. Mr Bingley shall be here before Christmas and shall answer every wish of your heart. However, I think it might be wise in the present circumstances not to tell our mother of the true contents of this letter. She has not yet recovered from my refusal to marry Mr Collins. A further setback in her matrimonial plans might be disastrous for her nerves.'

Jane was forced to smile. She knew exactly to what her sister referred. They would all have a wretched time of it, if that was the case. 'Well, she knows that I have received the letter. I had better tell her that they have gone to London for the Christmas period, but Mr Bingley should be back in the New Year and living at Netherfield.'

She did not like to deceive her dear mother; but she had no

wish for any other member of her family to be distressed by what had happened. It was going to be wearisome, waiting for him to return. She walked back to pick up the letter, but Elizabeth was there before her.

'I am going to burn this, Jane; you do not wish to keep rereading it and making more of it than it rates.' Before she could protest, the paper was on the fire. As it turned into ashes she hoped that her love for Charles would not suffer the same fate.

11

The days dragged miserably. Jane was determined to keep her distress hidden from the rest of her family. Even Elizabeth should not know how much she feared she had been mistaken, that Caroline's interpretation of the situation was the correct one: that Charles was not returning to Netherfield and would not be making her an offer.

They were sitting together in the drawing room when Sir William Lucas arrived for an unexpected visit. Jane listened in astonishment to him telling her mother that Charlotte was to marry Mr Collins.

Lydia, always unguarded and often uncivil, boisterously exclaimed. 'Good Lord! Sir William, how can you tell such a story? Do you not to know that Mr Collins wants to marry Lizzy?'

Sir William did not respond angrily to her sister's rudeness but took it in good part and merely repeated that he had just given his permission for Charlotte to become betrothed to Mr Collins. It was then Elizabeth spoke up.

'I beg your pardon, ma'am, but Charlotte told me this

herself. It is the truth: she and Mr Collins are to be married.' Elizabeth turned to Sir William. 'I must offer my congratulations to you, Sir William. I am delighted that Charlotte is to marry Mr Collins. I honestly hope that they shall be happy together.'

Jane had now recovered from the shock and knew that she must add her good wishes. 'And I, Sir William, I wish them every happiness. Mr Collins is a man of excellent character, and Charlotte will be happy in the union, I am sure.'

It wasn't until Sir William had left that her mother gave vent to her feelings. It took a considerable time to convince her that the information was indeed correct, that Mr Collins had indeed changed his allegiance from Elizabeth to Charlotte within three days. Next Mrs Bennet declared that she hoped they would never be happy together and that the match might be broken off.

'It is entirely your fault, Lizzy. If you had not refused him in the first place, then it should be we that are celebrating. I cannot bear to think of it. I shall not forgive you for your part in this; do not think I shall.'

Later, in the privacy of their sitting room, Jane was able to discuss the matter with her sister. 'I am a little surprised at the match, Lizzy, but I do hope they shall be happy. Did not Charlotte say to us a few weeks ago that she viewed matrimony quite differently? That as long as she was comfortable then she should be happy without having her affections engaged.'

'I cannot accept that someone I considered to be a good friend could make such a poor choice in a husband. She is not lacking in sense, Jane; how could she bear to be in permanent contact with that man? He is a pompous, conceited…'

'Lizzy, you must not speak so of him. He is a good man. Admittedly he has rather a lot to say on most subjects, but his heart is true. You did not wish to have him for yourself, so you must not deny Charlotte and Mr Collins happiness together.'

Lady Lucas appeared rather more often than usual, over the next days, to discuss the forthcoming marriage, and Jane could not help but notice her mother was finding the whole situation difficult. Elizabeth's disappointment in Charlotte had produced a restraint between the friends, pushing them apart. She was sad to see it when they had been such bosom bows before.

She could not have got through the week since Charles had left without a word to her if it hadn't been for the constant support of her sister. Jane had sent Caroline an early answer to her letter, and was now counting the days to when she might reasonably hope to hear again.

Even Mrs Bennet began to think there was something decidedly odd about Mr Bingley's continued absence. Day followed day without bringing any other tidings of him, other than a report which shortly prevailed in Meryton, as to him coming no more to Netherfield the whole winter. This report highly incensed their mother, and she never failed to contradict it as the most scandalous falsehood.

Jane knew that her first understanding of the situation had been the correct one. There was nothing that Elizabeth could say to her that would convince her otherwise. It was not his sister keeping him away, but that he was indifferent to her and would not return any day soon. She knew this to be true. He had gone, and as soon as she was not close he had forgotten her; moved on to charm and delight a more fortunate young lady.

Jane did her best to conceal her anxiety but knew that her sister was aware how painful it was. By mutual consent they decided not to allude to the subject, knowing that as the days passed there could only be one answer, and it was that Mr Bingley had left her.

Unfortunately such delicacy was not within her mother's nature, and an hour seldom passed on which she did not talk of

Bingley, expressing impatience for his arrival. Eventually Mrs Bennet was moved to say to Jane herself, that if he did not come back, she might think herself very ill used.

Charles found himself much preoccupied by affairs with his lawyers and realised that he would not be able to return, as he had hoped, to Netherfield until after the festive season. He decided that he would write to Jane – that could do no harm – and let her know that he was thinking of her and would come down to see her in the New Year.

My dear Miss Bennet,

I must apologise for not calling in to see you after the ball. There is something I most especially wish to ask you and I am intending to come down to Netherfield in order to speak to you as soon as Christmas is over.

We are all spending the holiday season at Pemberley. I am much looking forward to it, but would enjoy it so much more if you were with me.

I am counting the days till we are together again and pray that you are going to say that I am not presumptuous in my sentiments towards you. I look forward to your earliest reply on this matter.

I send you my warmest regards,

Charles Bingley Esq.

He read the letter through several times but on this occasion did not ask Mr Darcy's advice as to its content. He knew it was tantamount to a proposal but was determined not to lose the woman he wished to spend the rest of his life with; if that meant going against the wishes of his family and friends, then so be it. One thing he knew he would not do, however, would be to coerce Jane into accepting him out of duty and the expectations of her mother.

He sincerely hoped that the few weeks' interim before he arrived at Longbourn would allow the gossipmongers time to move on to something else. He intended to arrange it so that Jane met him secretly; then if she did not wish to marry him her family would never know that she had refused such a beneficial offer.

He folded the letter and addressed it carefully to Longbourn and then placed it in the silver salver on the side table adjacent to the front door. There were already several letters waiting to be taken to the post by one of his footmen.

Caroline was visiting him, but she had spent the entire morning trailing around after Darcy. He believed she was getting more strident, more desperate to attract his attention by denigrating any other young lady he might have met. He was certain that his friend had no interest in his sister; perhaps he should warn him of her intentions.

She appeared in the vestibule. Her bonnet and pelisse were on, and as she approached he heard her carriage pulling up outside. 'Caroline, we have spent little time together this morning. I am sorry I had letters to write. I believe that we are attending a soirée at the Ponsonbys' tomorrow?'

He saw her glance at the salver. 'Shall I take the letters for you, Charles? I have several of my own to deliver; it will save one of your men the journey. It is foul weather today.'

Surprised she should be concerned for the welfare of his staff, but pleasantly so, he immediately agreed. 'Thank you, sister, that is most kind of you. Take care, and I shall see you tomorrow, no doubt.'

He watched her gather up the letters and slip them into her reticule. Raising a hand in salute he strode off to the billiard room to join his friend.

* * *

It took all Jane's sturdy mildness of temperament to endure the separation from Bingley with tolerable tranquillity. The letter from Caroline she had been dreading finally arrived and put an end to any doubt on the subject. The very first sentence conveyed the assurance of the Netherfield party being all settled in London for the winter, and concluded with her brother's regret at not having had time to pay his respects to his friends in Hertfordshire before he left the country.

Jane was glad she read the letter in solitude. She could not have hidden her grief. Hope was over, entirely over. She would have to learn to live with the destruction of her happiness, to realise that she had misinterpreted everything that had transpired between them. It was not Mr Bingley's fault; it was hers. He had never said he loved her; indeed, she had never said she loved him. It was a misunderstanding of the most upsetting kind.

Elizabeth had been walking in the park and did not know the letter had arrived until she returned. When she came in, Jane handed it to her. She could not bear to read out the contents as she had done last time. 'I do not wish to discuss this, Lizzy. It hurts too much. I must adjust myself to the fact that my hopes are dashed. I am sure that very soon I shall be composed again, and everything shall be as it was before I met him.'

She raised a hand as her sister made a move to comfort her. 'No, Lizzy, leave me be. It is better if we do not dwell on it.'

A further two days passed before Jane had courage to speak

of her feelings to Elizabeth. She was finding it difficult to remain sanguine when her mother was constantly referring to Netherfield and Mr Bingley.

'Oh! How I wish my dear mother had more command over herself, Lizzy; she can have no idea of the pain she gives me by her continuing reflection on him. But I shall not repine. It cannot last long. He will be forgotten, and we must be as we were before.' She could see her sister did not believe her statement. 'Do you doubt me? Indeed, you have no reason. He may live in my memory as the most amiable man of my acquaintance, but that is all. I have nothing either to hope or fear, and nothing to reproach him with. Thank God! I have not had that pain. A little time, therefore, and I shall certainly try to be better.'

She knew her voice betrayed her misery and she made an effort to sound more positive. 'I have this comfort immediately, that it has not been more than an error of fancy on my side, but it has done no harm to anyone but myself.'

Her sister would have none of this. 'Dear Jane! You are too good. Your sweetness and unselfishness are really angelic; I do not know what to say to you. I feel as if I had never done you justice, or loved you as you deserve.'

'Lizzy, you must not say such things about me. I do nothing out of the ordinary, I assure you. I can only behave as I do because I know that you love me dearly.'

'Jane, this is not fair. You wish to think all the world respectable, and not to speak ill of anybody. I only want to think you perfect, and you set yourself against it. There are few people whom I really love, and still fewer of whom I think well. The more I see of the world, the more I am dissatisfied with it. Every day confirms my belief of the inconsistency of all human characters. I have met with two instances lately: one I will not mention;

the other is Charlotte's marriage. It is unaccountable! In every view it is unaccountable!'

'My dear Lizzy, do not give way to such feelings as these. They will ruin your happiness. You do not make allowance enough for the difference in situation and temper. Consider Mr Collins's respectability and of Charlotte's prudent, steady character. Remember that she is one of a large family; and as to fortune, it is a most eligible match. Be ready to believe, for everybody's sake, that she may feel something like regard and real esteem for our cousin.'

Elizabeth was not to be diverted and spoke most strongly about both Charlotte and Mr Collins.

'I must think your language, Lizzy, too strong when you speak of them both, and I hope you will be convinced of it, when you see them living happily together. But enough of this. You alluded to something else. You mentioned two instances. I cannot misunderstand you, but I entreat you, dear Lizzy, not to dismay me by thinking of *that* person being to blame, and saying your opinion of *him* is sunk. We must not be so ready to fancy ourselves intentionally injured. We must not expect a lively young man to be always so guarded and circumspect. It is very often nothing but our own vanity that deceives. Women sometimes find their attention means more than it does.'

Her sister snorted inelegantly. 'They take care that they should.'

'If this is done by design, then it cannot be justified. I have no idea of there being so much design in the world as some persons imagine.'

'I am far from believing any part of Mr Bingley's desertion done by design,' her sister said. 'I do not believe he schemed to do wrong, or to make you so unhappy; there may be error and there may be misery. Thoughtlessness, want of attention to other people's feelings, and want of resolution will do the trick.'

'And do you impute it to be either of those?'

'Yes: to the last. If I go on, I shall displease you by saying what I think of persons who you still hold in esteem. Stop me whilst you can.'

'You persist then, in your comments, supposing his sisters have influenced him?'

'Yes, in conjunction with his friend, Mr Darcy.'

Jane shook her head. 'I cannot believe that. Why should they try to influence him? They can only wish him to find happiness, and if he is attached to me, no other woman can secure it for him.'

'That position is false; they may wish many things besides his happiness. They may wish him to increase his wealth and consequence; they may wish Mr Bingley to marry a girl who has all the importance of money, connections and pride.'

'Beyond a doubt, they do wish him to choose Miss Darcy.' Jane was finding it increasingly difficult to talk about these things. 'But this may be from better feelings than you are supposing. They have known her much longer than they have known me; no wonder if they love her better. Whatever may be their own wishes, it is very unlikely they should have opposed their brother's.

'What sister would think herself at liberty to do it, unless his choice was something very objectionable? If they believed him attached to me, they would not try to part us; if he was so, they could not have succeeded. I suppose in such a situation, you see everybody acting unnaturally and wrong, and me most horribly unhappy.

'Do not distress me by the idea. I am not ashamed of having been mistaken, or, at least it is slight; it is nothing in comparison with what I should feel to think ill of him or his sisters. Let me take it in the best light, in the light in which it may be understood.'

Elizabeth came over and they embraced fondly. 'I cannot go against you in this, Jane. I promise, from this point on, I shall not mention *his* name again.'

Jane made every effort to appear unmoved by his having departed from the neighbourhood. She left it to her sister to convince Mrs Bennet that they had all been mistaken in what had taken place between herself and Mr Bingley. Mr Wickham's society was of material service in dispelling the gloom into which the late perverse occurrences had thrown everyone at Longbourn. They saw him often, and added to his other recommendations that of general unreserve.

Jane could not be happy that what he had told Elizabeth privately was now common knowledge. Now that the Netherfield party had gone the whole of Meryton appeared to openly acknowledge that Mr Darcy was the wrongdoer. And he was condemned as the worst of men by everyone apart from herself. Whatever they thought, she could still not believe ill of any of them, even when the evidence was so compelling to the contrary.

Mr Collins duly arrived on his second visit but this time spent most of his time at the Lucas house. Her mother was heard to lament on many occasions that it would have been better for him to have stayed there and not put her to all this trouble. When Saturday arrived, he took his leave of his relations with as much solemnity as before, and wished his cousin health and happiness and promised he would write another letter of thanks to Mr Bennet.

Jane had found his visit, this time, more trying to her nerves; outwardly she appeared as calm and unruffled as ever, and even to Elizabeth she did not reveal the depth of her suffering. Just the thought of spending time with others who were celebrating their happiness made her more aware of her own loss.

She no longer thought of him as Charles. She could not blame Mr Bingley, Caroline or Mr Darcy for what had taken place. It had been *she* who had mistaken things; she had placed too much weight on the attention he had shown her. She overheard her aunt, Mrs Gardiner, who had arrived to spend the Christmas week with them, talking to Elizabeth on the subject.

'It seems likely to have been a desirable match for Jane; I am sorry it went off. But these things happen so often! The young man, such as you describe, Mr Bingley, so easily falls in love with a pretty girl for a few weeks, and an accident separates them, then they as easily forget her. This sort of inconstancy is a very frequent.'

Jane could not bear to remain where she could hear the conversation further. Her mother always said eavesdropping brought no reward to the listener. She decided not to join her aunt and sister in the drawing room, but go to the kitchen to see if she could help Hill with the Christmas preparations.

The Gardiners were great favourites and Jane enjoyed their company. Mr Gardiner, who was her mother's brother, was a sensible man, who made his living within view of his own warehouses, but was both well-bred and agreeable. Mrs Gardiner, who was several years younger, was an intelligent, elegant woman and both she and Elizabeth were very fond of her.

Indeed, their aunt already knew what had taken place at Longbourn as they had told her in their frequent correspondence. Over the Christmas period they were so busy – what with the Philipses, the Lucases, and the officers – there was not a day without its engagement, and although Jane found this fatiguing, being busy gave her little time to dwell on her own grief.

She watched Elizabeth flirting with Mr Wickham and was glad to see her sister enjoying herself. If Elizabeth knew how low she felt, then she would not be happy either.

'Do you know, Jane, our aunt believed that I am in love with Mr Wickham? Do you consider that I am in danger of being so afflicted?'

'I should hope not, Lizzy. He is a charming young man, but not at all suitable for you. Perhaps, if he had his own fortune, then maybe you could consider him.'

She stopped, not wishing to continue on the subject, as to go further would lead them into discussion of Mr Bingley and Mr Darcy, and that she could not bear.

'Jane, why do not you go back to London with our aunt and uncle? A change of scene will be good for you. There are too many unhappy memories here for you at the moment.'

Jane felt her spirits lift a little for the first time in a long while. 'I should like that above everything, Lizzy. But it is not for *me* to invite myself.'

'Fustian! You know we are both welcome there at any time. I shall run down now and mention it to our aunt.'

Jane continued to stab at her embroidery. She no longer knew what the image should depict; it had become unrecognisable as the stitches had been placed so haphazardly, her concentration not on her work. She looked up when the door was pushed open and saw Mrs Gardiner there, not Elizabeth.

'My dear Jane, I had been intending to ask you to come back with us, but was not sure if you should feel obliged to accept when in fact you did not really wish to come.'

Jane put her stitching down, smiling faintly. 'I should love to come. Your house is such a happy one. And it is possible that I might be able to spend some time with my friend Miss Bingley.'

She knew that Caroline was not living in the same house as

her brother, so she might occasionally spend a morning with her without any danger of seeing him.

* * *

The day came for her departure and she embraced her sister fondly. 'I shall miss you, dearest one; perhaps you could come up and visit during my stay?'

'I shall do no such thing, Jane, at least not at first. You need to be away from us all, not be reminded of what has taken place here. You must correspond with me, and I will write back to you immediately. And you must promise me, Jane, that you shall not stay at home, but go out on every opportunity to enjoy yourself.'

'I do not believe that Mr and Mrs Gardiner go about a lot in company, Lizzy. However, I promise, that if I *am* invited to a party, or an assembly, I shall not refuse. I know that I must get on with my life, and be open to new experiences.' Neither of them mentioned Mr Bingley, and for that Jane was grateful.

12

Jane was determined to enjoy her extended stay with Mr and Mrs Gardiner and their four children. As their carriage trundled away from Longbourn, she had hoped to feel her spirits lift a little, to find herself anticipating the treats to come whilst she was in Town.

Unfortunately this was not the case. The further they travelled from the comfort of her own home, and the companionship and love of Elizabeth, the lower her spirits sunk. She made an effort to reply cheerfully to the kind enquiries of her aunt and uncle, but in spite of her best attempts they realised something was awry.

Her aunt asked solicitously. 'My dear Jane, do you have the headache?'

Jane nodded dumbly. 'I am afraid that I do, Aunt Gardiner. Pray forgive me for my lack of energy. I shall be perfectly well when we have arrived and I have had time to rest.' Jane hated to deceive her relatives even on so small a point.

She felt it was her just desserts that by the time they actually arrived in Cheapside she did indeed have a fearsome megrim.

She was almost incapable of speech, her stomach roiled, and she felt that the right side of her head was about to come asunder from the left.

'Do not try to speak, my dear, and leave your belongings in the carriage. A servant shall collect them for you. Come along, lean on your uncle. We shall take you in safely; never fear.'

Jane scarcely recalled her passage across the pavement, up the steps and into the house. She was aware of a blur of little faces peering at her eagerly through the banisters, but was far too wretched to acknowledge them. Without the physical support of her uncle, she was certain she could not have reached the bedchamber allotted to her.

'There you are, my dear girl, you shall be comfortable directly. A maidservant shall take care of you now. I hope you are recovered soon.'

Someone, she was not sure who, removed her garments and replaced them with a cool nightgown. Then she was between the sheets, the bed hangings drawn, the shutters closed and she was left in the peace and darkness she craved.

It was to be several days before Jane felt herself sufficiently recovered to do justice to her warm welcome, and the loving kindness off her aunt and uncle, by joining them downstairs.

She had the exclusive use of a maidservant, and it was a luxury she enjoyed but believed she did not deserve. The girl shook out the folds of Jane's skirt and stood back to admire her handiwork. 'There, Miss Bennet, you look a treat. That green gown is perfect.'

'Thank you; I believe that I am ready to face my little cousins at last. I have heard them clattering up and down outside, but until now have not felt well enough to greet them.'

She had visited the spacious house in Cheapside on many occasions, but this was the first time she had been on her own. It felt strange to descend the stairs without Elizabeth behind her. Her sister would be wondering how she did; she had promised to write as soon as she had arrived. The stairs curved round to end in a long, black-and-white-tiled passage.

'There you are, my dear Jane. You are looking a lot better this morning. You are still heavy-eyed and far too pale, but that is only to be expected, having been so sick for the past two days.'

'I do feel a little weak, but I believe that after I have broken my fast and stretched my legs a little I shall be recovered.' She looked around, expecting to see her cousins waiting to greet her.

'Are the children are not up yet?'

'Good heavens, they have been up for hours. No, I have sent them out for a walk with the nursemaid to view the ships on the river. They shall not return until midday, so we have the house to ourselves.'

Jane followed her aunt to the rear of the house to a small, sunny room in which the family took their meals during the day. There was a larger, more formal dining room, but this was only used in the evening when there were guests present.

There was no sideboard with a selection of dishes waiting under silver lids in this house. Here, you asked for what you wanted and it was prepared especially. She thought that her aunt and uncle were considerably better off than her family, but did not believe in conspicuous expenditure. They liked to live simply, and she loved them for it.

'I should like tea, and whatever bread your cook has baked this morning. I do not think I could face anything cooked today; I do hope I am not inconveniencing you by coming down at so late an hour when everyone else has finished their breakfast.'

Her aunt laughed heartily. 'You must stop apologising to me, Jane. You know how it is; we stand on no ceremony here. We treat our staff well, and in return they are happy to deal with our irregular habits. I have not eaten yet myself, so I shall join you.'

She picked up the little brass bell from the table and rang it loudly. Immediately the door opened and an elderly maid appeared, her apron pristine, her cap white. The woman bobbed in a curtsy. 'Are you ready to order your breakfast, madam?'

'We are. Miss Bennet would like fresh bread, butter, and honey.' She turned to Jane who nodded. 'Also we should like tea and whatever pastries are freshly made this morning.'

Jane was not sure that her stomach was ready for any sweet treats, but she did not wish to disappoint her aunt by refusing.

The tea, and other things, arrived within a few moments and she was pleased to find she was able to eat an acceptable amount of what was provided, even managing to eat one of the freshly baked scones; this, spread with strawberry conserve, was quite delicious.

'What do you wish to do today, Jane? I expect you would prefer to remain quietly in the house, but if you wish to go down to the Honey Lane market, I should be happy to accompany you.'

'That is kind of you, Aunt, but I have letters to write. I promised I should write to Lizzy when I arrived. She will be worrying if I do not send a note today.'

Jane sharpened her pen, uncorked the ink bottle and sat pensively, wondering what to write. She could not tell Elizabeth she felt so low in spirits that she was finding it an effort just to get out of bed. No, that would not do. She must forget about Mr Bingley. He was the most amiable man she had ever met, and was certainly the first gentleman she had been in love with. She had no notion how long the pain of losing him would remain with her, having not been unrequited in love before.

Her letter to her sister was brief, apologising for its tardiness, explaining that she had an unpleasant megrim from which she was now fully recovered. Jane said the house was, as usual, warm and comfortable, her aunt and uncle perfect hosts, and that she was eagerly anticipating being reintroduced to her young cousins. There was nothing else of importance to say. She sanded the paper, folded and addressed it.

She had brought with her a small amount of pin money. Her father was not ungenerous in this regard, but as she did not know how long her visit was to last, she had gratefully accepted the offer of having all her correspondence sent at the expense of her uncle.

* * *

A week passed before she received a reply from Longbourn. Jane occupied the time by entertaining the children. Her steady sense and sweetness of temper exactly adapted her to tending to children in every way: of teaching, playing with them and loving them. She did not go out on morning calls, and no one came to visit. She thought she would write to Caroline and tell her again that she was staying in London with her relatives. Jane spoke to her aunt about sending a note round to Grosvenor Street and it was soon done, but she waited in vain for a reply.

* * *

By Christmas Mr Bingley had given up hope of receiving a favourable reply from Jane. He could only believe that she had been so distressed by his letter that he could not bring herself to answer. He was so low in spirits that even his sister remarked upon it.

'Charles, you must make more of an effort to be sociable.

Upon my word, I do believe you are becoming as difficult to please as Mr Darcy. Will you not come and join Georgiana, Louisa and I for afternoon tea?'

The last thing he wished to do was make small talk with the painfully shy Miss Darcy. However, whilst he was staying in Pemberley he must make the effort; he was a guest in his friend's house and he did not like to think that he was being found wanting in his duties. He must push his own sadness to one side and pretend that he was enjoying the carol singers, figgy pudding and other festive treats.

They stayed up to hear the bells ring in the New Year and as he raised his glass of champagne with the others, he made his own resolution. He would leave Derbyshire as soon as the weather improved and ride down to see Jane. He would not believe she had rejected him until he heard it from her own lips.

Ten days later he cantered into Meryton, a groom in attendance. He was unrecognisable under his many-caped coat, tall beaver hat and muffler. He had deliberately taken a horse from his stables that had not been with him in Hertfordshire.

'Jenkins, you know what you have to do? Go into the general stores and enquire after the Bennet family at Longbourn. Remember, you have a parcel to deliver to Miss Jane Bennet.'

The man swung down from the saddle and nodded, touching his cap with his whip. 'I ain't to tell them who the parcel's from, nor say you's outside.'

'Exactly so. I shall walk the horses whilst I wait. Do not be long; it is perishing cold standing around.'

Ten minutes later his man emerged. 'It ain't the news you was expecting, sir. Miss Bennet ain't there. She's gone away with friends for a visit.'

Bingley tossed the reins down and, not waiting for his groom to remount, clattered back down the High Street, his hopes in tatters. He must put all thought of a union between himself and Miss Bennet behind him. It was time to get on with his life, however bleak it might seem to him at the moment.

* * *

Jane was in low spirits. Not hearing from Caroline, she had at last gone to see her and had met with unexpected coldness, and she knew her association with them to be at an end. She hoped to retreat to her bedchamber but her aunt heard her coming in and came out to greet her.

'My dear, let me assist you in removing your outdoor garments. You look half frozen after your visit to Grosvenor Street.'

She was gently directed towards the small parlour and did not have the energy to refuse. Her bonnet and cloak gone, she had no excuse to leave the room. Reluctantly she took her usual chair and waited for her aunt to order tea and pastries.

'You are so kind to me; I do not deserve it. As you have guessed I met with a miserable reception and my connection with the Bingleys is finally terminated. Lizzy was right: I do not believe Caroline and Louisa held any real affection for me. They were bored and so took me up.'

'I am sure that you are far too sensible to repine. These things can happen to anyone, even someone as sweet and kind as you. Young men frequently embark on a little flirtation in order to pass the time. They mean no harm, and if you read more into it than was intended I am quite certain you have the strength of character to put it aside and get on with your life.'

'It is easy for you to say, but I am in love with Bingley. I cannot put that aside so easily.'

'I am afraid, my dear, that you must try. You have four sisters behind you, and it is important for you to be settled. There are plenty of agreeable men in London. It is just a matter of you finding one that will suit.'

'I cannot easily forget him, but I promise I shall make an effort.'

'That is all that I am asking – just be prepared to accompany us when we go out.' A maid appeared with the tray and Jane was relieved the conversation turned to other topics. A while later she excused herself.

'I am going upstairs to write to Lizzy. She will want to know what happened this morning. She never liked Miss Bingley or her sister, and I am afraid that I now must accept her opinion of them both. It is hard to see people in a poor light, but on this occasion I believe that I must do so.'

'I am not surprised, my dear. A true friend would not have kept away so long. You have no need to be associated with someone as proud and disdainful as those two.' Her aunt did not add any condemnation of their brother, but she knew it was implied. It was small wonder he had not been to see her. She must try and forget about him; he had obviously forgotten about her.

She sat the small table and wrote to her sister.

My dearest Lizzy,

I am sure you will be incapable of triumphing at my expense, when I confess myself to have been entirely deceived in Caroline's regard for me. But, my dear sister, though the event has proved you right, I still assert that, considering what her behaviour was, my confidence was as natural as your suspicion. I do not at all comprehend her reason for wishing to be intimate with me, but if the same circumstances were to happen again, I am sure I should be deceived again.

Caroline did not come to see me; and not a note, not a line, did I receive in the meantime.

When I did see her, it was very evident she had no pleasure in it, and she said not a word of wishing to see me again, and was in every respect so altered a creature that when I departed I was perfectly determined to continue the acquaintance no longer. I will endeavour to banish every painful thought, and think only of what will make me happy, your affection, and the invariable kindness of my dear uncle and aunt. Let me hear from you very soon.

I am extremely glad that you have such pleasant accounts from our friends at Hunsford. Pray go to see them, with Sir William and Maria. I am sure you will be very comfortable there.

She must make the best of things; indeed, she had the children to entertain her and her aunt had promised her they would go skating on the Serpentine tomorrow. It was a considerable time since Jane had skated. She hoped she would not have forgotten how to stay upright. Uncle Gardiner was to accompany them and this made the outing extra special for the children.

'Jane, will you hold my hand? I'm not very good at skating.'

'I believe it will have to be the other way round, Lucy, for I am more likely to slip than you.'

'No one is going to take a tumble this morning. When your papa is present the morning would not dare to be anything but perfect.'

The children giggled and with a deal of pushing and excitement the three adults and four children squeezed themselves into the carriage. The temperature had been below freezing for several days and Jane had been assured that the ice would be more than thick enough for skating without fear of falling through.

The carriage bumped to a halt behind several others. She could already hear shouts and cries of excitement coming from the lake. The carriage door opened, the steps were let down and the children scrambled out eager to don their blades and slide upon the ice. The youngest, Edward, was to be pulled by his father on a sled that had been carried on the luggage box.

Jane strapped on her skates with some trepidation. She had never been an expert at this sport and was rather dreading being the only member of the party unable to glide gracefully across the frozen surface. Her aunt was not skating; she was to sit on a stool and provide encouragement and refreshments when required.

'I am not sure this is such a good idea, Aunt Gardiner. I feel decidedly unstable and I am not yet on the ice.' The others had already skated off, leaving her to make her own way to the edge of the water.

'Go along, my dear. It will come back to you, I am sure. If you stay close to the edge you can step back onto the grass if you feel insecure.'

'It does look such fun. Everyone is laughing and their faces are glowing with health and happiness.' She glanced down at her woollen gown and heavy cloak. 'At least if I do slip over I have several layers of material to cushion my fall.'

With a few tentative steps she was suddenly away and travelling with increasing speed towards the centre of the ice. She knew herself to be dangerously out of control, her feet moving of their own volition, her balance precarious. She heard a warning shout behind her but could not respond.

Suddenly there was a hideous cracking noise as the ice in

front of her gave way. There was nothing she could do. She was going to plunge into the icy depths and drown. Her arms waved frantically and she threw her weight backwards hoping to avoid catastrophe. Then from nowhere someone grabbed her cloak and she was hauled away from danger at great speed. Her feet flew from under her and she tumbled, her limbs entangled with her rescuer, to the ice.

The breath was knocked from her lungs and her head spun, but she was safe. Too shocked to move she lay cradled against the warmth of another skater.

'My dear Jane, are you hurt? Here, let me assist you to your feet. The gentleman who saved you is unable to move until you do.'

Her uncle reached down and she was upright again. She leant her weight against him, needing his comforting bulk to support her. She felt someone gently lift each foot in turn and unstrap her blades.

'There, you can take her to the side now, sir.'

'Come along, Jane, I shall guide you to the bank. I promise I shall not let you fall. You are quite safe now.'

It was not until she was sitting on a stool beside her aunt, cocooned in warm blankets, that her head cleared sufficiently for her to take in what had happened, how close to an icy grave she had come. She looked up to see a ring of anxious faces staring down at her.

'See, children, I am none the worse for my adventure. But I think in future I shall sit on the grass and watch you skate.'

Her four cousins smiled. With the drama over, they were obviously eager to get back on the ice.

'Is it safe to continue, Uncle?'

'Perfectly, not only is the ice thick on this side of the pond it is also shallow water.' He turned to speak to someone who was standing outside the circle. 'My dear sir, we cannot thank you enough for saving Miss Bennet. Only your quick action prevented a tragedy.'

Jane pushed herself to her feet. She wished to thank the man who had saved her life. Before she could speak, the gentleman exclaimed in surprise.

'Miss Jane Bennet? I cannot believe it is you. I had no idea I was rescuing an old acquaintance.'

'Mr Fox! Of course, we did not recognise you at first. My word, my boy, you have certainly improved with age. I swear you have grown over a foot since we knew you all those years ago.'

Her uncle smiled at Jane. 'Surely, my dear, you remember Mr Fox? He was forever at our door that spring that you and Lizzy came to stay.'

Jane stared in bewilderment at this strange young man who appeared to know her. Who could he be? Surely she would remember someone so personable; after all, she had not had so many beaus.

'You do not recall me, do you, Miss Bennet? I am Bertram Fox. We met when you were staying with Mr and Mrs Gardiner six years ago. I wrote you poetry.'

'I do remember. Forgive me, Mr Fox. You have changed out of all recognition. The only thing about your appearance that is similar is the colour of your hair.'

He grinned, quite unabashed by her comment. 'I must hope that you have forgotten the poetry. It was even worse than my youthful appearance. I can promise you I shall not be entertaining present company with anything *I* have written.'

Jane remembered her sisters' scathing comments about his verses. 'I am relieved to hear you say so. Such pastimes are best left to experts, such as Lord Byron, do not you think?'

She held out her hand and he clasped it warmly. 'Thank you

so much, Mr Fox. I am in your debt. I do hope I did not hurt you when I fell.'

He released her and bowed. 'Miss Bennet, you certainly did not. I shall not detain you longer. I see that your carriage is waiting to take you home. Do I have your permission to call tomorrow to see how you do?'

'I shall look forward to your visit, Mr Fox. I thank you most sincerely for saving my life.'

Mr Fox bowed and stepped back onto the ice to glide back to join his party who were watching from a distance. Jane could not believe the small and insubstantial youth who had written her appalling poetry all those years ago could have metamorphosed into a charming and handsome young man.

'I do not need to spoil everyone's fun, I am quite content to sit here and watch the children enjoy themselves.'

'Mr Gardiner is to remain behind with them, I shall accompany you home and then return to collect them.'

'No, please, I am quite capable of travelling by myself.'

Alone in the carriage Jane had time for reflection. Had this brush with mortality been a sign that she must move on with her life, be grateful that she had a life still to live? Whether it was a nudge from the Almighty or not, she was determined to forget about her heartbreak and from now on make an effort to enjoy her visit to Town.

* * *

The following day Jane was waiting in the drawing room when Mr Fox arrived. He seemed as charming as he had yesterday and soon she was conversing happily, giving him information about everyone at Longbourn. Naturally she did not mention Netherfield, or the reason she was staying in Cheapside on her own.

'Tell me, Mr Fox, where did you get to? One minute you were writing me verses stating your undying adoration, the next you had vanished into space.'

'I am afraid that I am not of independent means, Miss Bennet. My expectations are good, but I am at the beck and call of my grandmamma. It is from her that I shall inherit. I am sure you understand how these things work?' He smiled ruefully. 'I must dance to her tune whilst she is alive in order to live comfortably when she is not. I was called away by her, and by the time I returned you had gone home.'

Jane thought this rather cold-hearted. 'But you are fond of your elderly relative? I cannot imagine there is not a serious attachment on both sides.'

He smiled warmly. 'I apologise. I must have sounded an unloving grandson. You are quite right: I could not bear to do as I do if I disliked her. She is a delightful, if demanding, old lady.'

He stroked his waistcoat lovingly. 'Do you know, she called me a popinjay when I appeared in this, and she gave it to me herself and I had only worn it to please her.'

Jane giggled and took stock of the gentleman's attire; his waistcoat was red and gold stripes; however, his jacket was bottle green and quite inoffensive, as were his inexpressibles and shiny Hessians. 'I believe her judgement a trifle harsh, sir. Apart from your waistcoat there is nothing startling about your appearance.'

Mr Fox grinned. 'I must admit I have become inordinately fond of this lurid article. I love to see the shock on the faces of people when I turn round to greet them.'

The morning call passed far quicker than Jane could have anticipated. When he departed, he asked permission to call again the next day and she immediately agreed. He was delightful company, made no demands upon her, and was already a friend of the family. What harm could it do to get to know him a little better? For the first time in many weeks she had been able to forget her heartache. Her aunt and uncle were impressed with him too.

'Could I ask you a special favour? I should be most grateful if you refrained from mentioning in your letters to Longbourn about my meeting Mr Fox again. I do not wish to raise unnecessary expectations; I am sure you know to what I refer.'

'Of course, my dear girl – I fully understand your wish for discretion,' said her aunt.

But despite the need for discretion, Jane felt happier than she had in many days.

The next morning Jane was woken by all four children who had escaped from the nursery in order to tell her some wonderful news. Lucy led her siblings, and was the one who shook Jane by the shoulder.

'Jane, you must wake up; it is already past nine o'clock. We have something amazing to tell you.'

Instantly alert, Jane pushed herself upright to be confronted by four eager little faces. 'Good morning, children. I am tardy; that is quite clear. Now, what is it that could not wait until I came down?'

The smallest child, Tommy, broke free of the restraining hands of Emily, who was, as second oldest, delegated to take charge of him. He dodged under Lucy's outstretched arm and scrambled up onto the bed, his eyes sparkling with excitement. 'It's snowing! It is. There's lots and lots and lots.'

'How exciting! I cannot wait to go out into the garden and build a huge snowman with you all. However, I think I might be cold if I came in my nightgown.'

Tommy squealed with glee. 'Come, come, we don't mind. You can put your cloak and boots on top.'

Lucy took charge. 'Get down from that bed this instant,

Thomas Gardiner. We have told Jane about the snow; now we must let her get ready.'

Jane hugged the little boy and gently pushed him from the bed. 'I have a favour to ask all of you. Do you think you could do it for me?' A chorus of assent greeted this question. 'I should like you to run down and ask your mama, if I am not too late, if I may have toasted bread, tea and butter and honey for my breakfast.'

The children scampered off, eager to arrange her meal. They all knew that the sooner she breakfasted the quicker she would be outside playing with them. It was a long time since she had built a snowman and she was as eager as they to begin the task.

Dressed warmly and armed with spades, the intrepid party emerged into the rear garden to begin the construction. Jane had not been there long when she heard her aunt calling her from the back door. She glanced round to see Mr Fox emerge with what looked like a basket of vegetables and old clothes under one arm.

'Good morning, Mr Fox. You are most welcome here. I am unused to building snowmen. Let me introduce you to my cousins.' Each child bowed or curtsied politely, but then Thomas grabbed his hand.

'What have you got there, sir? Are we having a picnic in the snow?'

He dropped to a crouch, carefully placing the basket on the ground. 'No, Thomas, my friend, here I have the garments this gentleman shall require as soon as he is finished. I also have a carrot for his nose and two onions for his eyes.'

Jane watched him playing with the children. He was completely at ease in their company and very shortly her reserve dissipated and soon she was laughing as loudly as the children at his antics. When the snowman was complete, she stood back to admire it whilst the children put on its muffler and cap.

'I have so enjoyed this morning, Mr Fox. It was kind of you to give up your time to entertain the children.'

'It was entirely my pleasure, Miss Bennet. I love children and I can see that you do to. However, my feet are solid and I am in need of a hot drink. I do hope my hard work merits such a reward?'

'It does indeed, sir. Come along, children, it is time to go in and get warm.'

Elsie, their nursemaid, was waiting to collect them and whisked them back upstairs to get into dry garments. Her aunt was waiting to greet them both.

'Mr Fox, I have mulled wine and hot soup waiting in the breakfast parlour. I do hope you can stay and join us?'

Jane was pleased that he agreed. The more time she spent in his company, the better she liked him. It was obvious that her aunt and uncle approved of him as well.

13

'Darcy, I swear if I have to look at another statue or admire any more pictures I shall shoot myself,' Charles cried flinging himself into an armchair. His spirits had been low ever since leaving Netherfield, and although he had tried to fit in with his friend and put his gloomy thoughts behind him, enough was enough.

'Good God! I had not realised how bored you were today; you disguised your feelings admirably.'

'Georgiana was so happy to be there, I would not have dreamt of spoiling her pleasure in the occasion. She is a sweet girl, although she is rather too solemn. She rarely laughs out loud, and it was all I could do to prise the occasional smile from her.'

'I expect she will grow out of her shyness; she enjoys your company, and I thank you for coming with us today. Now, let us go to our club.'

They went to White's. They had no sooner settled themselves there than they heard the name Darcy spoken from an alcove behind them. Instantly alert, his friend sat up and deliberately eavesdropped on the conversation.

'I believe that Miss Darcy is to make her come-out next season; now she would be ideal for you, Winterton. She has an impeccable pedigree and over £100,000.'

Charles recognised the speaker; it was an acquaintance of his, Lord Rivenhall. His companion answered immediately.

'I do not take soiled goods, my friend. Did you not know I saw her last summer walking in Ramsgate, unchaperoned, and an officer from the militia with his arm around her waist. If she is already chasing officers, she will not do for me.'

Darcy's face blanched and his jaw became rigid. Charles knew what must come next. His friend stood up and stepped round to face the two gentlemen who had the temerity to slander his sister's name. He addressed the man who had just spoken.

'Sir, I overheard your comments. They are untrue and you will apologise immediately for casting aspersions on the good name of an innocent young lady.' He glared down at the man slouched in his chair, waiting for the retraction.

Slowly the gentlemen in question straightened until he was standing nose to nose with Darcy. 'I retract nothing. I know what I saw. Are you calling me a liar, sir?'

'I am. The lady is my sister, and I can vouch for her innocence. Such slander shall not be bandied abroad.'

Rivenhall attempted to smooth the situation. 'Darcy, I am sure there is an explanation. Lord Winterton is a friend of mine; he would not malign a lady unless he was certain of his facts. I expect it was not Miss Darcy he saw, but someone else entirely and it is a case of mistaken identity.'

Winterton, a tall thin gentleman of aristocratic mien, shook his head vehemently. 'I know what I saw. You shall apologise, Darcy, or name your second.'

'I certainly shall not apologise. Mr Bingley shall stand for me. He will attend on you and the time and date can be arranged.'

Lord Winterton nodded. 'Very well. Rivenhall, will you stand for me?'

'Are you sure this is the best way to proceed, Winterton? Can the matter not be settled any other way?'

'It cannot,' Winterton said firmly.

As they left the club, Charles recalled the dislike in which Darcy held Mr Wickham. His mouth became dry. Georgiana had indeed spent the summer in Ramsgate; had she become embroiled with Wickham and could this be what had caused the rift between this man and his friend?

* * *

Two days after the building of the snowman, Jane was eyeing the weather with disfavour. 'Do you think it is going to snow again, Aunt Gardiner? Mr Fox is calling for me later in order to take me for a drive in the park. I shall be disappointed if we cannot go.'

'The sky is overcast, but I do not think they are snow clouds overhead. If you wrap up warm, and put a hot brick at your feet, I am sure you shall come to no harm even if it does.'

'In which case, I shall go at once and get ready.' She paused at the door. 'You were quite right to insist that I make more effort. I am beginning to feel more myself every day. The charming company of Mr Fox is expediting matters.'

Muffled in extra clothing, including a red flannel petticoat that her aunt had produced from her own wardrobe, Jane scarcely recognised herself in the over-mantel mirror. 'Good gracious! I look quite stout dressed as I am. I do hope my strange appearance will not disappoint my escort.'

Her aunt laughed. 'I should think not. Dressed in a flour sack you would still look lovely. It's a great shame your pretty bonnet must be hidden under the hood of your cloak.' A knock on the door heralded the arrival of Mr Fox.

'I must not tarry. It is far too cold to keep his team standing.'

A parlourmaid already had the front door open and Jane ran lightly down the stairs. Mr Fox was waiting to hand her into his curricle.

'Good day, Miss Bennet. I am glad to see you are well wrapped up. I should hate for you to be cold. You will observe that the unfortunate boy who was sent out with your hot brick is now obliged to hold the horses for me.'

'I am sure you have given him recompense for his extra duties. I am so looking forward to this excursion. It is a long time since I have driven out with a gentleman.' She smiled shyly as he assisted her onto the seat. 'In fact, if I am strictly honest, apart from my father and uncle I have never been driven by a gentleman.'

He chuckled as she hoped he would, and by the time she had tucked herself under the rugs he was beside her, the ribbons in his hand.

'It is not far to the park, and I doubt there will be many taking the air today. Have you ever driven, Miss Bennet?'

'I have taken the gig around the neighbourhood on more than one occasion. It is something I always enjoy, but I must own I prefer to be in the saddle than behind the horses.'

'If the park is quiet, would you like to take the ribbons?'

She viewed the spirited chestnut geldings who were tossing their heads and stamping their hooves in their impatience to be moving. 'I should love to, but only if you think I am capable of controlling your team. Our docile mare is quite a different proposition to your animals.'

Holding the reins was an exciting experience and she was sad when a group of riders and a few assorted phaetons, plus several curricles approaching meant she had to hand them back to Mr Fox.

'Thank you; that was a most enjoyable experience. Look, two of the riders are coming over to us. Are they friends of yours?'

'I am afraid that they are. Would you object if I do not introduce you? I do not believe your aunt or uncle would wish you to be acquainted. They are a lively bunch, but harmless enough.'

Jane felt a moment's disquiet, but it was too late to complain as the men were upon them. She shrank back inside the protection of her hood and remained barely noticeable as the gentlemen exchanged pleasantries. She made an effort not to listen to their conversation but overheard something that filled her with trepidation. Surely Mr Fox would not be so foolish as to join in a race to Ryegate?

Before she could voice her objections, her companion snatched up the reins and flicked his whip. The horses sprang forward and she was forced to grip the side of the vehicle to avoid being tossed out.

'Mr Fox, I do not wish to be involved in any races and especially not out of town. Driving unchaperoned in the park is quite acceptable; anything else is not.'

He laughed and glanced across at her, his eyes glittering strangely. He was like a stranger to her, and she did not like what she saw. He ignored her protest and waved to his friends who were riding along beside him. 'Do not look so anxious, Miss Bennet. I'm an excellent whipster; you will come to no harm with me. It will be capital fun. My cronies have wagered a small fortune on the event. You shall be home before dark – never fear.'

With that he turned his attention to his driving and she was left to hang on as best she could. At least it was small comfort to know she was unrecognisable inside her dark cloak. She had thought when she had first seen him this morning that Mr Fox, in his many-caped driving coat, his beaver pulled down low over his eyes and his muffler tied several times round his neck looked a trifle rakish, but she had dismissed this as nonsense. She bitterly regretted her decision to accompany him now.

The first flakes of snow began to fall as he drove his curricle after the two phaetons. Jane called out for him to stop, but her words were whipped away by the wind. Too soon they had left the safety of London and were out into the countryside. The snow, after the first flurry, had stopped and the road was clear. The riders were ahead, the racing carriages almost out of sight. But a curricle pulled by matching greys edged closer. Jane's heart skipped a beat. Surely the driver did not intend to overtake on such a narrow road? She screamed a warning and Fox looked round. To her horror, instead of giving way he slapped the reins and cracked his whip, urging his team faster.

Suddenly Jane found herself a passenger in a second race and knew it might end in disaster for one or both of the vehicles. Frantically she grabbed at his hands, trying to make him give way, but he shook her off.

'Relax. Enjoy the experience. There are not many ladies who will have had the opportunity you're getting. Concentrate on staying on the seat. I should hate you to be thrown out; I should not be able to stop and collect you until the race is over.'

For a moment Jane thought he was serious, then he laughed at her shock, but did not rein back, in fact urged his team faster. Jane glanced sideways and froze, almost losing her grip. The curricles were racing wheel to wheel. The slightest error on either driver's part and they would all be killed.

She thought it better to close her eyes and pray. There was little else she could do of any benefit. The noise beside her lessened and she risked a look. Mr Fox had beaten his rival; they were pulling ahead. Thank God! Now perhaps he would agree to turn back, would listen to her pleas, remember he was a gentleman and not behave in this wild manner.

Then the carriage lurched and she was hurtling through the air to land in a deep ditch upon a soft bed of snow. As she lay there catching her breath, she heard several carriages thunder past and was not sure if she was scandalised or relieved that they did not stop to enquire if anyone was injured.

Carefully she flexed each limb in turn and was pleased to find them undamaged. She rolled over onto her knees and scrambled up. She could not see out of the ditch and found it was too steep for her to climb out unaided. She remembered the last thing Mr Fox had said to her and shivered.

A gaunt face appeared above her. 'I say, I am most dreadfully sorry. We hit a pothole, and before I could take hold of you, you vanished. Stretch up your hands. I shall have you out in a jiffy.'

Her fear vanished to be replaced by justifiable anger. She thought she had better wait until she was safely out of the ditch before she told him exactly what she thought of him. He was irresponsible, reprehensible, and she never wished to see him again.

Safely on the road she shook the worst of the snow from her person and glared at Mr Fox. She disliked being cross, but would make an exception in his case. She drew breath to begin, but he forestalled her.

'Do not look at me like that, as though you hate me. I deserve it. I have behaved appallingly. I cannot imagine what came over me. Please will you forgive me?'

He looked so wretched, she had not the heart to chide him. 'I accept your apology, Mr Fox. However, I wish to return home at once. You might not be aware of it, but it is snowing. If we do not set off immediately we might be unable to get home.'

They had been travelling a little over fifteen minutes when the blizzard arrived. Within moments the visibility was reduced to yards and Jane knew it was becoming dangerous to proceed. 'Mr Fox, it is getting thicker by the minute. Do you not think we should find somewhere to shelter until it stops?'

'I am not leaving my cattle out in this weather, Miss Bennet, so I suggest unless you see a coaching inn, or somewhere with a barn, you resign yourself to travelling in the snow.'

'I can scarcely see my hand in front of my face. How do you intend to drive safely if you cannot see?'

'I have told you already I am an expert. I should be grateful if you would remain silent and allow me to concentrate. If we come to grief because of your constant complaining, you shall only have yourself to blame.'

* * *

Charles went round to speak to Lord Rivenhall at his lodgings in Albemarle Street, in order to arrange a time and date suitable for both parties. As Darcy was the challenger, Lord Winterton had the advantage of being able to select his weapons of choice. Pistols were decided on but the date was not settled.

'It would be better to leave matters until the snow has cleared, don't you think, Rivenhall?'

'Winterton is out of town at the end of February, so it has to be before then.'

'Shall we say two weeks from today? Has your man any suggestions for the venue? I have never been involved in such an enterprise before and have no notion where it should take place.'

'Winterton has written the directions out for you. This is a bad business. I sincerely hope your friend Darcy comes out of it in one piece.'

'He is an excellent shot. It is Lord Winterton who should beware. Shall *we* bring the doctor?'

'Do that. Now that unpleasant matter is out of the way, would you care to share a bottle of claret with me at the club?'

Charles thought it would be helpful to learn more about Darcy's adversary and the best way to achieve that end was to provide Rivenhall with drink. When he was bosky he might let something of importance slip. 'Should be delighted. I have my carriage outside; I can give you a ride.'

All he had discovered by the time he returned home was that Winterton had fought three duels and come out the victor in each. Two of his victims had recovered; one had died several weeks later when his wound putrefied.

Although he had bragged about Darcy's ability, he was certain he had never used a weapon against a human being. When it came to it, would he be able to pull the trigger and watch a bullet enter another person?

It was too late to withdraw. Two weeks hence he must accompany Darcy to a deserted woodland on the outskirts of the city and stand by whilst someone was injured, possibly fatally. He blamed himself for not having prevented the challenge being issued. Darcy blamed Wickham. Charles prayed that his friend would emerge unscathed and would not have to flee the country for killing his opponent. He had not known how formidable Darcy could be when his family's honour was impugned, and was relieved that it was not he who would be fighting.

* * *

The snow was falling more heavily but still Mr Fox drove on. Jane caught a glimpse of something through the whiteness and tugged at his sleeve. When he looked round, she pointed.

'Mr Fox, I think I see a building just ahead. Could we not stop there until the worst of the snow has passed? Twice now your horses have slipped. Surely you do not wish to risk them breaking a leg?'

'You are right. I believe there might be some sort of dwelling ahead. I shall get down and lead my team. You remain here and try not to fall off again.'

With this brusque comment, he hooked the reins over the post and jumped down. She could hear him talking softly to his horses. It was obvious that he cared more about their welfare than he did hers.

With the collar of his coat turned up, his muffler wrapped around his face leaving only his eyes visible and his driving gloves protecting his hands, he was scarcely recognisable. Indeed, Mr Fox was *not* the kind of gentlemen she had supposed. She could see he was using the end of his whip to probe the road ahead, checking it was safe to proceed.

Enough was enough. Sitting on the box she got the full force of the blizzard in her face. She would be far better off walking beside the carriage as he did. She had stout boots on her feet, so she would come to no harm on the ground. The carriage lurched and halted, momentarily giving her the opportunity to scramble down before it moved off again.

Jane felt her way forward until she could grip onto the traces and steady herself. Perhaps it would be of help if she led the second horse? Her appearance beside Mr Fox so startled him he pitched forward into the whiteness, leaving the team to walk over him. She eased the carriage to a standstill. The horses were so demoralised by the conditions they showed no desire to continue without guidance.

She hurried back to find Fox spread-eagled in the snow. For a moment she thought him injured but then he was heaving himself up to his knees.

'I beg your pardon, Mr Fox. I could not see you in the blizzard.'

He spat out a mouthful of snow before answering. 'Good God, Miss Bennet, what are you thinking of? You should not creep up on a fellow. You scared me half to death. What are you doing down here anyway? Did I not tell you to stay where you were?'

'I thought I might be of more use leading the other horse.'

He brushed himself down angrily, but did not answer. Jane was unsure if she should try and placate him, or leave him to recover his temper. She did not like to be at odds with anyone, even someone like Mr Fox.

'How much further do you think it is to the dwelling?'

'Another two minutes at the most. If you are ready, Miss Bennet, we must press on.'

This was exactly the news she had been hoping to hear. The sooner they were inside the better. She was numb to the bone; his horses would be in a worse state. They were up to their hocks in snow. They were prime blood, not built to withstand this sort of weather. They needed to be out of the blizzard if they were going to survive this experience. She counted her footsteps in her head, having calculated it would be in the region of twenty paces to the farm. The horse she was leading was tiring, its head low, breath heaving in its chest. The farm had better be close. She doubted if any of them could continue for long in these conditions.

Suddenly the horses increased their pace and she was almost swept from her feet. A large black shape emerged from the swirling snow and she knew they had arrived. Thank God. It was a barn, not a dwelling, but it was ideal for their purpose.

Clinging desperately to the cheek strap of the horse she was leading, she prevented it from surging forward. Only one door was open. The carriage would be smashed if they tried to enter.

'Hang on, Miss Bennet, I shall have the door open in a second.' The barn had little snow in front of it; the blizzard was blowing from the rear. Mr Fox wrenched the door wide and the horses rushed in, carrying Jane with them.

Inside it was gloomy, but she could see at once that the roof was sound, the walls well maintained, and even better, there was a thick bed of straw across the far end of the structure.

'Miss Bennet, could I ask you to help me with the horses? It is imperative that we get them warm. We shall not get back to Town without them.'

By the time the animals were comfortable and contentedly munching on an armful of sweet-smelling hay, Jane was warm enough to remove her cloak. Mr Fox had ventured outside again to fill a pail with snow. He had said it would soon melt in the warmer temperature inside the barn.

Her hair was tumbling down to her shoulders, her bonnet hanging by its ribbons. She was hot and dirty but did not care. It was enough to be out of the elements and to know that the horses would not perish after all. Perhaps she had been mistaken about Mr Fox; he had been under great stress after all. Since they had arrived he had been everything he should be, enquired after her health, and praised her for her fortitude.

A cloud of snow blew into the barn as he returned from his errand. Triumphantly he waved his bucket. 'It is melting already, Miss Bennet. I shall be able to water the horses in a little while.'

Jane relaxed. Her charming companion was restored to her, the unpleasant hectoring stranger gone. 'It was fortuitous the farmer had left empty sacks in here. They are not pretty but serve to keep the animals warm.' She pointed to a space she had cleared. 'I have put the rest down there. We shall have somewhere dry to rest whilst we wait for the weather to clear.'

'An excellent plan – I am decidedly fatigued after all this unaccustomed exercise.' His teeth flashed white in the darkness. 'I declare, Miss Bennet, I much prefer building snowmen.'

'As do I. It is becoming cold in here; I am uncertain whether I should put on my cloak or wait until we go outside again.' She heard the clatter of the bucket being placed down and then he was beside her, standing uncomfortably close. He had somehow managed to discard his driving cape in those few seconds. She attempted to step away but he grabbed her arms.

'Come, my dear, I have a far better way of keeping warm. What harm is a kiss between friends?'

* * *

Charles slept little the night before he was to act as second at Mr Darcy's duel. He had inspected the box of duelling pistols to ascertain they were in perfect working order far more times than was necessary. Long before dawn he was downstairs, enveloped in a dark cloak, his hat pulled low over his eyes and the wooden box under his arm. His head groom had been taken into his confidence and was to drive the closed carriage to collect Darcy and the physician.

Outside it was still pitch-dark, but the weather had improved and the snow was long gone. There were few people about at this time of the morning and he was at his destination in good time.

Two similarly cloaked figures waited outside the house.

He unlocked the door himself and kicked down the steps to allow the doctor and Darcy to enter the carriage. They did no more than nod a greeting to each other; no one had any desire to converse this morning. The impending challenge weighed heavy on all their shoulders. All three of them could be arrested if discovered, and Darcy had the added burden of considering he could be killed.

The coach trundled through London, each gentleman resting in silence in their own corner of the vehicle. An hour after leaving Town the carriage slowed and Charles knew the moment had come. He leant across the carriage and gripped his friend's hand firmly.

'Good luck, Darcy. This is a wretched business.'

'I think you should both remain in the carriage whilst I go and talk to Rivenhall. There is no need for either of you to be seen until later.'

'Very well, Bingley. I have only to remove my outer garments; that will be the work of minutes. I am ready whenever you call me.'

The third figure in the carriage said nothing. No doubt he was praying that his skills would not be required that morning. Charles wondered how much Darcy had had to pay the man to get him to accompany them.

The first glimmer of light was coming over the horizon, sufficient for him to see that Darcy's opponent was already there. Across the clearing he could see a similar closed carriage. With the pistols under his arm, he marched towards it; he was no more than halfway there when a dark shape emerged from the gloom and almost ran towards him.

'Is that you, Rivenhall?'

'Of course it is, Bingley. Thank God you have come promptly.'

'I have to ask, is Lord Winterton prepared to apologise?'

'No, let's get this affair over.'

Charles opened the box of firearms. 'Do you select for your man, or must he do it himself?'

Rivenhall barely glanced at the weapons. 'I shall take one to him. We know that Darcy is an honourable man; he would not have tampered with either of them.'

With the remaining pistol Charles hurried back to the carriage. Darcy stepped out as he approached, dressed only in his shirt and breeches. He must be half frozen, but had insisted he could not aim true in his jacket.

'I have loaded and primed this for you. Lord Winterton will not retract so you must proceed. Do you intend to delope?'

'I shall not kill him; that is all you need to worry about.'

He saw a similarly garbed figure emerge from the other carriage. His hands were shaking. He hoped that Darcy's were steadier. He studied his friend. He appeared almost relaxed, no tension in his jaw, the hand holding the pistol resting casually at his side. One would think Darcy fought a duel every day of his life.

He watched him stride into the centre of the clearing where he halted. Not a word was spoken. Their breath clouded around their heads as the sun crept over the horizon. Darcy stood back to back with Winterton. Charles was to count the paces out loud. When he reached twenty, the men would turn and fire.

'One, two, three...' His voice was loud in the early morning silence. 'Eighteen, nineteen, twenty.'

Darcy turned slowly and raised his weapon. Winterton fired and Charles saw his friend sway slightly to the right and the bullet whistled harmlessly past his head. Good God! Winterton had aimed to kill. What would Darcy do in return?

A second explosion and this bullet found its target. A patch of scarlet stained Winterton's shirt and he staggered back. Darcy dropped his weapon and shouted for the doctor.

'Andrews, your services are required. Lord Winterton has a bullet through his shoulder.'

The doctor scampered past, his medical bag in one hand, his black cloak flying around him. Charles felt his pulse return to normal. 'My God, Darcy, that was the finest piece of shooting I've ever seen. You were magnificent. I was quaking in my boots, but you were as cool as if you were taking a morning stroll.'

'We must leave Andrews to return with Lord Winterton. We are finished here. Shall we find somewhere to breakfast?'

Charles slapped his friend on the back. 'I doubt we'll find anywhere satisfactory in this benighted place. However, the Red Lion is not too distant and they do a magnificent spread.' He was about to retrieve the pistol when he heard the sound of galloping horses. Good grief! The constables! Word of the duel had somehow reached the authorities; if they were apprehended all would be up for them.

'Run for it, Darcy; we are discovered.'

His friend was no more than three strides from the vehicle but he had further to go. He covered the last few yards in seconds, shouting to his driver to whip the horses up. The carriage was already in motion as he dived for the open door. Two strong hands gripped the collar of his cape and he was tumbled head over heels inside. The door slammed shut behind him. The chase was on.

14

Jane struggled but his fingers tightened, biting into her arms. 'Release me, sir. You forget yourself. I demand that you take me home at once. I have no wish to remain here with someone who is not a gentleman.'

'The road is impassable, my horses not fit to go out. You have no choice, so why not enjoy yourself?'

Her left foot connected sharply with his ankle and then with her right she stamped on his toes. Swearing volubly he staggered back and she was free, but for how long could she fend him off? If he was really determined to ruin her there was no one to hear her cries for help.

'You're mighty high in the instep for a provincial miss. Do not look so scared. I shall not touch you again. I'll not have you say I compromised you. I have no wish to be leg-shackled to a penniless young woman; I have grander plans.'

Retrieving her discarded cloak, she hastily slung it over her shoulders. She would not stay a moment longer with this monster. She would walk all the way back to London if he would not drive her. 'I insist that we return at once. I am sure that your horses are fit enough to resume their journey.'

'The road is impassable, you stupid girl. Why do you think we are marooned here in the first place? Go ahead, see for yourself.'

Jane inched the door open and to her delight the snow had passed, and she could see they had not been nearly as much fallen on the roads as she had thought. Triumphantly she turned to her attacker.

'The blizzard has gone. There is barely an inch on the road. It will be perfectly safe to return.' She glared at him, more angry than she had ever been in her life before. 'You are a perfidious gentleman. I have been much deceived by you. I pity the young lady who finds herself your wife.'

Not waiting for his assistance she pushed the doors wide open then stalked back to where the horses were standing and grabbed the bit of the nearest animal. If he would not harness his team, then she would do it for him.

'Very well, have it your own way. I can assure you I shall be as relieved as you to be back in Town. Do not think I shall call on you again, Miss Bennet. Our association is at an end.'

She bit back her pithy response; it would not do to anger him further, not when he was doing as she wished. She had no desire to be abandoned on the side of the road. She might freeze to death before another vehicle came along to rescue her.

The carriage was soon ready to depart and she scrambled up onto the box seat, leaving him to lead the animals outside. He joined her and in stony silence they returned to Town. It was getting late. Her aunt and uncle must be so worried about her non-appearance.

How she wished it was Mr Bingley sitting beside her, then today would have been an enjoyable adventure and not a hideous nightmare. The road was treacherous, the horses not able to travel at more than a walk, and the journey that had taken barely three-quarters of an hour in the other direction took one hour and a half to complete this time.

Mr Fox reined in outside the Gardiner house but he did not offer to assist her, and she certainly did not invite him in. Her aunt and uncle must have been watching through the window and the front door opened immediately.

'Stay where you are, Jane my dear. I shall come down to assist you.'

Her uncle reached up and she was lifted down. Now she was back safely her bravado evaporated. She felt wretched, ill-used and frozen to the marrow. 'Thank you, Uncle, I must apologise for being so tardy. I shall explain everything once I am inside.' Without a backward glance she moved away from the carriage, and if her uncle was surprised by her incivility to Mr Fox, he did not comment.

'Come in, come in, you poor thing. You are in a dreadful state. Let me take you upstairs. I already have hot bricks warming your bed, and a tray of something nourishing will be brought to you immediately.'

'You are too kind, Aunt Gardiner. I am ashamed of putting you through so much anguish on my behalf. I hardly know where to begin to tell you what has transpired. Mr Fox is not a gentleman. I do not wish him to be welcomed in this house again.' She ought not be issuing instructions in this way. She was a guest in their house, but she felt too dispirited to explain in detail what she had suffered at his hands.

An hour later she was feeling much more the thing, and ready to give the whole sorry story to her aunt.

'I cannot believe that we were so misled by that young man. You can be very sure he will no longer be received by any friends of *ours*. I blame myself for encouraging you to accept his invitations.'

'Please do not, I am a woman grown and can make my own decisions. However, from this point on, I shall not go out in society; I shall spend my time with you and the children.'

* * *

As Charles struggled to regain his feet the carriage rocked wildly. He could not believe their bad luck. The duel had been successful; it would be ill fortune indeed if they were apprehended by the constables. Again Darcy assisted him; his cloak was the problem, he was kneeling on the folds and this kept him trapped on the floor.

'Here, allow me to help you, Bingley.' His friend's strength was more than adequate to heave him onto the squabs. The carriage lurched violently to one side and he almost ended on the floor again. He hauled himself upright and hooked his hand into the strap.

'If we are stopped, Bingley, let me do the talking. What did you do with my pistols?'

'I am sorry, in the excitement I did not have time to retrieve them.'

'Excellent!'

To his astonishment his friend reached up and hammered on the roof; immediately the driver responded and the horses dropped to a less dangerous, collected canter. 'Darcy, we shall never outrun the constables now. What are you thinking of?'

'If there are no pistols in the carriage, and we have disposed of the doctor, there can be no proof we were doing anything illegal. The constables might suspect our purpose, but without evidence they can prove nothing. I shall tell them we have been visiting with friends but became lost in the dark. They will know that is fustian, but will be unable to prove it.' His teeth showed white in the gloom and Charles knew his friend was enjoying the experience.

He attempted to relax, but could not help himself from stiffening as two riders overtook the carriage and demanded it pull over. He was glad that Darcy intended to do the talking. He doubted he would make much sense; his nerves were all over the place this morning.

His friend lowered the window and stared out imperiously. 'What is the meaning of this? Can a man not go about his business without being waylaid in this outrageous manner?'

The coach door opened and two armed men waved them out. 'Out here, if you please, gentlemen. We wish to examine the interior of your vehicle. We have reason to believe you have been illegally duelling.'

Charles hesitated, waiting to see what Darcy wished him to do. He grinned and then indicated that he should follow him. 'I am Fitzwilliam Darcy of Pemberley. How dare you treat me in this fashion. Mr Bingley and I have been visiting friends, not that it is any concern of yours.'

The constable's air of authority began to deflate. Charles was lost in admiration for this handling of a difficult situation. As instructed he remained mute and left the talking to Darcy. The second man searched the inside of the vehicle and emerged shaking his head at his associate. This was exactly as Darcy had said it would be.

'If you have finished your investigation, my man, we wish to return to Town. Kindly remove yourselves at once.'

'I beg your pardon, Mr Darcy, it appears our information was incorrect. You may continue on your journey.'

Charles wanted to leap back in and demand that the horses

were sprung, but Darcy stared superciliously down at the two constables and then sauntered back to the carriage. The driver snapped his whip and they rolled away.

'My God, that was a close-run thing. You were magnificent. You fobbed them off perfectly. Now I can look forward to my breakfast.'

'It is not over yet. I expect Winterton will have been apprehended by now. There were six men. I expect the other two to arrive imminently, baying for our blood.' He smiled. 'It is time to spring the horses, my friend, unless you wish to spend a night in jail.'

Immediately Charles was on his feet and craned out of the window. 'Get moving; they will be after us again.' There was no sign of any pursuit behind them, but he trusted his friend's judgement and if he said they needed to make haste that was good enough for him.

He was thrown back as the horses were urged into a flat gallop. He braced his feet against the far seat, rather enjoying the excitement. He had left the window down, and with some difficulty stuck his head out without losing it. He dropped back in shock.

'They *are* onto us. I spotted four horses in the distance. Do you think we can outrun them?'

'We must hope that we do. Is your driver resourceful?'

'In this sort of situation? I have no idea, Darcy. I believe there is a crossroads the other side of these trees. If we can get there before them, with luck the dust will have settled and they won't know which direction we took.'

He had no notion what being taken into custody might mean for him. Acting as a second did not hold such a high penalty as actually fighting. Amidst the bouncing and jolting it was difficult to see how his friend was dealing with the thought that he might imminently be removed to prison.

'Will Winterton be taken in? Do you think he gave us up to the law in order to get his own back?'

'A gentleman would not do that. Unless they have both of us, he can tell them it was an accident. Absolute balderdash, that they will not be able to disprove if I am out of reach.'

This time Darcy risked his neck to see if their pursuers were gaining on them. The carriage veered wildly to the left; the right side of the carriage was airborne. For a moment Charles thought he was about to meet his maker. Then the wheels crashed back, the vehicle righted itself, and they continued at breakneck speed.

Darcy laughed out loud. 'We have just safely negotiated the crossroads. With luck they will think we continued on to Town. God knows what lies in this direction, but I am sure your driver knows his business.'

This proved to be the case. A short while later the carriage slowed to a more decorous trot and then dropped to a walk before turning into the cobbled yard of a substantial coaching inn. However, it did not stop there, but continued under a second archway where it finally halted.

'We are safe. Your driver and groom can take care of the team back here whilst remaining out of sight. Are you ready, Bingley? I could do with my breakfast; I am sharp-set.'

Two hours later they left the inn and returned at a more leisurely pace. Charles was to leave his friend where he had collected him. 'I think it is a good thing you are going to Kent to visit your relatives. It would be better if you are out of town for a while.'

'Thank you for your support this morning. I had a capital time. I cannot remember when I was so energised. When I return from Rosings, remember you and your family are to come to me at Pemberley for a visit.'

When Charles returned, his house was awake, but fortunately Caroline was not in residence at present or he would have had a deal of explaining to do. That evening he was to dine at Grosvenor Street and he believed that Georgiana would be accompanying Darcy. He hoped she would not mention her brother's strange behaviour to Caroline or Louisa.

He arrived early that evening and was greeted warmly by Caroline.

'My dear Charles, did you know that we are all invited to go back to Pemberley when Mr Darcy and Georgiana return after Mr Darcy's visit to Rosings?'

'Yes, Darcy mentioned it to me. However, I think I might remain in Town this time. Although society is a little thin at the moment, it is not long to the start of the season and I already have several invitations from families who have returned from the country.'

He saw his sister frown and wondered at it. The invitation had been issued and Darcy would not change his mind, because he did not intend to accompany them on this occasion. He would reassure her on this matter when he got a moment to be private with her. There was also something he wished to discuss with his sister that he could not do in public.

Georgiana volunteered to play the pianoforte and, whilst the others gathered to listen, he drew his sister to one side. 'Caroline, have you heard from Miss Bennet since you were in Town?'

'No, why should I? I cut the connection immediately we arrived here. Charles, I do not think you should stay in Town whilst we are at Pemberley. You are Mr Darcy's closest friend. I am sure he only invites us to stay because of your connection.'

He thought she was probably correct but it would be insensitive to say so. He knew it was her dearest wish to become mistress of Pemberley and he did not have the heart to tell her it would never happen.

'I am sorry that you felt obliged to drop Miss Bennet,' he said to Caroline. 'I believed you had a genuine fondness for her. I would not like to think my disappointment had spoiled your friendship.'

'You must not worry on my account, Charles. She was never anything more than a casual country acquaintance – someone to enliven my days whilst we were at Netherfield.'

He turned away, disappointed in her. He loved Jane, believed he always would, and did not like to think that his beloved had been used in this cavalier fashion by his sisters. He was determined not to go to Pemberley. He needed to keep busy, be surrounded by noise and bustle, and not be constantly reminded of what he had lost. There was too much time spent in silent contemplation in the countryside.

* * *

Two weeks after Jane's unpleasant experience, it was as though it had never happened. The snow had all but gone, and Mr Fox's name was no longer mentioned. Her relatives were kindness itself, and at no time made her feel she was being ungracious by remaining at home when they went out to dine.

When a letter from her sister arrived saying that on her way to visit Charlotte and Mr Collins in Hunsford, Sir William had agreed to call in at Cheapside and stay the night, she was overjoyed. Such excitement! It had been too long since she had spent time with her sister. She could scarcely contain her eagerness to be reunited with her Lizzy. It was noon when Jane, who was watching from the drawing room window, saw their visitors arrive.

'Oh good, they are here at last. I shall go and meet them myself.' She glanced up to see her little cousins hiding halfway up the stairs, waiting to greet the visitors. They had not seen her sister for a twelvemonth, and they were too shy to come lower.

'Lizzy, I am so happy to see you.' Jane held out her hand and Elizabeth took it. She turned and curtsied politely to Sir William. 'I am pleased to see you, Sir William. It is so kind of you to break your journey here so that my sister and I can see each other.'

All was joy and kindness. The guests were shown to their rooms and her sister into her own chamber. After a cold collation, the day passed most pleasantly away; the morning in bustle and shopping, and the evening at one of the theatres. This was a treat for all of them. Even the children were included.

Somehow, Jane found herself separated from Elizabeth, and obliged to sit between Sir William and Maria. She glanced across several times and saw her sister happily conversing with their aunt during the intervals between the acts. She knew she would have time, when they were alone in her bedchamber, to share any secrets they had been holding back from their letters; perhaps she might even mention Mr Fox.

However, Elizabeth had nothing much to say about Longbourn, apart from the fact that Mr Bennet missed Jane and was looking forward to her return. Elizabeth was full of excitement as she had been invited by their aunt to travel to the Lakes in the summer and the opportunity to share her own news did not arrive.

Jane listened to her sister talking rapturously about the treats to come. 'Oh, Jane, what delight! What felicity! This treat will give me fresh life and vigour. Adieu to disappointment and spleen. What are men, to rocks and mountains? Oh! What hours of transport we shall spend!'

The fact that Mr Wickham had abandoned her sister to pursue a young person called Miss King who had recently inherited £10,000, seemed not to bother Elizabeth one jot.

Jane found it hard to sleep. She heard her sister's steady breathing, and it gave her comfort. She wished that she had felt so little for Mr Bingley that she could accept his moving on to someone else as easily as Elizabeth had accepted Mr Wickham's defection for another. She did not have the heart to spoil her sister's happiness by discussing her own continued sadness.

The house in Gracechurch Street seemed empty and flat after Elizabeth, Sir William and Maria left; Jane did her best to appear in good spirits, offering to take her little cousins on frequent outings. The boys were delighted to accompany her to the River Thames to watch the ships go by. The eldest, Lucy, informed Jane that the tide would be turning by the time they arrived, and they would see the coal and timber lighters, as well as larger ships, sailing past. Plenty to entertain them for an hour or more.

The children were accompanied by their nursemaid, Elsie, a jolly girl, who knew her charges well, and left Jane with little to do but hold hands and answer questions. When they returned from the excursion she was pleasantly fatigued, and having passed an unsettled night, knew next time she retired to her bed she had a fair chance of sleeping soundly.

Mrs Gardiner attempted to fill the afternoon with another visit to the circulating library. Jane had little appetite for novels at present; in fact, she had very little inclination for anything frivolous.

'Jane, if you wish to return to Longbourn, I shall be happy for you to use the carriage. It is not more than a few hours' drive.

You seem so dispirited now that Lizzy has left. Would you not feel happier at home?'

Jane was aghast. The last thing she desired was to be at Longbourn without dearest Elizabeth at her side. The very thought of listening to Kitty and Lydia's silliness made her shudder. No, she had much rather stay where she was until Elizabeth returned with Maria in six weeks' time; then they should travel back together.

Longbourn would not be the same. She tried not to think that it would never be the same now that *he* had left the area. 'Thank you, aunt, but I am very content to remain here.'

'The remaining six weeks of your visit shall pass quickly, Jane. I know you do not wish to go out in the evening, but the weather is improving every day, and I intend for us to go and visit the menagerie at the Tower, and we shall visit the museums, and perhaps we can discover a lecture or two you might enjoy.'

'You do not have to inconvenience yourself on my behalf. I do not wish to be a trial.' She saw her words had disappointed. 'However, if you really have the time and energy for so much activity it will make the weeks fly past.'

'In that case, my dear, we shall begin with the menagerie. The children would enjoy a trip to the Tower; and we could certainly drive around to see the sights. When it is warmer we could take a picnic to Hyde Park or Green Park.'

'That sounds delightful. I am feeling better already. Perhaps, if there is time, we could visit an area which has a milliner's, a drapery shop, and a general stores. I should like to buy the children a small something before I depart, and also purchase gifts for my family.' With the matter decided satisfactorily for both parties, no more was said about Jane's low spirits.

The trip to the Tower – with four children, the nursemaid, and her aunt – was declared a resounding success by all who attended. The lions were fearsome, the ravens large and black, and the Tower itself a salutary reminder of times past.

When she returned home, to her delight, there was a letter from Lizzy waiting for her. Eagerly she opened it and scanned the contents.

My dearest Jane,

I must tell you that I am well settled here in the vicarage with Charlotte and Mr Collins. Although the house is small, it is well appointed and has a great air of comfort throughout. It would seem to me that Charlotte is content with her marriage but even happier when Mr Collins is absent. He is often away at Rosings visiting with his patron, Lady Catherine, and I believe that this lady is talked of far more than his work with the church.

I have come to the conclusion that Lady Catherine is more conceited and proud than her nephew Darcy. I know you will laugh at this, for no one could be more haughty than he. We are obliged to visit almost daily, and are treated to as great a display of incivility as any I observed at Netherfield.

Since I began this letter you will never guess, my dear Jane, who is visiting at Rosings. Mr Darcy himself! For some reason he is forever visiting the vicarage and putting himself out to be pleasant. I much prefer Colonel Fitzwilliam, who, I believe, has joint guardianship of Georgiana Darcy…

Jane replied immediately. She regaled Elizabeth with an amusing account of her visit to the Tower, glad that she had something to enthuse about, and give her sister no reason to suppose that she was not feeling in good spirits.

But in reality she was now counting the days till May, which would herald the return of her sister and Maria. It would be a full four months by the time she returned to Longbourn. The noise and press of people in Town had become more oppressive as the weeks passed by. She longed for the tranquillity of the countryside, to be able to walk or ride freely, to visit with friends and neighbours and be in no danger of being accosted or having to take a footman or maid every time you left the house. She loved her aunt and uncle dearly. They could not have treated her with more affection had she been their own daughter; however, since her unfortunate experience with Mr Fox, she no longer felt comfortable in Town.

15

Charles did not allow himself to be persuaded to accompany Darcy and the others to Pemberley after Easter. He remained in Town and kept himself fully occupied with visits to his club and other masculine entertainments. Despite telling his sister to the contrary, he had not attended any of the events to which he had been sent invitations. He found such occasions flat, the conversation insipid and none of the young ladies half as pretty as Jane.

When Elizabeth eventually arrived in Cheapside, Jane detected a certain reserve in her sister. Several times she appeared about to tell her something important, but then could not quite bring herself to do so. The four days they spent gallivanting around Town passed in a flash and before Jane knew it they set out together from Gracechurch Street for a small town in Hertfordshire. Here they were to meet Mr Bennet's carriage, transfer their trunks and belongings, then complete the journey, allowing Mr Gardiner's vehicle to return to Town in good time.

It was Elizabeth who pointed out Lydia and Kitty waving from an upstairs window at the inn. 'Look, Jane, the girls are here before us. I do wish Papa had not allowed them to come on their own. I shudder to think what they might have been doing to disgrace themselves whilst they have waited for us to arrive.'

They made their way upstairs where Lydia and Kitty proudly displayed a table set out with such cold meat as an inn larder usually affords.

Kitty exclaimed. 'Look, is this not nice? Is not this an agreeable surprise?'

'And we mean to treat you all,' added Lydia, 'but you must lend us the money, for we have just spent ours at the shops out there.'

In and amongst her talk of bonnets, Lydia told them that Miss King had been sent away and so Wickham was still single. Jane looked at Lizzy to see what effect the news had on her sister, but to her surprise she did not look pleased. Jane had thought that Lizzy had had a tendre for him, but perhaps she was mistaken. To this news, Lydia added that the regiment were removing to Brighton and that she longed to go. Jane exchanged glances with her sister. Lydia in Brighton did not bear thinking about.

'Have you seen any pleasant men? Have you had any flirting? I was in great hopes that one of you would have got a husband before you came back. Jane will be quite an old maid soon, I declare. She is almost three-and-twenty!'

Jane recalled her experiences with Mr Fox and thought she would rather die an old maid than marry for the sake of it.

Their reception at home was most kind. Mrs Bennet rejoiced at seeing Jane in undiminished beauty; and more than once during dinner did Mr Bennet say voluntarily to Elizabeth, 'I am glad you have come back, Lizzy.'

After supper that evening she was eventually alone with Elizabeth in their sitting room. Jane turned to her sister with a smile. 'Lizzy, you must talk to me. I have known since we met at Gracechurch Street that there is something you wish to tell me and have not had the opportunity to do so.'

'Not tonight. I shall tell you tomorrow, when my head is clear.'

With that Jane had to be content. The following morning she was dressed and ready in their parlour to hear what her sister had to say.

'Jane, you had better be seated before I begin, for I am sure that you shall not believe what I am going to reveal.'

Jane sat and waited expectantly. What her sister then told her did indeed astonish.

'You well know, for I mentioned it in my letters to you, that Mr Darcy was frequently with me whilst I was at Hunsford. What I did not tell you was that the day before he left he proposed to me.'

'Lizzy, I am astounded. How did this come about? I thought that the gentleman did not admire you.'

'I shall tell you. I was never so angry in my life. I shall try and remember exactly how he phrased it. Yes, I have it. *"In vain have I struggled. It will not do. My feelings will not be repressed. You must allow me to tell you how ardently I admire and love you."* There! What do you think of that?'

'Good gracious! That is hardly a romantic proposal. I cannot understand it, Lizzy. Why should he have to struggle against his feelings for you? You are everything that is good, and as intelligent as you are lovely. You are his equal in everything apart from fortune.'

'You have not heard the best of it. He went on to tell me that in spite of my inferiority, and the family obstacles caused by having relations that were not to his liking, he had eventually decided that he loved me sufficiently to ignore these drawbacks.'

Jane was scandalised. 'What did you reply?'

Her sister became so agitated she jumped to her feet. 'I told him that I *should* feel gratified by his proposal, but I was not in any way pleased. I said that I had neither desired nor sought his good opinion and that I was sorry to hurt his feelings.' Elizabeth moved around the room whilst she gathered her thoughts. 'I also said that as he had fought so hard against his feelings for me I was sure that it would not be long before he was able to forget.'

'Lizzy, to have turned down such a man as that! He being so sure of succeeding was wrong; but consider how much it must increase his disappointment.'

'Indeed, I am heartily sorry for him; but he has other things that will probably soon drive away his regard for me. You do not blame me, however, for refusing him?'

'Blame you! Oh, no!'

'But you do blame me for having spoken so warmly of Wickham.'

'No – and I do not know that you were wrong in saying what you did.'

'But you *will* know it, when I have told you what happened the very next day.'

When Jane heard of the perfidy of Mr Wickham she was most distressed. 'To think that Darcy treated Mr Wickham well, gave him the value of the living instead of the living itself. And for that young man then to have attempted to elope with Georgiana Darcy; well, I can hardly credit it. How could someone be so wicked? And he appears such an amiable person.'

They sat in silence whilst Jane digested this unpleasant information. 'Is there not some possibility of error? I am pleased that Mr Darcy has been vindicated. I always believed him to be an honest man, as you know. But Mr Wickham such a villain? It cannot be true.'

'This will not do,' said Elizabeth. 'You never will be able to make both good for anything. Take your choice, but you must be satisfied with only one. There is such a quantity of merit between them; just enough to make one good sort of man; and of late it has been shifting about pretty much. On my part, I am inclined to believe it all Mr Darcy's, but you shall do as you choose.'

Jane did not know how her sister could view the matter so light-heartedly. 'I do not know when I have been more shocked. Wickham so very bad! It is almost past belief. And poor Mr Darcy! Dear Lizzy, only consider what he must have suffered. Such a disappointment. And to know that you think so ill of him too. And imagine having to relate such a thing about his sister; it is really too distressing. I am sure that you must feel it so.'

'Oh no, my regret and compassion are all done away by seeing you so full of both. I know you will do him such ample justice, that I am growing every moment more unconcerned and indifferent. Your profusion makes me sanguine; and if you lament over him much longer, my heart shall be as light as a feather.'

'Lizzy, you must not make a jest of this. Poor Wickham! To think there is such an expression of goodness in his countenance, such an openness and gentleness in this manner, and it is all a sham.'

'I wish I had not been so vehement in my support of him. But Darcy had all the appearance of being a villain and Wickham the innocent party.'

'Lizzy, when you first read that letter, I am sure you could not treat the matter as you do now.'

'Indeed, I could not. I was uncomfortable enough. I was *very* uncomfortable, I may say, and unhappy. With no one to speak to of what I felt, no Jane to comfort me and say that I had not been so very weak and vain and nonsensical as I knew I had. Oh! How I wanted you.'

'How unfortunate that you should have used such very strong expressions when speaking of Wickham to Mr Darcy, for now they *do* appear wholly undeserved.'

'Certainly. But the misfortune of speaking thus is the most natural consequence of the prejudices I had been encouraging. There is one point on which I want your advice. I want to be told whether I ought or ought not to make our acquaintance in general understand Wickham's character.'

Jane pondered for a moment before answering. 'Surely there can be no occasion for exposing him so dreadfully. What is your own opinion?'

'That it ought not to be attempted.'

What exciting times they had both had, thought Jane.

* * *

The first week of Jane's return to Longbourn was soon gone and the second begun. She rather believed her sister and herself were the only females in the vicinity not sunk into deepest dejection at the imminent departure of the regiment from Meryton. Lydia and Kitty were inconsolable and neither girl could comprehend how anyone with any sensibility could continue to eat and drink as normal.

'Good heavens! What is to become of us! What are we to do?' Lydia frequently exclaimed. 'How can you be smiling, Lizzy?'

Their affectionate mother shared all their grief; she remembered what she had herself endured on a similar occasion, five-and-twenty years ago. There were constant lamentations about not being able to visit Brighton, and Mr Bennet remained firmly in his library.

'If I was not so ashamed of their behaviour, Jane, I should be able to find all this amusing. I am beginning to believe that Mr Darcy was right to object to the behaviour of our family,' Elizabeth said.

'It is never right to criticise one's *own* family; however, I believe it must be difficult for someone from such a superior background to understand that there is no malice intended in the silliness. If Papa could only take more interest in Lydia and Kitty, I am sure they would not behave in this way.'

'Dear Jane, you are so right. A great deal of the blame must rest on our parents.'

'I do not intend to lay blame upon anybody's shoulders, Lizzy. Now, let us go outside and forget about the fuss.'

They returned from their promenade to discover that events had changed in their absence. Lydia had received an invitation from Mrs Forster to accompany her to Brighton. Jane turned to Elizabeth in surprise when she heard this news.

'How can this be? Why should Lydia be invited by the new wife of Colonel Forster? She is younger than Kitty; surely *she* should have received the invitation?'

'It would seem that Lydia has become an invaluable friend to Mrs Forster and although they have only known each other for three months they have been intimate for two.'

'Poor Kitty! She will be inconsolable. It is a great shame that Mrs Forster could not invite both of them to accompany her to Brighton.'

'It is a great shame, Jane, that either of them are allowed to go. Can you imagine how Lydia will behave when she is away from Longbourn? I shall speak to Papa, implore him to stop her from going. Can you imagine the great disadvantage for us all, which must arise from the public notice of Lydia's unguarded and imprudent manner; nay, which has already risen from it?'

'You are no doubt considering Mr Darcy's feelings when you say that, are you not? Do you regret it, Lizzy, refusing him?'

'No. But all the same I do not wish our sister to disgrace us any further.'

Jane watched her sister leave to speak to their father and although she would not like to see Lydia disappointed, she was certain a visit to Brighton by someone of Lydia's disposition was not a sound idea. Unfortunately, their father did not see it that way.

'Papa refuses to become involved,' said Lizzy with a sigh. 'He says that Lydia, Kitty and Mary are all very silly and that we shall have no peace at Longbourn if Lydia is not allowed to go to Brighton. He insists that Colonel Forster is a sensible man and will keep her out of any real mischief.'

Much relieved by her sister's reassurance, Jane was able to enjoy the walk and felt ready to face Lydia's overexcitement and Kitty's excessive complaints. At least all the noise and fuss involved with Lydia's departure meant she had less time to think of what *she* had lost. Time had not lessened her grief over the departure of Bingley from her life. She had thought on her return that things would be as they were before she had met him. The opposite had been the case. She could not stop thinking about him. Everywhere she went she was reminded of past happiness.

Jane rather believed that her four months in London had aggravated her loss and not alleviated it in any way. She wished she could forget him as he had obviously forgotten all about her. He had known she was in Town and could easily have visited her if he had so desired. There could be no other explanation for his absence; like his sisters, he had put her to one side when he had left Hertfordshire.

Her mother's preoccupation with Brighton meant she no longer referred to him and Netherfield so frequently, and as she had not mentioned meeting Mr Fox again, at least her mother could not plague her about that episode of her life which was now, thankfully, closed.

'Lizzy, shall we walk in the shrubbery? I need to get away from all this talk about the military.'

'It is tiresome listening to Kitty wailing and Lydia screeching. I should much rather converse with you.'

'We do not need to bother to go upstairs to find our bonnets, Lizzy; the sun is almost set.' Jane linked her arm through her sister's and they exited through a side door, not wishing to alert their mother of their intended escape.

'It is strange to see Lydia so set on her course to find a husband. Do you feel the need to do so?'

'You know that I do not, Jane. It is a great pity that we have not an independent income, then we could set up in our own establishment, two old maids together.'

'One thing is for certain: I shall not do as Charlotte has. I would rather remain single than tie myself to a man I could not love with all my heart.' She sighed. 'I fear I shall never meet another man like Mr Bingley, so I am destined to be a spinster all my life.'

'You would not marry in order to leave Longbourn? Can you imagine spending the remainder of our days here? And what when Papa dies? Do we ask Mr Collins to take us in?'

'Pray, do not even consider a situation such as that. One of us will marry for love and must promise to take care of the other.' Jane knew she would never be the one to wed, so she must rely on Lizzy to find someone she could love well enough to share her life.

On the very last day of the regiment's remaining in Meryton, Mr Wickham and some other officers, were invited to dine at Longbourn. Jane still found it hard to credit that this charming young man had behaved so badly; she sincerely hoped that Elizabeth was able to contain her disgust and not reveal to the assembled company that Wickham was no longer a favourite of theirs.

She saw them talking together earnestly and something Elizabeth said made him appear alarmed and agitated and his complexion was heightened somewhat. For a few minutes he remained silent, then he appeared to shake off his embarrassment and turned back to her sister to speak to her quietly.

When they were preparing for bed that evening, Jane asked her sister what Wickham had told her. 'We discussed Lady Catherine and I told him that I had spent three weeks in the company of Colonel Fitzwilliam and Mr Darcy.'

'Oh dear, Lizzy, I hope you did not speak of what you had been told in confidence.'

'Of course I did not. I merely hinted to him that I saw through him and knew him for the charlatan he was. He is not a stupid man; he understood to what I was referring.'

'It will be a relief, Lizzy, when the regiment has left and we can forget all about Mr Wickham.'

The house was quiet after Lydia's departure. She had promised to write frequently but letters were always long expected and always very short. Her correspondence with Kitty was longer, but was so full of intimate revelations that Kitty was not prepared to share them with the rest of the family.

Even Jane noticed the difference in Meryton now that the regiment had left. Their parties abroad were less varied than before and the constant complaints of Mrs Bennet and Kitty about how dull everything had become cast a real gloom over their domestic circle. It was a full three weeks before health, good humour and cheerfulness began to reappear at Longbourn.

'It is going to be very odd here when you are away,' said Jane. 'It is a great shame that your plans had to be altered, but my uncle must, of course, put his engagements first. I know how you were looking forward to going as far as the Lakes, but I am sure Derbyshire will be just as pleasant. I know what you are thinking: that you might run into Mr Darcy, but Derbyshire is a large place and I am sure you will not see him.'

'I pray that you are correct. Jane, I do so wish you had been included in the invitation. But I believe that our aunt is relying on your taking care of the children for her. I am quite certain I do not have the patience that you do.'

'I spent many months in London with them; it is only right that you should have your turn. I love the children and cannot wait to see them running about at Longbourn.'

The time fixed for the beginning of her sister's northern tour was fast approaching; Jane, in spite of her protestations that she had no wish to accompany them and would be perfectly happy at home, was rather dreading the separation.

Although they never spoke of Bingley, or indeed of Mr Darcy and his refused proposal, Jane was aware that Elizabeth knew how much she was suffering and made every effort to keep herself cheerful and take her mind off what she had lost. It was not her intention to reveal her distress, but when one was so close, it was impossible for the other not to know that her high spirits and smiles were often forced.

She had taken to riding every morning and sometimes her excursions took her past Netherfield. It was little comfort to see the handsome building empty; she wondered what would become of it. Would he sell the lease? It was not her concern any more what he did; she must get on with her life and learn to be happy again.

* * *

Four weeks passed before the arrival of their uncle and aunt and their children. Jane was fully occupied settling her young cousins and Elsie into the nursery. Elizabeth was to depart the following morning and she was dreading the separation. She kept her disquiet to herself and was able to embrace her sister lovingly and wish her a happy holiday. They promised to exchange a frequent correspondence; Elizabeth vowed she would write as soon as they were settled and left her with an address in Lambton to which she could send her first missive.

She had no time to dwell on her sadness at being parted from her favourite sister as the children demanded her full attention. Mrs Bennet had declared she was far too old to be bothered with them, that her nerves could not take the strain. Mary and Kitty had no interest in their young cousins and her father was, as usual, closeted in his library.

It had been her intention to devote the morning hours to lessons but seeing a row of expectant faces, all eager to get outside and run about, she had not the heart to insist that they study their books that morning.

'I believe that I shall allow you one week without schoolwork; and after that you must promise to apply yourselves every morning. I have given my word to your parents that I shall not neglect your studies in their absence.'

Within twenty minutes they were clattering down the stairs and heading for the garden. She had no leisure to think about her own problems, or even to miss her sister very much. She threw herself enthusiastically into the entertainment of the children and was frequently as wet and muddy, after one of their excursions, as they were.

When the children were safely installed in the nursery she had to bathe and change and be ready to attend a variety of little parties and social engagements. Her days were full and so were many of her evenings. The letter she had promised to send to Elizabeth was started and then put by until she could find the time to complete it.

The house was quiet, everybody asleep when Jane was awakened by a thunderous knocking at the front door. She scrambled out of bed, fumbling with a tinderbox in order to light a candle. She slipped into her robe and held the candle aloft to see that the mantel clock said it was midnight.

Had no one else heard the knocking? Should she go down herself and see who it was? No, she would go to her mother's apartment and rouse her. Mama could wake Papa and *he* could go down and deal with whoever was outside the door.

Jane was halfway along the passageway when she heard a door open at the far end and her father appeared, nightcap askew, his bed robe hastily tied.

'Go back to your rooms, Jane. I shall deal with this. If it is anything that requires Mrs Bennet to be told, I shall send word to you.'

'Yes, sir. I shall wait in my sitting room.' Jane knew that it had to be bad news; no one would send good tidings with such urgency.

16

It was some time before Jane received her summons. Hill had appeared at her sitting room door, her hair stuffed higgledy-piggledy under her cap and her bombazine dress pulled on over her nightgown.

'The master asks that you come down and join him in the library directly, if you will, Miss Bennet.'

Jane's heart plummeted. He must require her to speak to Mama; the news must be dire indeed to consider waking her. The housekeeper led the way through the darkened house and along the corridor to the library.

Her father was standing, a letter in his hand, and his expression filled her with foreboding. 'Jane, I am relieved that you are here. This is an express come from Colonel Forster. Your sister has run off with Wickham. She left a note for Mrs Forster informing her of their intention. They are on their way to Scotland in order to get married.'

'That is the most parlous news, sir. Poor Lydia! Whatever could have possessed her to do something so disastrous?'

'I have no idea; I had no inkling that Wickham was interested in Lydia. For if I had, I certainly would not have allowed her to go to Brighton.' He rubbed his eyes and stared again at the letter as if he could not believe what was written there. 'Colonel Forster is on his way to Longbourn and it is up to you, my dear girl, to go and break the news to Mrs Bennet. I think we shall have to rouse Kitty and Mary. It is possible that one of them knows more about this question than we do.'

'I shall go up at once; I must stay with Mama. I am certain that she will be prostrate at this news. Do you think it might not be better to leave the girls in ignorance until morning? Mama will be suffering from her nerves, and Kitty and Mary's distress will not help.'

He shrugged, as if indifferent to the anxiety of his wife. 'Do as you think best, Jane. If you are not to get the others up then I shall retire to my chamber. We shall all need our wits about us to face the morning.'

As Jane ran back upstairs, her immediate thought was that it was fortuitous she and Elizabeth had decided not to inform the rest of the family about Wickham's true character. If they knew what sort of man Lydia was to marry it would make matters so much worse.

She paused for a few moments to compose herself, before quietly knocking on her mother's door. There followed half an hour of noise and hysterics, after which Jane felt able to leave her mother with the housekeeper and go down to the kitchen and make herself a drink of hot milk. The room was once more in darkness, the tea, for her mother's nerves, having already been made and taken up. Placing her candlestick on the dresser she busied herself finding milk from the slate shelf in the pantry and a copper pan from the rack on the wall.

Taking her drink, she returned to her apartment. She would write to her sister before she went back to bed; no one else would think to do so, she was sure. This information was going to spoil Elizabeth's trip, but although it pained her, she knew Lizzy would want to know immediately what had taken place.

She found the half-written letter she had started the previous night and decided she would continue on the same sheet of paper. Her thoughts were in a jumble; she was bewildered by what had happened. It was so imprudent a match on both sides, but she was willing to hope for the best, and that somehow Wickham's character had been misunderstood. He was thoughtless and indiscreet, but she did not think that this elopement indicated anything bad at heart.

She found it difficult to compose herself sufficiently to write without alarming her sister. The letter was blotted, with many crossings-out, and she feared Elizabeth would not be able to decipher it. After quickly folding it she wrote the address, hoping it would arrive without delay at its destination.

The night was warm, her windows open to let in what little breeze there was. Jane removed her night robe and climbed back into the bed she usually shared with her sister. It was impossible to sleep. Whatever reassurances her father had given to the contrary, it did not seem to be a satisfactory conclusion to Lydia's impulsive behaviour. How could a girl so young and inexperienced make a success of married life? And Wickham? Although his choice had been disinterested at least, he must know Lydia brought nothing with her.

The runaways must have passed within ten miles of Longbourn. If only they had stopped to consider how wrong were their actions, her poor parents would not have to endure the worry of a missing daughter.

* * *

Pemberley in July was the perfect place to be, Charles decided, as his carriage rolled to a halt outside the magnificent edifice. There were no importunate young women hoping for a smile from him, and with his closest friend on hand to entertain him, he was as content as he would ever be without Jane at his side. Since the duel, his admiration for his friend had grown. He was a man of many parts, able to extract himself from difficult situations and enjoy so doing.

Liveried footmen raced to let down the steps, and his friend strolled round from the stables to greet him in person. 'Did you have an uneventful journey down? Miss Bingley and the Hursts arrived earlier today. They are already making themselves at home.'

'I am glad to be here, and to see you looking so relaxed, my friend. Indeed, I can safely say I have never seen you look so well.'

Darcy smiled. 'We are not the only ones in Derbyshire, Bingley. Elizabeth Bennet and her uncle and aunt, Mr and Mrs Gardiner, are staying at Lambton. I am taking Georgiana to meet her tomorrow.'

Charles thought that his friend's buoyant mood was quite out of proportion to his having a chance encounter with a mere acquaintance. Were his earlier suspicions correct? Did Darcy have an interest in Elizabeth after all? He hoped that might be so. Whatever the outcome of that relationship her unexpected appearance in Derbyshire would give him the opportunity to enquire how Jane was doing.

If he could manoeuvre the conversation in the correct direction, he would ask Elizabeth why Jane had not replied to his letter; perhaps he might discover there was an innocent explanation.

Charles felt happier than he had in months. To be able to

talk about the woman he loved to someone who loved her too! He was overjoyed at the prospect.

The next morning he waited until Darcy and Georgiana had left and then followed on horseback. His subterfuge was pointless as his friend saw him arrive at the inn; at least his arrival would not be a surprise to anyone.

He hurried up the stairs and into the room. He could not help greeting Elizabeth with warmth. He had grown fond of Jane's sister the few times they had met last year. However, he could not ask the questions he most desired the answers to, at least not yet, but he was determined to speak to her in private as soon as possible and find out more about Jane.

'Miss Elizabeth, how is everybody at Longbourn? I do apologise for not having returned to Netherfield; I have been much involved with business and other things. You know how it is: when in Town and involved in society the months fly by.' He hoped he sounded like a man who had not been pining for an unrequited love.

'My family are well. Thank you for your kind enquiry, Mr Bingley.'

'I hear that Miss Lucas is now married to Mr Collins and residing in Hunsford?'

'Yes, I spent some weeks with her and am pleased to report that she is happy in her new life.'

'Are you staying long in Derbyshire?' Miss Elizabeth answered that they were to return in two weeks as Mr Gardiner had urgent affairs in Town. He had no opportunity to ask directly how Jane was, if she still remembered him with kindness, until just before they left.

'I am very sorry that it has been so long since I have had the pleasure of seeing you. It is about eight months. We have not met since the 26th of November, when we were all dancing together at Netherfield.'

The mere mention of that evening reminded him how lovely Jane had looked, their shared amazement at their extraordinary supper and the way she had felt in his arms when they had danced. That night he had been so happy believing the next day she would agree to be his wife. Was it possible he could start to hope again? He did not allow her to comment but continued, hoping she would understand his meaning.

'Are all your sisters at Longbourn at present, Miss Elizabeth?'

'Lydia is in Brighton with Colonel and Mrs Forster, Kitty and Jane are at Longbourn looking after my little nieces and nephews whilst my aunt and uncle are here with me in Derbyshire.'

Charles felt his heart swell inside him at the mention of the woman he loved. He knew that Jane would be affectionate with children. She was the sweetest girl imaginable.

Darcy came across to interrupt their conversation and Charles had never been less pleased to see him. He could have sat and talked to Elizabeth about Jane all day. 'I have invited Mr and Mrs Gardiner and yourself to dine with us at Pemberley, ma'am. I hope that is acceptable?'

Bingley saw her cheeks colour as she answered in the affirmative. The party were taking their leave, but he bowed and spoke quietly to her. 'I am delighted that you are coming to Pemberley the day after tomorrow. I have many enquiries to make after *all* my Hertfordshire friends.'

He was satisfied that she understood his oblique reference to Jane; when they met next he would make his questions more direct. He wanted to know which friends Jane had been staying with in January when he had visited Meryton and found her absent.

He rode home in high spirits and was pleased to see Darcy as happy as he had ever seen him. Was there a romance in the wind between Elizabeth and his friend? It would be interesting to study them when they were together at dinner in two days' time.

Charles spent a restless night, unable to sleep, his head full of images of Jane. His life had taken on a new purpose, and he had begun to hope again. He dressed in good spirits and was downstairs breaking his fast when his sisters came in.

'Good heavens! I did not expect to see you two down so early.'

'Good morning, Charles. We intend to take the barouche into the village and wish to be there before it gets too hot.' Caroline helped herself to a tiny portion of mushrooms and tomatoes and took it to a place at the table.

'The village? What can be there be in such a tiny place to get my two sisters out of bed before noon?'

Louisa laughed. 'The housekeeper informed us there is to be a fair on the green this morning and there will be a fortune teller. I have always wanted to visit such a person and now have the ideal opportunity.'

The very idea of either of his elegant sisters allowing a gypsy lady to touch them made him smile. 'In which case I shall accompany you. I should very much like to know what fate has in store for me.'

His sisters returned vastly disappointed by the excursion as the promised clairvoyant had failed to appear. Nothing could dampen his enthusiasm for the day. Darcy met him in the entrance hall, his face white and strained.

'Bingley, thank God you are back at last. I have to go to London immediately but I did not wish to leave until I had spoken to you personally.'

'Can it not wait until Miss Elizabeth and her relatives have dined tomorrow?'

'Mr Gardiner has been called back so they would not have been able to come anyway. You are very welcome to remain here in my absence and keep Georgiana company.'

Charles heard the travelling carriage pulling up outside and then noticed Darcy's trunk was packed and waiting by the door. 'Take care, and do not worry about us; we shall entertain ourselves quite happily.'

However, his pleasure in the day had vanished now he knew he was not going to be able to talk to Elizabeth about Jane. It was curious that both she and Darcy had been obliged to leave so suddenly, but it was none of his concern. He decided to go out for a ride. It would give him time to think about his next move.

On his return he was met by Caroline. 'Charles, did you know that Darcy has deserted us? It is the outside of enough to invite us here and then abandon us to our own devices.'

'He had to go to London, but you have Georgiana here to entertain you. I thought you loved being at Pemberley.'

She scowled at him. 'I do hope Miss Elizabeth and her dreadful relatives shall not turn up to dine tomorrow. I could not bear it, not without Mr Darcy to deflect their common behaviour.'

Charles stared at his sister with dislike. Had she always been so supercilious and he had never noticed? 'As it happens Mr and Mrs Gardiner have also returned to Town and Miss Elizabeth has obviously gone with them.'

Her mouth pinched. 'Good, that, at least, is something I can be pleased about. And you are quite right, I do love Pemberley. I wish I could live here always. I shall go at once and tell Georgiana that I am to take charge of her in her brother's absence.'

This was the last thing Darcy would want. He had no intention of staying at Pemberley himself. He would ride to London and see if he could find the courage to visit Longbourn and try to persuade Jane to reconsider.

* * *

Jane did not close her eyes all night. She could think of nothing else but the disaster that had overcome the family. If only Wickham's character had been revealed this would never have happened. The next morning was no better. It was her duty to tell her sisters what had happened.

When Kitty heard she was not surprised and Jane realised her sister had known all along what Lydia had planned. She could only pray that Colonel Forster might bring encouraging news when he arrived that morning. However, the information he brought was far worse than she could ever have supposed. Wickham had no intention of going to Gretna Green and there was no sign of the runaways anywhere.

For the second time she was obliged to break terrible tidings to her mother and further hysterics and upset followed. Her father was determined to search for Lydia himself and he left for London with Colonel Forster immediately after breakfast, leaving Jane to manage the household as best she could.

She had never seen her mother so unwell. It was some time before she was able to control her weeping and then she did not seem able to converse coherently. Hill sent up a special tisane and after much coaxing Jane was able to get her mother to swallow it. This draught soothed her distress, and Jane was relieved to see her patient fall asleep.

There were things she had to do; she must speak to Kitty and Lydia and reassure them. The children might be aware that matters were unsettled, so it was imperative that she run up there and instruct Elsie to take them for a picnic. It would be better if her little cousins were elsewhere today. Then she must go down to the kitchens and make sure that meals would be prepared as usual.

All this must be done as if *her* heart was not breaking too. What she had suffered when *he* had left Netherfield was nothing in comparison to what poor Lydia must be feeling at this moment. She must be so ashamed and so sorry to have caused her family such distress. And now what was to be hoped for? At best, that her sister would marry a man who did not love her. At worst, she would be ruined. Poor, poor Lydia!

17

Jane knew there was only one person who could make this more bearable. She needed Lizzy to come back to Longbourn. She would write at once explaining the whole and telling her how much she longed for her return.

Dearest Lizzy,

I hardly know what I would write, but I have bad news for you, and it cannot be delayed.

Her pen flowed over the paper as she revealed the dreadful story. She then wrote quickly about all she knew of Lydia and Wickham's whereabouts and told her sister she still could not believe that everything would not somehow be put to rights.

I am truly glad, dearest Lizzy, that you have been spared some of these distressing scenes; but now as the first shock is over, shall I own that I long for your return? I am not so selfish, however, as to press for it, if inconvenient.

Adieu

Jane read what she had written and decided that it would not do. She snatched up her pen and begged Lizzy to come back at once, bringing her uncle and aunt with her. Her uncle would know what to do. He could go to Town and help Papa with his search.

* * *

Several days later the little Gardiners, attracted by the sight of a chaise, were standing on the steps of the house in order to see the spectacle, thus they were the first to see their parents enter the paddock. Jane, who was in her mother's apartment, heard them calling out in excitement and ran down the stairs in order to be in the vestibule when Elizabeth came in.

Her eyes were tear-filled as she embraced her sister affectionately. 'Lizzy, I cannot tell you how pleased I am to see you.'

'Has there been any news of the fugitives?'

'No, there has not. But now that my dear uncle has come, I hope everything will be well.'

Mr and Mrs Gardiner approached and Jane embraced them fondly. 'I was never so glad to see anyone in my life. Thank you so much for coming.' She smiled through her tears. 'Please, come into the drawing room and I shall tell you all I know.'

When she had completed her tale, her uncle shook his head. 'It is a bad situation, and I shall be glad to help in any way I can.'

When they visited her mother in her sitting room she took great comfort from her brother's timely arrival. 'Brother, I do not know how I should go on without you! I am all to pieces; I am suffering most dreadfully from my nerves, but I shall be better now that you and my sister are here to comfort me.'

'You must not give way to useless alarm, but it is right to be prepared for the worst; however, there is no occasion to look on it as certain. It is not quite a week since they left Brighton. In a few days more we may gain some more news of them. Until we know that they are not married and have no design of marrying, do not let us give the matter over as lost. As soon as I get to Town, I shall go to my brother and make him come home with me to Gracechurch Street, and then we may consult together as to what is to be done.'

'Oh! My dear brother, that is exactly what I would most wish for. Now do, when you get to Town, find them out wherever they may be; and if they are not married already *make* them marry. And as for wedding clothes, do not let them wait for that, but tell Lydia she shall have as much money as she chooses to buy them *after* they are married. And, above all things, keep Mr Bennet from fighting.

'Tell him what a dreadful state I am in, that I am frightened out of my wits and have such tremblings, such flutterings all over me, such spasms in my side and pains in my head, and such beatings at heart, that I can get no rest by night or day. And tell my dear Lydia not to give any directions about clothes until she has seen me, for she does not know which are the best warehouses. Oh, brother, how kind you are! I know you will contrive it all.'

Jane caught Lizzy's eye. She could hardly credit the extent of her mother's folly. Her sister gestured that they should go outside and she willingly followed her.

'It was most unfortunate, Jane. I was reading your letter when Mr Darcy arrived and I was obliged to tell him the whole story.'

'Mr Darcy! I had no idea you had renewed your acquaintance with him.'

'Yes, we met quite by accident. My aunt and uncle and I were looking around Pemberley, having assured ourselves that he was not in residence, of course. I cannot tell you how mortified he was to meet me.'

Jane noticed that her sister's cheeks were flushed. 'What happened next?'

'He could not have been more kind and charming and came to visit me with Georgiana the next day and issued an invitation for all of us to dine with him.'

'I knew Bingley could not have a friend who was not as good a person as he is.'

'As you have mentioned that gentleman, I have to tell you that I spoke to him as well and he was most insistent that I tell him about Longbourn. He knew the exact date that he had last seen me. I thought that quite significant.'

It was Jane's turn to flush with pleasure. 'I think about him all the time, Lizzy. Do you think there is a chance that he might have changed his mind?'

'A very strong chance, my dear Jane.'

The thought that Charles (dare she call him that again in her heart?) might be thinking of her made it easier to bear the matter of Lydia and Wickham.

* * *

Caroline was not at all pleased by being abandoned so cavalierly by Mr Darcy and despite telling him that she would now enjoy her stay by entertaining Georgiana, she would not let the matter drop.

'Charles, surely you know why he has gone like this? We have come down to Pemberley expecting to spend several weeks with dear Georgiana and Mr Darcy, and what has happened?'

Charles was almost certain this was a rhetorical question and did not bother himself to answer. He had not liked the way his sister had behaved when Elizabeth and her aunt and uncle had come over for a visit. They were all delightful company and he had been uncomfortable on their behalf at her disdainful comments. Certainly Darcy had been most displeased; his sister would find herself ostracised by his friends if she did not learn to curb her tongue and be more civil.

'We were not here even a day before Miss Elizabeth Bennet and her dreadful relatives were being entertained. Mr Darcy is all politeness, but I do think he might have considered his other guests before inviting such people here.'

He had had quite enough of this nonsense. He stared at her and instead of seeing a fond and loving sister sitting there, he saw a jealous harridan, a spiteful woman interested only in furthering her own advantage. Disgusted by his discovery he turned away, not bothering to answer. He heard her calling after him but continued his journey out of the house and ran to the stables.

What he needed now was a good gallop across the moors to clear his head.

When he returned he had come to a decision. He no longer had any interest in his sister's opinion; she had lost his respect. It was only Darcy he had to convince and he rather thought that his friend might be in love with Elizabeth. Why else had he made such a point of introducing Georgiana to her? Something had happened between them – he was sure of that – and whatever the outcome it gave him the go-ahead to return to Netherfield. He did not care any more about Jane's relatives, or whether she loved him as much as he loved her, he was determined to see how the land lay and take it on from there.

He was bereft without her; if Jane was prepared to marry him for whatever reason, that was good enough to him. He was sure in time he could persuade her to love him in full measure.

* * *

Every day at Longbourn was now a day of anxiety; but the most alarming part was when the post was expected. The arrival of letters each morning found the entire company gathered expectantly in the front hall.

Mr Gardiner did not write again until he had received an answer from Colonel Forster and then he had nothing of a pleasant nature to report. Mrs Gardiner read the letter to herself and then shook her head sadly.

'I am not sure if I should read you this missive; there is nothing to encourage us to hope.'

'Please do, Aunt Gardiner; we must hear the news however parlous it might be,' Jane said glancing anxiously at her sister for support.

'Well, he says that Wickham's former acquaintances are numerous, but since he has been in the militia he does not appear to have been on terms of close friendship with any of them.

'Therefore they cannot find anyone likely to give any news of him. And the wretched state of his own finances was a very powerful motive to secrecy, in addition to his fear of discovery from Mr Bennet. It transpires that he has left gaming debts behind of a very considerable amount.' Mrs Gardiner looked around at the others before completing her tale of woe. 'It would seem that although he owed a good deal in Meryton, his debts of honour are still more formidable.'

Jane heard this with horror. 'A gamester! This is wholly unexpected. I had not an idea of it.' She looked to Elizabeth for confirmation and her sister nodded.

'Oh! There is some good news for you; Mr Bennet is expected to return to Longbourn tomorrow. It would seem that he has done as much as he can and is feeling very downhearted about his lack of success. Mr Gardiner has convinced him that he would be better at home and leave him to pursue the enquiries on his own.'

Jane immediately stood up. 'Poor Papa! He did so want to find Lydia and bring her home to us. I shall go at once and tell our mother that he shall be home tomorrow. She has been so concerned he might find Wickham and become involved in a fight. She will be relieved to know he is unscathed.'

That evening Jane and Elizabeth took a stroll in the garden after supper. They had scarcely had time to continue their discussion of the Derbyshire trip, when Jane took the opportunity to ask her sister what Pemberley had been like. She already knew that Mr Darcy had been there.

'It is as wonderful as Miss Bingley told us, Lizzy?'

'Yes, indeed it is. We were shown around by the housekeeper, and very civil she was. The rooms are well proportioned and spacious, and their furniture suitable to the fortune of their proprietor. I must say it was neither gaudy nor uselessly fine, and with far more real elegance than the furniture at Rosings.'

'And to think, Lizzy, you might have been mistress of all that splendour. Do you not regret, even a little bit, having refused Mr Darcy?'

'No, I do not. The house is very fine, the grounds impressive, but if I had agreed to be mistress of Pemberley House I should not have been able to see my aunt or uncle again. They would have been lost to me. I should not have been able to invite them to visit.'

'I cannot imagine that Mr Darcy would be so proud; but I am sure that *you* know what is best for you. Did he not invite you all to dine with him?'

'That is very true, but at *that* time I did not know he was going to do so. Do you know, Jane, that his housekeeper spoke of him so highly that I began to doubt my own judgement? She insisted that everybody who knew him, liked and respected him. That she had never had a cross word from him all her life, and she had known him since he was four years old.'

'We have both been mistaken in our assessment of more than one gentleman recently, have we not? I believed that Bingley was going to make me an offer, and you believed that Wickham was a gentleman and not a rogue.'

'I believe that I have certainly mistaken Darcy. He could not have been more charming and civil the three times that I met him. However, I refused him, and that is the end of the matter. A gentleman like him would not ask a second time.'

'We Bennet girls do not appear to be successful where men are concerned. Perhaps we are all destined to be still here when Mr Collins comes to take up residence.'

'We have already talked of this. I cannot see any way out of this situation unless we are left a fortune by an unknown relative.' Lizzy squeezed her arm and they laughed together. The future would have to take care of itself; there were more than enough problems to deal with in the present.

* * *

Charles received a brief letter from Darcy a few days after his friend's sudden departure from Pemberley. He scanned the contents quickly. It said little about why he had left or what he had been doing in London but asked him to come to join him as there was something of importance he wished to discuss and it could only be done in person. Georgiana was to be left in the capable hands of her companion, Mrs Annesley, and he was to tell both his sisters that as Darcy was not intending to return anytime soon, it would be better for them to terminate their visit to Pemberley also.

He smiled grimly; it could not have been made more clear. Darcy no longer wished Caroline to have free access to his home. He folded the letter and pushed it into his waistcoat pocket to peruse in more detail at a later time. Although he now saw both his sisters in a different light, he had no wish to cause them unnecessary hurt by this curt dismissal.

He would tell them Darcy was not returning and that Georgiana and her companion were to go to stay with friends in Bath. They could hardly remain alone in Pemberley under those circumstances. He immediately sought out Mrs Annesley and explained what he required her to say and for some reason she appeared delighted to be involved in the small deception.

He realised Caroline was not popular with the staff; they would be happy to see her depart immediately.

* * *

Two days following Mr Bennet's return, Jane and Elizabeth were walking in the shrubbery behind the house enjoying half an hour's respite from their duties.

'Lizzy, is that not Hill approaching? I do hope Mama is not unwell.'

'Miss Bennet, I beg your pardon for interrupting you, but I was in the hope you might have got some good news from Town, so I took the liberty of coming to ask.'

'What do you mean, Hill? We have heard nothing from Town.'

'Dear madam, don't you know there is an express come for master from Mr Gardiner? He has been here this half hour, and master has had a letter.'

At once Jane thanked the housekeeper and she and her sister ran towards the house, both too eager to hear the news to have time to discuss what they had heard. They ran through the vestibule and into the breakfast room. It was empty.

'The library, let us try there, Jane.'

Their father was not in their either. 'Perhaps he has gone upstairs to speak to our mother, Lizzy.'

They turned and were on the point of ascending when they met the butler. 'If you are looking for my master, ma'am, he is walking towards the little copse.'

Upon this information they instantly passed through the hall once more and ran across the lawn after their father, who was deliberately pursuing his way towards a small wood on one side of the paddock.

'Run ahead, Lizzy, you are fitter and lighter than I. I shall make my own way in my own time.' She watched her sister race ahead and saw her catch up with their father. A lively exchange took place and then he took a letter from his pocket and Elizabeth impatiently caught it from his hand. It was at this juncture Jane came up with them.

'Read it aloud, Lizzy, for I hardly know myself what it is about.'

'Gracechurch Street, Monday,
'August 2

'My dear brother,

'At last am able to send you some tidings of my niece, and such as, upon the whole, I hope shall give you satisfaction. Soon after you left the vicinity, I was fortunate enough to find out which part of London they were in. The particulars I

reserve until we meet. It is enough to know that they are discovered and I have seen both Lydia and Wickham.'

'Then it is, as I always hoped,' Jane interrupted. 'They are married! I beg your pardon, Lizzy, please read on.'

'I had seen them both. They are not married, nor can I find there was any intention of being so; but if you're willing to perform the engagements which I have ventured to make on your side, I hope it will not be long before they are. All that is required of you is to assure to your daughter, by settlement, an equal share of the five thousand pounds, secured among your children after the decease of yourself and my sister. Moreover, to enter into an engagement allowing her, during your life, one hundred pounds per annum.

'These are conditions, which, considering everything, I had no hesitation in complying with, as far as I thought myself privileged, for you. I shall send this by express, that no time may be lost in bringing me your answer.

'You will easily comprehend from these particulars that Mr Wickham's circumstances are not so hopeless as they are generally believed to be. The world has been deceived in that respect, and I am happy to say, there will be some little money, even when all his debts are discharged, to settle on my niece, additional to her own fortune. If, as I conclude will be the case, you send me full powers to act in your name, throughout the whole of this business, I will immediately give directions to Haggerston for preparing a proper settlement.

'There will not be the smallest occasion of your coming to Town again; therefore, stay quietly at Longbourn, and depend on my diligence and care. Send back your answer as soon as you can, and be careful to write explicitly. We have judged it

best, that my niece should be married from this house, which I hope you will approve. She comes to us today. I shall write again as soon as anything more is determined on.

'Yours, etc. EDW GARDINER'

Elizabeth was astonished by the contents of the letter. 'I cannot believe it. Can it be possible that Wickham will marry Lydia?'

'Wickham is not so undeserving then, as we have thought him,' Jane added. 'My dear father, I congratulate you.'

'Papa, have you answered the letter?'

'No, Lizzy, but it must be done soon.'

'Oh! My dear father, come back and write immediately. Consider how important every moment is in such a case.'

Jane added her entreaties. 'Let me write it for you, if you dislike the trouble yourself.'

'I dislike it very much, but it must be done, I suppose.' And so saying, he turned back with them, and walked towards the house.

Elizabeth was curious about the terms mentioned in the letter. 'It is good news, indeed; Lydia and Wickham must marry and I am pleased that it took so little to persuade him to comply.'

Mr Bennet became quite agitated. 'There are two things that I want very much to know: one is, how much money your uncle has laid down to bring it about; and the other, how I am ever to repay him.'

When Jane and Elizabeth were together after supper they discussed what had taken place that day. 'I do wish, with hindsight, Jane, that I had not told Darcy about Lydia and Wickham. Now that she is to marry, he need never have known.'

'It is a pity, but surely Mr Darcy will not discuss the matter?'

'I am certain that he will not; he is a man of the utmost

probity and I totally rely on his secrecy in this. But I must wish he did not know about it.'

'He will not think less of you, I am sure.'

'Dear Jane, how can he not? He is such a proud man. I thought he was softening in his behaviour towards me, but this has spoilt everything. We can never be more than strangers now.'

'But you do not want to be more than that.'

'No, of course not, but I would rather he did not think badly of our family.'

'Poor Lizzy. Yet we must be happy that Lydia is to marry. I wonder how long it will take our mother to persuade Papa to relent on the matter of them visiting here. He says he will not allow it but I think he must change his mind.'

'He will agree either to the wedding clothes or the visit, but I doubt that he will do both. I am certain that even Mama shall settle for a lack of new clothes in order to be reunited with Lydia.'

'Then we should speak up for them. It will give our sister's marriage a validity it will not otherwise possess.'

'Very well. Let us go and talk to him.'

They were soon with their father.

'Dear Papa, I understand how you must feel on this matter; of course neither Lydia nor Mr Wickham deserve to receive your approval. They have both behaved disgracefully. However, would it not look strange to the neighbourhood if we did not bid them farewell before they set off to the north of England?' Jane smiled sweetly and looked at Elizabeth for support.

'Only think, sir, they shall both be so far away you will not be obliged to receive them again in the foreseeable future. This will give closure to the matter, allow Lydia to say goodbye to Kitty,

Mary and her mother. Could you not reconsider for our sakes, if not for theirs?'

He sighed and raised his hand in a gesture of defeat. 'Very well. I am not happy about it, do not expect me to be pleased to see either of them. I shall let them come for your sakes, but it will be this once only; be very clear on that.'

With that Jane had to be satisfied. Now that their aunt had returned with the children to Cheapside, both she and Lizzy were much involved with duties around the house but nevertheless found time to take a daily constitutional in the garden. On one of these occasions their conversation returned to their own future.

'I still cannot quite believe that our youngest sister is to be married first. That is turning precedence on its head, is it not, Lizzy?'

'Indeed it is. It could have been me if I had not been so mistaken in Bingley's feelings. Do you think that we might both be invited to London next year? It would be so much more enjoyable to have you at my side.'

'Perhaps next summer they might decide to go to the Lakes after all, and I shall insist that you come too. If we are to be left firmly on the shelf we must, at least, make an effort to see a little more of the world.'

Jane smiled. 'That is another thing, to think that Lydia will be going to the north of England. Indeed, being the wife of a regular soldier, she could be sent to the Americas or even India, could she not?'

'Travel would be wasted on her. As long as there are parties and pretty dresses she is unaware of anything else.'

18

The day of Lydia's wedding arrived and Jane and Elizabeth walked in the shrubbery after they had completed all the little tasks Mrs Bennet deemed necessary to prepare for the arrival of Mr and Mrs Wickham.

'It must be so difficult for Lydia, to be married without the support of her family. I do feel for her. To feel herself so shamed, to have let down her family in this way, to have put everyone to such a deal of trouble, I could not bear it myself. Poor Lydia to have her wedding day spoilt by such feelings as those.'

'Jane, you repine too much on the matter. She has the support of her aunt and uncle, and she will be with us by dinner time. I doubt not that the reception she will receive from our mother, Kitty and Mary will more than make up for their absence at the church.'

'I wonder if she shall be very much changed by the experience, Lizzy. I am dreading how Papa will be with them both; also I shall not know how to speak to Mr Wickham.'

'Knowing Lydia as I do, I should very much doubt that the experience will have altered her much. Remember, Jane, according to our uncle she was perfectly happy living out of wedlock with Wickham and not in the slightest hurry to leave.'

'I cannot understand how a girl with Lydia's upbringing could have become embroiled in such a scrape. Come, Lizzy, I think we should return to the house. We do not wish to be tardy.'

They hurried back in order to be in the breakfast room to receive the young couple. Although Jane and her sisters were concerned, their mother was beside herself with excitement. Jane could not help but notice her father looked impenetrably grave; he had not forgiven Lydia for her behaviour.

She could hear Lydia's voice in the vestibule and the door was thrown open and she ran into the room as though she had just returned from a delightful visit. Their mother stepped forwards and embraced her and welcomed her with exclamations of rapture, and even gave her hand, with an affectionate smile, to Wickham.

'My dear Lydia, Wickham, I am so happy to see you both and do most heartily congratulate you on your nuptials. Imagine that! You are Mrs Wickham now. Who would have thought it? Married at sixteen, and to such a handsome man, an officer and a gentleman.'

Mr Bennet did not greet them quite so cordially. Jane was glad it was not she who had to face his disapproval. His countenance rather gained in austerity and he scarcely opened his lips. The easy assurance of the young couple, the way they behaved as if nothing untoward had occurred, as though they had been married with everybody's full support and approval, deeply shocked her.

She could scarcely credit that Lydia had changed not one bit. She was still as unabashed, wild noisy and fearless as always.

'Well! Have I not done exactly as I said I would? It was always my intention to be married first and see what a delightful husband I have. Do you not congratulate me on my wedding day?'

Reluctantly, it seemed to Jane, all of them offered their felicitations. Even Kitty and Mary were subdued in the face of Lydia and Wickham's blatant disregard for everybody's feelings. Eventually they all sat down and Lydia glanced around the room, commenting on some little alteration to it, and observing that it was a great while since she had been there.

Jane sat listening to them both and blushed. She was aware that Elizabeth was equally uncomfortable. Neither Wickham nor Lydia felt the need to apologise for their behaviour. They seemed both of them to have the happiest memories in the world; nothing of the past was recollected with pain.

Several times Jane shuddered and looked to Elizabeth for reassurance when Lydia alluded quite happily to subjects that neither of them would have dreamt of mentioning.

'Only think of its being three months since I went away; it seems but a fortnight, I declare; and yet there have been things enough happened in that time. Good gracious! When I went away, I am sure I had no more idea of being married till I came back again! Though I thought it would be very good fun if I was.'

Jane felt herself colour and shifted with embarrassment in her chair. How could Lydia be so thoughtless? Her sister – apparently unaware of the distress she was causing to all who listened, apart from her husband – continued gaily in the same vein.

'Oh! Mama, do the people hereabouts know I am married today? I was afraid they might not; and when we overtook William Goulding in his curricle, I was determined he should know it and so I let down the side glass next to him, took off my glove and let my hand just rest upon the window frame, that he might see the ring, then I bowed and smiled like anything.'

This last statement proved too much for Elizabeth and she scrambled to her feet and ran from the room; Jane wished she could go with her but felt duty-bound to remain where she was and offer support to her parents at this difficult time.

It was not until they were passing through the hall go to the dining parlour that her sister rejoined them. Lydia at that moment walked up to Jane and said with a condescending smile, 'Ah! Jane, I take your place now. You must go lower, because *I* am a married woman.'

All through the meal Lydia's ease and good spirits increased. She told her assembled family that she longed to see Mrs Philips, the Lucases, and all the other neighbours, and hear herself called Mrs Wickham by each of them. It was insupportable, but worse was to come when they were reassembled in the breakfast room.

'Well, Mama, and what you think of my husband? Is not he a charming man? I am sure my sisters must all envy me. I only hope they may have half my good luck. They must all go to Brighton. That is the place to get husbands. What a pity it is, Mama, we did not all go.'

Mrs Bennet nodded vigorously. 'Very true; if I had my will, we should. But my dear Lydia, I don't at all like you going such a way. Must it be so?'

'Oh Lord! Yes, there is nothing in that. I shall like it above all things. You and Papa, and my sisters, must come down and see us. We shall be at Newcastle all winter, and I dare say there will be some balls, and I would take care to get good partners for them all.'

Mrs Bennet trilled happily. 'I should like it beyond anything.'

'And, then when you go away, you may leave one or two of my sisters behind you; and I dare say I should get husbands for them before the winter is over.'

Elizabeth could remain silent no longer. 'I thank you for my share of the favour, Lydia, but I do not at all like your way of getting husbands.'

Even this direct reference to her sister's indiscretion did not repress Lydia's buoyant spirits.

When eventually Jane was able to retire to the blessed silence of her shared apartment, she turned to her sister in despair. 'Lizzy, how shall we support it? They are to be with us a full ten days; imagine the embarrassments, the indiscretions we shall all have to endure before they depart.'

'We must thank God, Jane, that they do not stay above ten days. If Mr Wickham had not received his commission before he left London, and have to join his regiment at the end of a fortnight, they might have been with us for weeks.'

One afternoon Wickham came to walk beside her in the garden. 'Miss Bennet, or should I call you Jane, now that I am your brother?'

'It is permissible for you to call me by my given name, but I would prefer it if you did not.'

She had surprised herself by speaking so sharply to a man she had used to think charming and reliable. His expression changed and for a moment he looked uncertain.

'In which case, I would not dream of offending you. No doubt you are unhappy that I cannot provide for Lydia as well as you might have hoped. If Mr Darcy had not deprived me of my living, matters would be very different.'

'I understand, sir, that things are not quite as you would have me believe. Mr Darcy is an honourable man and treats everyone with respect.'

He looked shocked, but rallied and smiled his usual superficial smile and walked away. Jane watched him go. She could not help comparing him with Charles. Now *he* was a true gentleman in every respect.

A few days after Elizabeth and Jane heard such news from Lydia, they could scarcely credit it. The girl was determined to share with them every last detail of her wedding day in spite of their discouragement.

'No really, we have no wish to hear of it. I think there cannot be too little said on the subject.'

'La! You are so strange! But I must tell you how it went off. There was my aunt, all the time I was dressing, preaching and talking away just as if she was reading a sermon. However, I did not hear but one word in ten. I was thinking, as you may suppose, of my dear Wickham. I longed to know whether he would be married in his blue coat.'

Jane made a desperate attempt to stop her sister's flow of words. 'Lydia, I believe I heard Kitty calling you. Do you not think you should go and see what she wants?'

'Fiddlesticks to that! I should much rather be here with you to and tell you exactly what took place. Just as the carriage came to the door, my uncle was called away and I was so frightened that he would not be back in time and we would not be married that day. Luckily he came back again in ten minutes time and then we all set out.'

She smiled round at her sisters, seemingly unaware of their disinclination to listen to her account. 'However, I recollected afterwards, if he had been prevented from going, the wedding need not be put off, for Mr Darcy might have done as well.'

'Mr Darcy!'

Jane looked up in surprise and Elizabeth jumped to her feet in utter astonishment.

'Oh, yes – he was to come there with Wickham, you know. But, gracious me! I quite forgot! I was not to have said a word about it. I promised them so faithfully! What will Wickham say? It was to be such a secret!'

'If it was to be a secret,' Jane said hastily, 'say not another word on the subject. You may depend upon my seeking no further information.'

'Oh! Certainly,' said Elizabeth, but Jane could see her sister was burning with curiosity. 'We shall not ask you any questions on the subject.'

'Thank you,' said Lydia, 'well, if you did, I should certainly tell you all, and then Wickham would be angry.'

Jane watched Elizabeth hurry away and was obliged to sit and endure a further thirty minutes of tedious details before she could escape to join her sister in their private sitting room. As she walked in Elizabeth was folding a letter. She could guess to whom it was addressed, but her delicate sense of honour would not allow her to speak on the subject, even when they were private. If the matter was confidential then it would not be she who would ask impertinent questions.

However, it did not stop her wondering exactly what Elizabeth had written to her aunt.

19

Charles returned to his town house four days after receiving the letter from Mr Darcy, leaving his sister Caroline to travel back with Louisa and Hurst. He had no wish to be cooped up in his carriage with her, listening to her complain and criticise everyone she knew. No, he was much better travelling speedily from Derbyshire to London; the closer he got to his destination the more determined he was to send instructions to Nicholls to have her prepare Netherfield for his arrival.

However, when he reached home he was immediately embroiled in various matters with his lawyers and was unable to send word to Netherfield for a further two weeks. He advised Darcy that he was back, but received a short note in reply saying he would contact him as soon as he was free to do so.

Charles was puzzled as to why he had been asked to return to Town in order to talk to his friend, when Darcy refused to come and see him. He was in the drawing room reading a newspaper when the visitor he had been expecting these past two weeks was finally announced.

'My dear Darcy, I have been kicking my heels in Town when

I could have been in Derbyshire enjoying my visit to Pemberley in your absence.'

'I do apologise, Bingley. My business has been satisfactorily concluded. I am now here to make a suggestion. I think it is time that we returned to Netherfield. I should like to accompany you, if you would allow me to.'

This was unexpected but pleasing news. It was exactly what he wished to do himself. He felt sure his friend intended to pursue Elizabeth and that would give him the opportunity to renew his acquaintance with Jane without revealing his intentions. He did not wish Darcy to know he still loved her. If he discovered that she had no feelings for him then it would be him alone who suffered from the rejection.

'I should be delighted to go back to Hertfordshire for a week or two; I made good friends there and felt that I came away too quickly, without saying my farewells. I believe that there has been sufficient time passed by for me to return without exciting undue comment.'

'Excellent! When shall you go down?'

'I should send word to Nicholls tomorrow. If I allow her three days to remove the covers and fill the larder, that should be sufficient. I have only a skeleton staff at Netherfield; I shall send down my people from here. Although there will only be the two of us in residence, the house is far too large to be run without a full complement of servants.'

The letter was duly written and sent the following morning; he was not sure if he was excited or fearful to be visiting Longbourn again after so many months' absence. His future happiness depended on the reception he received from a certain member of the Bennet family.

* * *

Jane was relieved when the day of Lydia's departure finally arrived. Even at the last, Lydia had made a jibe about her sisters not being married, saying that she would not have time to write to Longbourn now that she was married. She suggested that her sisters might like to write to her as they had nothing else to do.

But life had barely settled down to normal when news arrived that Charles was to return to Netherfield! And all the hopes she thought she had put aside rose up again. Could he be returning for her?

'I saw you look at me today, Lizzy, when Aunt Philips told us of the present report; and I know I appeared distressed. But do not imagine it was from any silly cause. I was only confused for the moment because I felt that I should be looked at. I do assure you, the news does not affect me either with pleasure or pain. I am glad of one thing: that he comes alone, because we shall see the less of him. Not that I am afraid for myself, but I dread other people's remarks.'

'I am glad to hear you say so, Jane. You have had more than enough upset over the past few weeks and it will do you no good to have more. Although, I do feel it is a shame that Mr Bingley cannot come to a house, which he has legally hired, without raising all this speculation.'

'I do agree with you, and I, for one, shall not be expecting to see him at all. I have nothing against Mr Bingley, although I no longer wish to be intimate with his sisters, but neither do I wish to renew our acquaintance.'

Jane was almost convinced that what she had said to Elizabeth was the truth. It had been nine months or more since she had set eyes on Charles, quite long enough to have recovered from her misapprehension. However, she knew herself to be affected by it. She jumped at every loud noise, felt her eyes fill with tears for no reason at all and was well aware that her sister knew how disturbed she was.

It did not help that her mother began again on the subject that had been discussed at length almost twelve months ago. 'As soon as ever Mr Bingley comes, my dear, you will wait on him of course.' Mrs Bennet cried to her husband.

'No, no. You forced me into visiting last year, and promised if I went to see him, he should marry one of my daughters. But it ended in nothing, and I will not be sent on a fool's errand again.'

Although her dear father did not mean to distress her by his remark, Jane could not help but feel this referred to her dashed hopes. Her mother continued to demand that it was absolutely necessary for a call to be made to Netherfield; that all the other gentlemen in the neighbourhood would be visiting with their cards on Mr Bingley's return.

'It is an etiquette I despise. If he wants our society, let him seek it. He knows where we live. I will not spend *my* hours running after my neighbours every time they go away and come back again.'

Mama would not give up the subject and Jane wished she could leave the room without drawing attention to herself.

'Well, all I know is that it will be abominably rude if you do not wait on him. But, however, that shall not prevent my asking him to dine here. I am determined. We must have Mrs Long and the Gouldings soon. That will make thirteen with ourselves, so there will be just room at table for him.'

Jane was able to talk privately to Elizabeth on the matter. 'I begin to be sorry that he comes at all; I could see him with perfect indifference, but I can hardly bear to hear it thus perpetually talked of. My mother means well; but she does not know, no one can know how much I suffer from what she says. Happy shall I be when his stay at Netherfield is over.'

'I wish I could say something to comfort you, but it is totally out of my power. You must feel it; and the usual satisfaction of preaching patience is denied me, because you have always so much.'

Jane believed that she had revealed far too much of her feelings already and hastily changed the subject. When Charles arrived at Netherfield her mother continued to fret over how soon she could send the invitation to dinner, but the third morning after his arrival they were all gathered in her mother's dressing room when Mrs Bennet cried out in delight.

'Oh! Do come and look, girls. Just see who is riding towards the house at this very moment. I cannot believe Mr Bingley should come and see us before I had sent him his invite. I wonder what that can mean?'

Jane clenched her fingers in her lap and remained where she was; Elizabeth, to satisfy her mother, went to the window, looked and hastily returned to her place. Jane noticed that she looked almost as disturbed as she by the visitor.

'There is a gentleman with him, Mama. Who can it be?' Kitty cried.

'Some acquaintance or other, my dear, I suppose; I am sure I do not know.'

'La! It looks like that man that used to be with him before. Mr what's his name? That tall, proud man.'

'Good gracious! Mr Darcy! And so it does!. Well, any friend of Mr Bingley's will always be welcome here, to be sure; but else I must say that I hate the very sight of him.'

Jane turned and looked at Elizabeth with surprise and concern. She felt the awkwardness which must attend her sister in seeing him after she had revealed so much about Lydia's disgrace. It was no wonder that Elizabeth had returned to her seat with such alacrity.

Jane touched her hand and smiled sympathetically. It must be very difficult for her sister to be obliged to meet a man whose merit she had undervalued. Her face, which had lost its colour, now took on an additional glow, and Jane could see Elizabeth's lips trembling in a smile, and there was an added lustre in her eyes. She was at a loss to know what this could signify.

She had no time to ponder on her sister's reaction to the news that Mr Darcy was coming, as the two gentlemen arrived in person. Jane greeted both guests politely and returned to her embroidery, and was embarrassed by the way that her mother treated Charles with such civility and was so cold to his friend.

Jane hardly dared to raise her eyes, making random stabs at her sewing, knowing very well that she would have to unpick them when their visitors had gone. He seated himself next to her mother and she listened eagerly to what he said. Just hearing him speak was a pleasure indeed.

'It is a long time, Mr Bingley, since you went away.'

'Indeed it is, Mrs Bennet, but I am here again now.'

'I began to be afraid you would never come back. People did say you meant to quit the place entirely at Michaelmas; but, however, I hope it is not true. A great many changes have happened in this neighbourhood, since you went away. Miss Lucas is married and settled. One of my own daughters, Lydia, married Mr Wickham. I suppose you have heard of it; indeed, you must have seen it in the papers. It was in the *Times* and the *Courier*, I know; but it was not put in as it ought to be. Did you see it?'

'I did, madam, and may I offer congratulations on your youngest daughter's wedding.'

'It is a delightful thing, to be sure, to have a daughter well married, but at the same time, Mr Bingley, it is very hard to have her taken away from me. They are gone to Newcastle, a place quite northward, it seems, and there they are to stay. I do not know for how long. His regiment is there; I suppose you have heard of his leaving the militia and of his being gone into the regulars? Thank heaven he has *some* friends, though perhaps not so many as he deserves.'

Jane saw Elizabeth flinch at these words and then her sister hastily joined in the conversation. 'Mr Bingley, how long do you expect to stay in the country at present?'

He smiled pleasantly. 'A few weeks, I believe, Miss Elizabeth.'

He had not changed; perhaps he looked a trifle older, but he was still the man she loved and she could not help herself from responding to his warm regard. On seeing her expression, Charles moved across and took the seat that her sister had just vacated.

Jane was anxious that he perceive no difference in her at all and was determined to talk as much as ever, be as open and amiable without showing any partiality, even though *he* seemed less chatty than she recalled.

'Miss Bennet, I hope I find you well?'

'Yes, Mr Bingley, thank you for enquiring.' Jane searched her mind for something else to bring into the conversation as he seemed not to have anything further to say. 'And Mrs Hurst, and Miss Bingley, they are both well?'

'Yes, they shall not be joining me on this visit. They are busy in Town.'

Jane risked a glance at him and thought she saw admiration reflected in his eyes. Surely, after so long, she could not be so foolish as to believe him interested? 'It is quiet at Longbourn now that Lydia has gone.' She bit her lip in vexation. What had possessed her to mention the subject that must be embarrassing to both of them?

'I must own, I was surprised to hear that your sister had

married Wickham. But Darcy assured me it was a love match, so I wish them well.'

It was then that Jane realised Charles did not know the full story; Elizabeth had been correct in believing that Mr Darcy would not reveal what he knew about Lydia's disgrace. She was relieved. Such knowledge might have made him think less of the family.

'As do we all, of course. You are here for the shooting?'

'I am, but I hope that I might be permitted to call at Longbourn as well?'

Jane did not know how to answer; she dared not look at him in case her expression revealed her excitement at his words. Her feelings had not changed over the months they had been separated; could it be that he had reconsidered? That the intervening time had made him realise she was more to him than a friend?

She was not aware that she sat in silence for much of the remainder of the visit. Her mind was so busily engaged in speculation that she forgot to speak. When the gentlemen rose to go away, Mrs Bennet was mindful of her intended civility, and they were engaged to dine at Longbourn in a few days' time.

'You are quite a visit in my debt, Mr Bingley, for when you went to Town last winter, you promised to take a family dinner with us as soon as you returned. I have not forgot, you see; and I assure you, I was very much disappointed that you did not come back and keep your engagement.'

Jane saw Charles shift uneasily on his feet and his cheeks coloured. 'I must apologise for not returning, but I was prevented by pressing affairs. I look forward to making up for my omission in a few days.'

The gentlemen departed and Jane immediately followed her sister, who had left the room abruptly. She knew that her expression reflected her pleasure in the visit having passed so successfully without her having revealed to anyone her feelings.

'Now, Lizzy, that this first meeting is over, I feel perfectly easy. I know my own strength, and I shall never be embarrassed again by his coming. I am glad he dines here on Tuesday. It will then be publicly seen that, on both sides, we meet only as indifferent acquaintance.'

Elizabeth laughed, seeing through her words with ease. 'Yes, very indifferent indeed! Oh, Jane, do take care.'

'My dear Lizzy, you cannot think me so weak as to be in danger now?'

'You are in very great danger of making him as much in love with you as ever.'

Jane hurried away to the kitchen to collect the trug in which she was to pick plums for Hill to make a crumble. Once outside in the tranquillity of the orchard, she thought back to what her sister had just said. Could Lizzy be right? Had Charles come back to Netherfield just to resume his courtship of her?

She must not get her hopes raised, she could not bear to have them dashed a second time.

But if this was true, why had he not come to see her while she had been staying in London? The only explanation could be that Caroline had not told him she was there.

As Charles rode away from Longbourn, he was well pleased with how the visit had progressed.

'Miss Bennet looks remarkably well, and Miss Elizabeth also, do not you think so, Darcy?' he called across as they exited the paddock.

'I do, my friend. I have never seen two more healthy young

ladies. I am, this time, anticipating our next visit here.' Darcy kicked his horse into a canter, making further conversation impossible.

After dinner Darcy said he had letters to write and would join him in an hour, leaving Charles to his own devices. He settled in his favourite armchair in the library to think about what had happened that day. Jane was a little thinner than she used to be, but still as lovely. He was certain he had not imagined her pleasure in his company and he had loved every moment he had spent with her.

This time he would not leave Netherfield until he had asked her to marry him. If she refused, then so be it. He had had enough of being solitary. He would go and find Darcy immediately and insist that they play a game of billiards and talk about Jane and Elizabeth.

Not liking to presume, Charles decided not to call again at Longbourn until they were to dine. Instead he spent his time visiting old friends and very soon realised the pleasures of Hertfordshire had not faded in his absence. He would rather be there than anywhere else, even Pemberley. He knew the fact that the woman he loved resided close by made Netherfield the most attractive place in the world.

He had been unable to ascertain from their brief visit exactly how Jane felt about him. She had looked at him as she always had, but she had often fallen silent and that was something he was not used to in her company. He did not like to ask his friend what that might signify; if it meant she was not interested he did not wish to know.

* * *

On Tuesday, the day that Charles and Darcy were to come to dine, there was to be a large party assembled at Longbourn. Jane had done her best to appear unmoved by all the preparations and knowing winks and arch looks that her mother sent in her direction. She took no more time on her preparations that evening than usual.

'Jane, you look lovely tonight. Your eyes are sparkling and your complexion perfect,' her sister said to her as they were leaving their chamber, 'and I have always loved that leaf green gown on you.'

'Thank you, Lizzy. It is a favourite of mine, but I have worn it many times before. However, I do not believe I have seen *your* gown before this evening? I believe that we *both* look our best.' Jane slipped her arm through her sister's. 'I intend to enjoy this evening. It is such a relief that neither of us are embarrassed to meet the Netherfield gentlemen.'

Those who had been invited to dine gathered in the drawing room to sip sherry wine and exchange pleasantries. When the butler announced that dinner was served they repaired to the dining room. Jane headed towards her usual position at the far end of the table, and as she reached her place she happened to glance round and saw Charles hesitating in the doorway. She could not help herself, she smiled and he took that as an invitation.

Politely he pulled out her chair and, when she was seated, he sat next to her. As the rest of the party found their places she was aware that Elizabeth glanced towards Mr Darcy and Charles did the same. Then she forgot about the other guests as he turned to her with the sweet smile she remembered so well.

'Miss Bennet, it has been far too long since we had occasion to be together. I cannot tell you how pleased I am to be back at Netherfield, and able to see you again.'

'I am glad that you have returned. It is a great shame to have such a grand house standing empty.'

'Well, I am back now and considering holding another ball. Do you think this a good idea?'

Jane glanced at him, smiling. 'As long as we do not receive a plate of apple pie and roast beef.'

He chuckled. 'I remember. I should certainly not employ a groom to wait at table again. Neither shall I have Caroline as my hostess. I am hoping…' He stopped abruptly and looked conscious. Jane's heart lurched. She was almost sure he had been going to ask her to stand in Caroline's place.

'Perhaps you could have something less formal than a ball. Remember the delightful evening we spent at Lucas Lodge? We danced and enjoyed our supper on that occasion.'

'Then that is what I shall do. As long as I can dance with you, I shall be content.' The warmth in his expression was unmistakable.

The conversation was interrupted by the arrival of the soup, which was followed by venison and partridges and various other side dishes, which Jane scarcely noticed. When her mother rose to lead the ladies into the drawing room she thought that Elizabeth seemed a little quiet. But she had no time to dwell on that as her mother asked her to preside over the tea and for her sister to pour the coffee.

After the tea things were removed, the card tables were placed and Jane had no further opportunity for private conversation with Charles. However, she was conscious of his eyes turning frequently in her direction, and he smiled whenever she looked his way. Jane nodded and smiled whenever she was addressed but had no recollection of what had been said to her. All she could think about was the possibility she could hope again. That Charles was going to spend all winter at Netherfield and hold parties and soirées. How different her life was today. A few short weeks ago she could never have imagined such happiness ahead.

There was no further opportunity for private conversation as Charles and Darcy were obliged to leave first when their carriage arrived before the others. No sooner had they departed than her mother smiled across at her.

'Oh, my dear Jane, I never saw you looking in greater beauty. Mrs Long said so to me when I asked her whether you did or not. What do you think she said besides? *"Ah! Mrs Bennet, we shall have Jane at Netherfield at last"*.'

Later in their apartment, Jane turned to her sister with a degree of satisfaction. 'It has been a very agreeable day. The party seemed so well selected, so suitable one with the other. I hope we may often meet again.' Her sister smiled knowingly. 'Lizzy, you must not do that. You must not suspect me. It mortifies me. I assure you that I have now learnt to enjoy his conversation as an agreeable and sensible young man without having a wish beyond it. I am perfectly satisfied from what his manners now are, that he never had any design of engaging my affection. It is only that he is blessed with greater sweetness of address, and a stronger desire of generally pleasing than any other man.'

'You are very cruel. You will not let me smile and are provoking me to it every moment.'

'How hard it is in some cases to be believed!'

'And how impossible in others!'

'But why should you wish to persuade me that I feel more than I acknowledge?'

'That is a question that I hardly know how to answer. We all love to instruct, though we can teach only what is not worth knowing. Forgive me; and if you persist in indifference, do not make *me* your confidante.'

* * *

Charles bounded out of bed believing his life was about to change for the better. He had not mistaken Jane's affection. She had responded with such enthusiasm to his every word. He was almost certain she loved him.

Downstairs he headed for the breakfast room, for the first time in many months actually looking forward to his meal. The room was empty. Darcy not yet come down. There was enough food laid out on the sideboard to feed ten people, but he knew it would not go to waste. What he and Darcy did not consume would feed his staff.

He had piled ham, scrambled eggs, grilled mushrooms and tomatoes upon his plate when the door opened and his friend walked in. He turned to greet him cheerily and was surprised by how serious he looked.

'I intend to return to London, Bingley. I have things to attend to, but there is something I must tell you before I leave.'

'You look so grave, Darcy. I do hope it is not bad news.'

'I have a confession to make, my friend, something I should have told you long ago. Do you remember that it was my persuasion that led you to think that Jane Bennet did not hold you in the same esteem as you held her?'

'Indeed I do. Have you now come to a different conclusion?'

'I am ashamed to admit that I have. My interference in your affairs was both absurd and impertinent.'

'What are you telling me? Those are strong words indeed. You had no right to interfere in my concerns. I would not dream of doing so in yours.' He slammed down his plate on the table and two slices of ham shot off onto the floor. He glared at Darcy. 'I cannot believe you would deliberately mislead me.'

'No, at least I do not have that on my conscience. At the time I honestly believed Miss Bennet did not hold deep and lasting feelings for you. I am now certain that I was incorrect; and I do most humbly apologise for causing you both so much unhappiness.'

'From your expression I gather there is more you have to tell me. I am waiting.'

Darcy continued to look sombre. 'You are correct. I have not told you the whole, Bingley. There is more, and this you will not accept with equanimity, I am sure.'

'What else did you do to keep us apart?'

'I knew that Miss Bennet was in Town for three months last winter, and I purposely kept it from you. I thought it better; it was none of my business. And I fully understand if you no longer wish to call me friend.'

Charles could not understand that Darcy had actually deceived him; that Caroline had done so he could more readily accept. He turned aside, too angry to trust himself to speak. He strode away, wishing to be on his own, to digest this unpleasant information. To think, that Jane had been in Town and he had not known! What she must have thought of him to have ignored her in that way!

He remembered the letter he had written and knew without doubt that his sister had not posted it. Jane had never received it, had not known how he felt. What Caroline had done was far worse. It was done for selfish reasons, out of jealousy. Had Darcy acted out of regard or pride? Did his dislike of Jane's relatives mean he could not contemplate his closest friend becoming part of the Bennet family?

Darcy could go to the devil. He strode out of the house and

ran to the stable shouting for his horse to be saddled. Once mounted he dug in his heels. His mount reared and took off at such speed he covered the groom in dirt. He drove the animal faster and faster until his anger began to dissipate.

After a mile or so he drew rein and allowed his horse to drop back into a canter. He began to take stock of his surroundings, to think rationally again. He recalled the most important thing that Darcy had told him: Jane loved him, had always done so. He could not imagine how miserable she must have been imagining herself cruelly abandoned. Poor Jane, it was small wonder she treated him with some reserve when they were together this time.

'Time to go back, old fellow. I must mend fences with Darcy and then get over to Longbourn and speak to Mr Bennet.'

The horse flicked its ears in response and seemed as eager to return to Netherfield as he was. There was no sign of his friend when he returned. The butler told him Darcy had gone out looking for him. He grinned. He would wait in the library. Shortly afterwards there came a quiet knock on the door and he was happy to greet his friend without animosity.

Charles went over and gripped his hand. 'It is all water under the bridge. You have told me the very thing that I most wanted to hear. I had not been able to decide, even after seeing my darling Jane twice, whether she is in love with me. I have no wish to make her an offer that she might feel obliged to accept because of her mother's influence. I shall go tomorrow and speak to her.'

Darcy, not normally a demonstrative man, shook his hand vigorously and then embraced him. 'I cannot tell you how relieved I am that you have forgiven me. I have felt wretched indeed since you rode off without me.'

'We shall put it all behind us, Darcy. All that matters now is that I love Jane and that it is likely she returns my affections.' He grinned at the look of comical relief on his friend's face. 'Pray, correct me if I am wrong, but I believe that I am not the only one in love with a Miss Bennet.'

Charles was delighted to see Darcy colour and turn away without denying the statement.

20

Having bid his friend goodbye, Charles immediately made ready to ride over to Longbourn. His step was light, his demeanour so happy, all of the staff he encountered appeared to feel their spirits lift on seeing him. It wasn't until he was in the saddle that he realised Jane thought he had behaved badly. Although she had seemed happy in his company the other evening, was this just because she was being civil to a guest? She had certainly been quiet on their first meeting. Now he was not so sure he would get a favourable reception.

However, he was warmly greeted by all the Bennet family, but it was towards Jane that he constantly turned. Did her blushes mean that he was a welcome visitor or that she was displeased with him? When Mrs Bennet made a pointed comment she looked away, as if not pleased by her mother's references. Did this mean he was still unforgiven? Had he and Darcy mistaken her feelings?

But then each time she smiled, he was sure he could see love in her eyes and could not understand how he had been so blind last year as to have missed what was so obvious to him now.

If Mr Bennet had appeared to join the merry party in the drawing room, he would have asked to speak to him, but he did not wish the lady of the house to be forewarned of his intention. Jane must be the first to know how much he loved her. Having spent more than an hour at Longbourn, he knew it was time to leave or he would be accused of outstaying his welcome.

'Mr Bingley, would you care to dine with us tonight? Remember you are still in our debt on that score.'

'I am afraid, Mrs Bennet, that I have a prior engagement that I cannot cancel. If I had known that you intended to ask me to dine I can promise you I would not have accepted another invitation.'

'Next time you call, Mr Bingley, I hope we shall be more lucky.'

'I should be very happy at any time to join you here. It is only this evening that I am unable to come.'

'Can you come tomorrow?'

'I should be delighted. I have no engagement at all for tomorrow. I thank you most heartily and look forward to coming to Longbourn.'

With their good wishes ringing in his ears he departed. Tomorrow evening he would find a moment to be private with Jane and declare himself; he was eager for that moment to arrive after having delayed so long.

* * *

Jane waited until Sarah had left the bedroom before turning to her sister. 'Lizzy, do *you* think that Charles loves me as much as I love him?'

'Of course he does, you peagoose. He could not take his eyes from you; I have never seen a man so besotted.'

'In which case why has he not spoken to *me* of his feelings? And if he intends to make an offer why hasn't he spoken to Papa? After all, he has visited here several times already. If he had intended...'

'Dearest Jane, you are working yourself up unnecessarily. He is as insecure as you are, but he will speak to you as soon as he is certain that he will receive a favourable answer.'

'But I love him so much, surely he must see that in the way I behave with him? I could not survive another disappointment.'

Her sister rushed across to enfold her in her arms. 'Enough of this, you must go to sleep. All will be well in the morning, I promise you.'

It seemed an eternity to wait until the evening when Charles was to dine with them. Somehow she muddled through the day until it was time to get ready. She was in her bedchamber when her mother ran into their room, in her dressing gown, with her hair half finished.

'My dear Jane, make haste and hurry down. He is come; Mr Bingley is come. He is, indeed. Make haste, make haste. Here, Sarah, come to Miss Bennet this moment, and help her on with her gown. Never mind Miss Lizzy's hair.'

'We will be down as soon as we can, but I dare say Kitty is more forward than either of us. She went upstairs half an hour ago.' Jane was relieved her voice did not reflect her excitement at his early arrival.

'Oh! Hang Kitty! What has she to do with it? Come, be quick, be quick! Where is your sash, my dear?'

Their mother left them together. 'Lizzy, I shall not go down until you are ready to come with me. I do not like the way Mama is trying to force me into his company. It is most distressing; I will not be party to it.'

'My dear Jane, we all know why Mr Bingley has arrived so

early. For exactly the same reason that our mother wishes you to go downstairs alone. He has come to make you an offer.'

'Please, do not say such things to me. I have been disappointed once before; I could not bear to have my heart broken for a second time. If Charles wishes to speak to me then I am sure that the occasion shall arise without my being pushed in his direction in this embarrassing manner.'

Mr Bennet was in fact the first to greet their guest and when Jane arrived on her sister's arm she had no more to do than curtsy and smile warmly at him. The same anxiety by her mother to get them by themselves was visible again during the evening.

After tea, her father retired to the library, as was his custom, and Mary went upstairs to play her instrument. Jane tried to ignore her mother's nodding and winking at both her sisters. Eventually Kitty spoke innocently to their mother. 'What is the matter? Why do you keep winking at me? What am I to do?'

'Nothing, child, nothing. I did not wink at you.' A further five minutes passed without interruption until Mrs Bennet could contain herself no longer and jumped to her feet. 'Come here, Kitty my love, I want to speak to you.'

Jane looked at Elizabeth in distress, knowing that her sister would not give in to such premeditation. However, moments later the door half opened and her mother called out loudly.

'Lizzy, my dear, I want to speak with you.'

Jane watched in despair as her sister was obliged to go, leaving her alone with Charles for the first time in almost a year. She could not remain seated. She believed he would think she was sitting there waiting for him to drop to one knee and propose.

'Miss Bennet, please do not be alarmed. I have no wish to

embarrass you in any way. Come, sit down again and let us talk of commonplaces until the others return.'

'You are too kind, sir. I do most heartily apologise for Mrs Bennet. It is not my doing, I can promise you.' Jane glanced up and was reassured by what she saw. His expression was bland, his manner relaxed. He had not been embarrassed or put out in any way by her mother's machinations. She returned to her seat and soon the conversation flowed as it always had, his ease and cheerfulness making him a most agreeable companion.

When he was invited to stay for supper, he accepted happily and before he went away Jane heard him arrange to go out shooting with her father the next morning. She could think of only one reason why he would wish to abandon his plentiful coverts in order to shoot at Longbourn.

No sooner were they private and the bedchamber door firmly closed behind them, than Jane grabbed her sister's hands and spun her around the bedroom. 'Lizzy, I am so happy I believe that I might burst from it. Charles is to speak to Papa tomorrow when they are shooting together.'

Dizzy from the twirling, Lizzy tumbled onto the bed. 'At last, you shall have the happiness you deserve. He is the perfect man for you and I am only sorry that it has taken almost a year for him to make up his mind. He could have saved you so much unhappiness if he had spoken after the ball as we had all expected.'

'It is forgotten. Our time apart has merely served to prove that we are steadfast in our love. Unlike poor Lydia, who scarcely knows Wickham and is unlikely to be happy in that relationship.'

'I suppose that could apply even more to Charlotte and Mr Collins.' She jumped up and ran to embrace Jane. 'But they are not our concern now. We have a wedding to plan.'

'Good heavens! He has not asked me formally. I cannot possibly think so far ahead. Can you imagine Mama's delight when she hears? Two daughters married in the space of a few months! She will be in high alt indeed.'

'And Papa, I am certain, will not quibble about bride clothes this time. Think of the excitement of visiting the warehouses in Town. I do hope I shall be included in all the planning.'

Jane kissed her sister before turning to blow out her candle. 'I should not enjoy it half so much if you are not by my side throughout.'

* * *

Charles was up betimes and had rehearsed the speech he was going to give to Mr Bennet many times. He had no appetite and did not even visit the breakfast parlour before taking his gun to the stable. The head groom was somewhat startled to see him there.

'I shall have the curricle harnessed in no time at all, sir. I beg your pardon for not having it ready.'

'No need to apologise. I am unpardonably early. I shall assist you; then it will be done all the sooner.' Placing his guns to one side, he followed the man into the coach house. When the horses were in place and his guns beside him on the seat, he decided he needed to change his garments as they were now mired with stable dirt.

'Take them round to the front in ten minutes. I must return to the house temporarily.'

What the man thought of his strange behaviour he had no notion, but he could not arrive at Longbourn dressed anything but perfectly. His valet greeted him with his usual aplomb and made no comment about redressing his master.

Charles glanced at his reflection, finally satisfied that he could do no more to improve his appearance. He raced downstairs and into his waiting carriage. He grinned as his team trotted down the drive. At least he would not be embarrassingly premature.

His host was waiting for him in the stable yard and he had a sudden moment of apprehension that he was, in fact, late. He glanced nervously at the stable clock and saw that it was exactly the appointed hour. Now it was almost the time to ask for permission to marry Jane he began to worry that after the way he had treated her, her father might regard him with disapproval. He knew it was essential that he had his future father-in-law's complete support. Jane would not be happy otherwise.

'Good morning, Mr Bennet; it is a wonderful morning to be out with our guns, is it not?'

The older man nodded. 'Indeed, sir. If you are ready, let us be off before the ladies descend on us. I am surrounded by clucking hens, but of course I do not include Jane or Lizzy in that clutch.'

Charles had been shooting with little success when his host leant his gun against a fence post and turned to him, a quizzical expression upon his face. 'My dear young man, your aim has been so far off this morning as to be dangerous to anyone within one hundred yards of you. Come now, we both know why we are out here this morning. Let us get the matter done and then we can both concentrate the better.'

He felt his cheeks burn. He had no idea his nervousness had been so obvious. Hastily propping his own gun next to Mr Bennet's he straightened his shoulders and looked his future father-in-law directly in the eye.

'Mr Bennet, I am here this morning, as you have already surmised, to ask your permission to marry Jane. I have been in love with her since the first time we met, but did not appreciate that she had feelings for me. I believe that you know my circumstances very well; I am in a position to give your daughter everything she needs in life.'

'My dear boy, all my Jane ever wanted was for you to love her. She has been unhappy these past months, but I shall not hold that against you. Yes, speak to Jane, and the sooner the better. Mrs Bennet is like to have an apoplexy if she is kept dangling without the news she craves. I apologise in advance for the excesses you will have to suffer at her hands once she is aware you are to become part of the family.'

'Thank you, sir. I shall speak to her this evening.' He grinned, recalling the stratagems employed by Mrs Bennet to leave them alone last night. 'I am certain I shall be given ample opportunity to make my offer.'

Charles offered his hand and Mr Bennet shook it warmly. Neither man had any desire to kill further game birds so, tucking their shotguns under their arms, they spent the remainder of the morning wandering around Longbourn getting to know each other better.

* * *

Jane toyed with her food and was relieved when the maid removed her plate. Her mother led the ladies into the drawing room and they were followed almost immediately by Charles and her father. Elizabeth had a letter to write and went into the breakfast room after tea whilst the others got out the card table.

Charles spoke quietly to her. 'I have no desire to play cards, Miss Bennet. I have something most important that I wish to ask you.'

Jane knew what it was and was as eager as he to have the card players remove from the room. It was her turn to stare pointedly at the door and Kitty, whose behaviour had much improved since Lydia was no longer there to influence her, smiled and instantly got to her feet.

'Mama, I have the headache and think I would feel so much better if you and Mary were to walk with me in the garden for a short while.'

Her mother glanced up and understood the situation perfectly. 'My poor dear, of course we will accompany you.' She gripped Mary by the elbow and Jane watched with amusement as the girl found herself bundled unceremoniously from the room.

The door closed behind her family and for a moment she was at a loss as to how to position herself to make things easier for Charles. 'Shall we be seated, Mr Bingley? I certainly shall feel more comfortable that way.' Never having received a proposal of marriage before, she was unsure what would happen next, but rather thought being seated the best way to go.

Immediately he joined her, sitting far closer than she was accustomed to. 'Look at me, my love. I wish to see your lovely face when I ask you my question.'

She turned her head and gazed, radiant, waiting him to speak.

'I have loved you since the day I first met you at the Meryton assembly last year. I wish I had had more confidence in my ability to win your affections; then I could have asked you this last year.' He reached out to take her hands and held them gently in his own. Jane stared down; her fingers trembled at the intimacy.

'My darling girl, will you make me the happiest man alive? Will you do me the inestimable honour of becoming my wife?'

'I will. There is nothing I should like more. I have loved you this age; I have been so miserable since we have been apart.'

'I hope you can forgive me for not speaking to you after the ball last year; if I had known how you felt, nothing could have stopped me coming to your side. I had no idea you were in London. My sister and Darcy kept the information from me.'

Jane reached out and tenderly touched his face. He stopped talking and his hand came up to stroke her hair. 'I do not care about any of that; it is in the past. We shall be together and that is all that matters.'

'There is more. I shall keep nothing back. I wrote a letter telling you how I felt and Caroline kept it from you. I came down to Meryton to speak to you in January, only to find that you had gone away. If I had known it was to London I should have sought you out.'

Jane did not care about the past – she was enjoying the present too much and she had her future to consider now. His proximity would give rise to comment if anyone were to come in and see them, but more importantly she knew herself to be in danger of doing something decidedly indecorous. The closer Charles was to her the more she wished he would kiss her.

'I think that we should walk around the room. I hope you understand, I would prefer to inform my mother before...' Her words trailed away and her cheeks flushed. How could she have been going to say something so indelicate?

He smiled and her knees trembled. He held out his hands. For a moment she hesitated, then placed her own in his, and he pulled her gently to her feet. They moved towards the fireplace where Jane halted. To her astonishment his arms came around her waist, and he drew her closer.

'Now that we are betrothed, my darling, I believe that I am allowed to kiss you.'

Jane was not sure he was allowed to do any such thing, but she tilted her head and felt the gentle pressure of his lips on hers. She had never experienced anything so wonderful. She had a strange desire to close the remaining gap between them. He did not take advantage of the situation, immediately releasing her, but remaining so close she could almost feel his heart beating.

The door opened and Elizabeth appeared. Instantly he stepped away and she knew her face revealed what had taken place. They both sat down, not knowing what else to do. Jane could think of nothing appropriate to say, so for a moment they all waited in awkward silence.

Then Charles stood up, bending down to whisper in her ear, 'I spoke to Mr Bennet this morning. I shall go at once and tell him you have accepted me. We have matters to discuss, settlements to make, and the sooner we do it, the sooner we can be married.'

Jane watched him hurry out and immediately scrambled to her feet and ran across to embrace her sister. 'Lizzy, I am the happiest creature in the world. It is too much! I do not deserve it. Oh! Why is not everybody as happy?'

'I cannot tell you how delighted I am, Jane. He is an excellent man and will make you a good husband. I could not have chosen a better brother if I had searched all year.'

'He has gone to speak to Papa; he asked his permission this morning but is now gone to talk about arrangements. All the sadness of the past few months is as nothing; I did not know it was possible to feel such joy. How I wish you could experience the same, dearest Lizzy.'

'You must not worry on my account. I shall share in *your* happiness and that will be enough for me.'

'I have so much to tell you. You would not believe what Charles has said. But I cannot do so now; I must get instantly to my mother. I would not any account keep her waiting for the good news. I shall not allow her to hear it from anyone but myself. Oh! Lizzy, to know that what I have to relate will give such pleasure to all my dear family! I do not know how I shall bear so much happiness!'

* * *

Charles left the library with the arrangements made. He returned quickly to the drawing room to find that Jane had gone and only her sister was there.

'Where is your sister?'

'With my mother upstairs. She will be down in a moment, I dare say.'

'Miss Elizabeth, has Jane told you our good tidings? I hope that you approve her choice of husband. I know that you are very close and she would not wish to do anything that upsets you.'

'Mr Bingley, my only quibble with you is that this matter was not settled months ago. I am delighted that finally you have resolved your differences. I am certain that you will be happy together.'

Charles walked over and offered his hand and they shook with great cordiality. 'I can promise you that I shall make your sister content. We shall be the happiest couple on this earth. I insist that you are not a stranger to Netherfield. My dearest Jane will not wish to be apart from you for long.'

She indicated that they be seated and he was grateful for her consideration, for his legs had taken to trembling like a blancmange. He told her that he believed his marriage would be a happy one because her sister and he were so much alike, and she agreed most heartily.

He hardly knew what he was saying, for his eyes were fixed

on the door waiting for his beloved to return. When she did, she was accompanied by Mrs Bennet and her two sisters. He was aware that there was a glow of such a sweet animation on Jane's face that she looked handsomer than ever.

* * *

Jane spent the remainder of the evening in a daze of happiness. She did not mind that her mother spoke her approbation and approval without a pause for breath for more than thirty minutes. She hardly noticed that Kitty simpered and smiled and whispered loudly to Elizabeth that she hoped it would be her turn soon.

When her father joined them at supper, he did not allude directly to the engagement but she could tell from his voice and manner how happy he was. When Charles eventually left, promising to return first thing in the morning, Mr Bennet turned to her. 'Jane, I congratulate you. You will be a very happy woman.'

This was exactly what she wished to hear. She went to him instantly, kissed him and thanked him for his goodness.

'You are a good girl, and I have great pleasure in thinking you will be so happily settled. I have not a doubt of your doing very well together. Your tempers are by no means unalike. You are each of you so complying, that nothing will ever be resolved on; so easy, that every servant will cheat you; and so generous, that you will always exceed your income.'

She smiled at his jest. 'I hope not so, sir. Imprudence or thoughtlessness in money matters would be unpardonable in *me*.'

Mrs Bennet took the matter seriously. 'Exceed their income! My dear Mr Bennet, what are you talking of? Why, he has four or five thousand a year and very likely more.' She beamed at Jane. 'Oh! My dear, dear, Jane, I am so happy! I am sure I shall not get a wink of sleep all night. I knew how it would be. I always said it must be so at last. I was sure you could not be so beautiful for nothing! I remember, as soon as I ever saw him, when he first came into Hertfordshire last year, I thought how likely it was that you should come together. Oh! He is as handsome a young man as ever was seen!'

Mary immediately joined in the conversation. 'I do hope, Jane, that you shall allow me the use of the library at Netherfield? I am sure there must be hundreds of books that I have not read before.'

Jane nodded. 'You may all come as often as you wish; after all, we are only three miles away from Longbourn. I am not going far.' She had been about to mention Lydia's departure with Wickham to Newcastle, but thought it better not to.

Kitty, not to be outdone by her sister, immediately demanded that there should be several balls held at Netherfield during the winter, and Jane said she would discuss it with Charles once they were married.

21

Longbourn was a home filled with excitement and anticipation. Jane had little time to spend with Elizabeth that evening and they had so much to make up for after their long separation. After everybody else had retired, she finally had time to share what she had learnt from him.

'Lizzy, he has made me so happy. He was totally ignorant of my being in Town last spring. I had not believed it possible.'

'I suspected as much, but how did he account for it?'

'It was his sisters' doing. They were certainly no friends of his acquaintance with me, which I cannot wonder, since he might have chosen so much more advantageously in many respects. When they see, as I trust they will, that their brother is happy with me, they will learn to be contented, and we shall be on good terms again; but we can never be what we once were to each other.'

'That is the most unforgiving speech that I have ever heard you utter. Good girl! It would vex me, indeed, to see you again the dupe of Miss Bingley's pretended regard.'

'Would you believe it, Lizzy, when we went to Town last

November, he really loved me, and nothing but a persuasion of my being indifferent would have prevented his coming down again!'

'He made a little mistake to be sure; but it is to the credit of his modesty.'

'Charles is a not a proud man; he is everything that is good and amiable and is constantly telling me he cannot believe his good fortune in having *me* love *him*.'

'I suppose it will not be long before news of your engagement will be all over the neighbourhood. You must brace yourself for visits and congratulations.'

'I shall not mind at all, Lizzy. I am in good humour with the whole world. I am certainly the most fortunate creature that ever existed. Why am I thus singled from my family, and blessed above them all! If I could see *you* as happy, if there were but such another man for you.'

'If you were to give me forty such men, I never could be so happy as you. Till I have your disposition, your goodness, I never can have your happiness. No, no, let me shift for myself; and perhaps, if I have very good luck, I may meet another Mr Collins in time.'

* * *

Charles was tempted to disturb Nicholls when he returned that evening, but restrained himself. He would gather the staff on the morrow and make a formal announcement. After all, Jane would be their mistress now. It was to her they must defer on all domestic matters.

Darcy would be returning that afternoon as well. He could not wait to share his news with his dearest friend. He smiled in the darkness of his bedchamber; maybe it would not be so long before he was congratulating Darcy on *his* engagement.

At eight o'clock he was in the hall with his servants assembled. He had also summoned the outdoor staff to hear his announcement. He stood on the stairs and surveyed them. They were shifting uncomfortably, especially those not used to being inside. He noticed the outside men had been obliged to remove their footwear. Nicholls would not allow mud on her pristine floors.

He smiled and cleared his throat. Every eye swivelled to stare at him. 'Thank you for coming in so promptly. I have important news that I wish to share with you. Yesterday I became engaged to Miss Jane Bennet, who is known to all of you, and she will be mistress of Longbourn before Christmas.'

His announcement was greeted by a second of silence and then the hall erupted in a roar of congratulation. Caps were hurled into the air and several of the girls embraced each other. He could not have hoped for a better reception. Jane was obviously much loved by all who resided at Netherfield.

The butler waved his hand and instantly there was order. 'Mr Bingley, sir, may I offer you, on behalf of the entire staff, our sincere congratulations. Miss Bennet will find us all eager to work with her.' He snapped his fingers in the air and there was a rousing cheer, rapidly followed by two more.

'Thank you; Miss Bennet and I shall make this our principal home, and I am sure that we shall entertain all our neighbours when we return from our wedding trip.' He nodded to the butler and like magic the crowd of people vanished. 'Nicholls, I should like to speak to you after I have had my breakfast.'

He intended to discuss the possibility of holding an engagement ball or some such celebratory event. He did not wish to do anything that might offend his future mother-in-law, and his housekeeper would know what would be appropriate in the circumstances.

* * *

That afternoon Darcy arrived and Charles was waiting in the hall to greet his friend. 'You are to congratulate me, Darcy, on my good fortune. Jane has made me the happiest of men.'

'I am delighted and wish you every happiness with your lovely bride. I am hoping that you will be able to offer *me* congratulations of a similar sort very shortly.'

'I knew it! You are going to offer for Elizabeth; I know you have been interested in Jane's sister almost as long as I have been in love with Jane. Does your arrival here have anything to do with your aunt's visit to Longbourn three days ago?'

Darcy grinned and slapped Charles vigorously on the back. 'It does indeed, Bingley. I shall tell you the whole. I proposed to Elizabeth when she was at Hunsford but she turned me down. But when she came to Pemberley I thought I could persuade her to reconsider.'

'Let us repair to the library; we can be private there. I am astounded that she should have turned you down.'

'It was a salutary lesson, well learnt I can assure you. My damnable pride got in the way, as usual, and I made a complete mull of the whole situation. I am surprised she is still speaking to me.'

Charles walked over to the table and poured them both a generous measure of brandy. He offered one to his friend who took it gratefully. 'Here, Darcy, drink this. You are in need of a restorative.'

He sat and his friend followed his lead. 'I was able to be of some assistance to the Bennet family and this, I believe, stood me in good stead with Elizabeth. However, I was not brave enough to consider trying my luck a second time until Lady Catherine's visit.' He sipped his brandy, lost in thought, and Charles waited patiently for him to continue his extraordinary story.

'My aunt tried to persuade Elizabeth to renounce me totally; when she refused to do this I knew it was probable that she had changed her mind and would receive my second proposal favourably.'

Charles was puzzled. 'I do not see how this would make you think she had reconsidered.'

'I know her so well; if she had no interest she would not have hesitated in agreeing to renounce me. The fact that she refused to do so has given me hope. Wish me luck, my friend; tomorrow I hope to have the opportunity to speak to her alone.'

'I shall propose that we all go for a walk, and then Jane and I shall lag behind and you can walk on with Elizabeth. Hopefully, Mary shall not wish to join us on the excursion, and Kitty can be persuaded to visit her friend Maria Lucas. I suggest we walk in that direction.'

This scheme was declared by Darcy to be exactly what was needed; Charles arranged to meet his friend first thing next morning to ride to Longbourn.

It was a fine morning, ideally suited for taking a long country walk, Charles thought happily. 'Darcy, I wish you good fortune this morning. I want you to be as happy as I am.'

'I think that an impossibility. I am more reserved than you, cannot show my feelings as easily.'

He smiled and Charles could see the difference in Darcy. His friend no longer had an austere look. His expression was relaxed; there was a definite spring in his step. 'That does not mean you do not feel as deeply. Come, the horses are outside and I cannot wait to see my betrothed this morning.' He loved being able to use that phrase. Jane was going to marry him; he was the luckiest man on the planet.

This time it was Darcy who looked nervous. It was a new experience for him to see his friend discommoded in this way. As soon as he saw his darling girl waiting on the steps of Longbourn he forgot about anything else, other than how much he loved her and how soon he could persuade her to set a wedding date.

Vaulting from the saddle he tossed the reins to a waiting groom and, risking the displeasure of his future relatives, stepped forward and took her hands in his. 'My dearest, I cannot tell you how long the night has been without you. I have Darcy with me this morning.'

She giggled and peeped over his shoulder to nod to his friend. 'I had noticed that, my love. Mr Darcy is not a gentleman one could easily miss.'

He wanted to pull her into his arms and kiss her smiling mouth. She was adorable, but somehow he restrained himself. 'Jane, sweetheart, I am going to propose that we all go out walking; I shall need your support in this scheme.'

She nodded; whatever he demanded of her, he knew she was willing to give without question.

The sun was out and the weather pleasant, so a walk would be no hardship at all even so early in the day. His suggestion was eagerly seized upon and soon afterwards Elizabeth and Darcy, accompanied by Kitty (Mary was too busy with her books), set off towards Lucas Lodge with Jane and Charles. The party had not walked far when he spoke quietly to Jane.

'Let us allow the others to outstrip us. You and I can walk slowly together.'

This ploy suited Jane exactly; the more time she spent alone with him the happier she was. She watched Elizabeth, Darcy and Kitty forge ahead and soon they were out of sight. They strolled hand in hand for a while in silence.

'Jane, my darling, do you wish me to buy Netherfield for you? I shall do so at once if that is what you want.'

'It is a lovely house, and it is where we first fell in love, but it *is* very close to Longbourn.' She hesitated and then continued earnestly. 'I love my family dearly, and I know that my mama is so looking forward to being able to see me regularly.'

Mrs Bennet and her younger sisters would be forever visiting. They would have no time to themselves; perhaps she would grow tired of seeing them so often and might consider moving later. 'I have the lease for another year. That should give us ample time to decide if we wish to stay at Netherfield permanently.'

The look of gratitude she gave him made him feel a giant among men. He wanted to sweep her up in his arms and show her how much she meant to him. Instead he contented himself with squeezing her hand and dropping a feather-light kiss upon her parted lips. For a moment he thought he had offended her. She dropped his hand and turned away from him.

'My darling, I must beg your pardon most humbly. I promise you I shall not take such liberties again until we are married.'

Instantly she spun round. 'Oh no! You misunderstood me, my love. It is exactly the opposite. I know we must not... must not be intimate, but when you touch me it makes me feel warm all over. I really think it best we do no more than hold hands for both our sakes.'

'In which case I think we must set the date of our wedding. How soon do you think you can prepare your trousseau?'

Trustingly she slipped her hand back in his and they continued their walk. 'We shall have to go to the warehouses in

London; then everything has to be made.' She glanced at him mischievously from under her bonnet brim. 'I do not think that could be achieved in less than six months.'

'Baggage! Do not tease me, I could not wait that long. Six weeks will seem like an eternity, but I can just manage that.'

'Then six weeks it shall be. I do not require that many new gowns, my love; I am perfectly content to wear what I have. However, if I do not have bride clothes my mother would think me not properly married.'

Charles glanced at his pocket watch and saw to his astonishment they had been walking for over an hour. 'Jane, we must turn back. We must be several miles away from Longbourn. They will be sending out search parties if we do not go back soon.'

On their return he discovered that his friend and Elizabeth were still absent. He and Jane had been gone almost three hours, but there was no sign of the others returning.

* * *

'Charles, where can Lizzy and Mr Darcy have got to? I am certain they would not have continued on to visit Maria with Kitty. I do hope they have not met with a mishap. Do you think you should go out and look for them?'

He shook his head. 'I do not think Darcy would appreciate my appearance as if he is not capable of conducting a walk without assistance. I am sorry, my dear, but I cannot stay with you longer at the moment. I have business to attend to in Meryton, but, as always, I shall join you for dinner and spend the evening in your company.' He raised her hand to his lips and pressed a gentle kiss upon her fingers.

Surprised that he had abandoned his friend in this peculiar

way, she went inside, avoiding the breakfast room where she could hear her mother talking to Mary. Instead she retreated upstairs and sat in the window seat, watching the paddock to catch a glimpse of her sister and Mr Darcy returning.

As it happened she was with Sarah, getting ready for dinner in her dressing room, and did not see Elizabeth arrive. By this time she was most concerned that her sister had been absent so long, for Kitty had returned some time ago. They met on the stairs.

'My dear Lizzy, where ever can you have you been walking to for so long?'

'We wandered about and lost track of both place and time. I must hurry upstairs and change for dinner. Mr Darcy has galloped off to do the same.'

With that unsatisfactory answer, Jane had to be content for the present. On joining her family in the drawing room, she was not surprised to see that neither Charles nor Mr Darcy were yet present. Kitty was full of details about the time she had spent with Maria and this filled the time until Elizabeth came in.

Jane had already explained why her sister had been so long away and little more was said on the subject. Charles and his friend arrived shortly afterwards and she became so immersed in conversation with him that nothing else was of any importance.

'It is very mysterious, my love. Lizzy will not tell me where she went all day with Darcy. Did he tell you why they were gone so long?'

He glanced in their direction and smiled knowingly. 'I have no idea, but I am sure that your sister will explain it all to you when you are private. Now, can you guess where it was I went this afternoon after I left you?'

She shook her head. 'Tell me at once. You know that you are bursting with news.'

'I have spoken to the vicar and the wedding date is set for the end of October. We have to decide where we shall go for our wedding trip. Do you have any preferences, my darling?'

'I do not wish to go too far. November can be treacherous. Perhaps we could stay in your town house? I should love to visit the theatre and opera with you at my side.'

'Are you sure? Would you not like to travel to Scotland and see the mountains? We could spend Christmas and the New Year in Edinburgh. It is a grand city, albeit somewhat cold.'

'A month in Town is all that I require; then we can return to Netherfield and plan our celebrations. I would like to have my first Christmas with you in our own home, with my family around me. By the by, we must now think about wedding guests. Do you have many relatives you wish to ask?'

'My two sisters and Hurst are the only relatives I have. Apart from Darcy and Georgiana, of course; they are as close as family to me.'

'I am afraid that I have dozens that will expect to be invited, most of which you have already met. Mama will wish to organise that, so I must leave it all to her. As long as we are married, I care little about the details.'

The evening came to a close far too soon for her. With promises to be at Longbourn immediately after breakfast, Charles took his leave. She was still thinking about her wedding tour and whether she should be more adventurous in her choice when she retired.

'Tell me, Lizzy, what do you think? Should we go to the Lakes or perhaps to the coast, or remain in London as I have suggested to Charles?' To her surprise, she found that Lizzy was not listening to her. 'Lizzy? Lizzy? Are you wool-gathering?'

Lizzy looked up, her expression distracted. 'I have something to tell you, Jane, that I am certain will astound you. I hardly know how to begin. It is very difficult, but still I must, and I am sure that as you love me so you will want me to be happy.'

Jane was bewildered. What could Lizzy mean?

'Well, the truth is... Darcy and I are engaged.'

She could not believe what she had heard. She had had no suspicion that her sister was in love with Darcy. 'You are joking, Lizzy. This cannot be! Engaged to Mr Darcy! No, no, you shall not deceive me. I know it to be impossible.'

'This is a wretched beginning indeed! I am depending on you, as I am sure nobody else will believe me, if you do not. Yes, indeed, I am in earnest. I speak nothing but the truth. He still loves me, and we are engaged.'

Jane looked at her doubtingly. 'Oh! Lizzy. It cannot be. I know how much you dislike him.'

'You know nothing of the matter. *That* is all to be forgotten. Perhaps I did not always love him so well as I do now, but in such cases as these, a good memory is unpardonable. This is the last time I shall ever remember it myself.'

Jane still could not believe her sister now loved Mr Darcy. 'Are you quite sure you are not jesting?'

'Oh! Jane, why should I wish to do so? No, it is the truth. I see I will have to convince you. You know that I took a great dislike to him in Hertfordshire, but you know also that my feelings to him started to change when he told me the truth about Wickham, and again when he helped Lydia.'

'Yes, but I did not know they had changed so much.'

'I hardly realised that I had fallen in love with him myself, until recently. I am not surprised that you are disbelieving.'

'Was it the fact that he helped our sister that changed your mind about him?'

'Not really, it is because he is the most honourable, decent and wonderful man I have ever met. I cannot understand how prejudiced I was against him when we were first acquainted. After all, did you not tell me often enough that Bingley would not have him as a friend if he was in any way unpleasant?'

'It was not a sudden thing, Lizzy? I knew the first moment I set eyes on Charles that he was the one for me.'

'I know you did, but we are not alike in that respect. But we have arrived at the same destination nevertheless. Darcy and I have both changed over the year and are finally of the same opinion: that we love each other and wish to be wed.'

'Good heavens! Can it really be so? Yet now I must believe you. My dear, dear Lizzy, I would, I do congratulate you, but are you quite certain? Forgive the question, are you quite certain that you can be happy with him?'

'There can be no doubt of that. It is settled between us already. We are the happiest couple in the world. But are you pleased, Jane? Shall you like to have such an impossible brother?'

'Very, very much. Nothing could give either Charles or myself more delight. We considered it; we talked of it as possible. Do you really love him quite well enough? Oh Lizzy! Do anything rather than marry without affection. Are you quite sure you feel as you ought to?'

'Oh, yes! You will only think I feel more than I ought to do, when I tell you more.'

'What do you mean?'

'Why, I must confess to loving him better than I do Bingley. I am afraid you will be angry.'

Jane threw her arms around her sister and kissed her. 'My dear sister, now please be serious. I want to talk to you in earnest. Let me hear everything that I am to know, without delay. Will you tell me how long you have loved him?'

The rest of the night was spent in exchanging secrets with her sister. When Elizabeth told her that Darcy had been Lydia's saviour, not their Uncle Gardiner, she was not surprised.

'He is a good man, and I am delighted for you both. If you love him half as much as I love Charles then you shall be happy indeed. Lizzy, let us insist on having a double wedding. As soon as Mr Darcy speaks to our father, we can start planning.'

'Are you sure, Jane dearest? I do not wish to intrude upon your special day. I should be happy to wait until after you and Bingley have married.'

'No, Lizzy, we shall do it together. I am certain that both Charles and Darcy shall be as happy at the suggestion as we are. And it will mean our father only has to provide one wedding breakfast, and not two. However, we have set a date for the end of October. Will that be too soon for you?'

She saw her sister blush becomingly. 'It cannot be soon enough for me.' Giggling together they fell into bed, not voicing what had caused the laughter but both knowing they were eagerly anticipating sharing *everything* with their husbands.

Eventually conversation was at an end and Jane fell asleep, her head full of plans for their shared nuptials, trips to London to purchase the materials for their bride clothes and whether she should change her mind and ask Charles to take her to the coast. She had never seen the sea. Even in the winter it would be an exciting prospect, especially if she was sharing it with him.

* * *

Charles was already dressed and pacing the drawing room at

Netherfield when Darcy eventually returned. One look at his face was enough to tell him his mission had been successful.

'Congratulations, I wish you happiness. Elizabeth will make you the perfect bride.'

'Do you know, Bingley, until she accepted my offer I was still uncertain. I begin to feel the same euphoria as you. I can scarcely gather my thoughts. I am to be married to the most beautiful woman in Hertfordshire, and to my astonishment she loves me as much as I do her.'

Charles slapped him vigorously on the back. 'I beg to differ, my friend. *I* am marrying the most beautiful girl in Hertfordshire, but Elizabeth comes a close second. Now, you must go and change. The carriage is outside and we are going to be embarrassingly tardy.'

Eventually, when they were on their way, Charles had questions he still needed answers to. 'Well, my friend, when are you to speak to Mr Bennet? It is going to be difficult maintaining the pretence that you are at Longbourn to accompany me and for no other reason?'

'I think after supper, when he retires to his library, I shall follow him. If we spend the day out of the house, on another long walk, it might be possible to maintain the fiction for a while longer.'

'Mrs Bennet holds you in extreme dislike, and the two younger sisters are too afraid of you to speak in your presence. It is hard to tell Mr Bennet's opinion, but I think he is a sensible man, it is from him both Elizabeth and Jane have their good sense and impeccable manners.'

Mr Darcy laughed out loud. 'I do not think you understand your future mother-in-law, Bingley, if you do not realise that as soon as I become her daughter's intended her dislike of me will vanish. The thought of my wealth and status will turn me instantly into her favourite person.'

He grinned, not sure if it was quite proper to poke fun at what was soon to be his family, after all. 'It will be hard for you, enduring the eulogies from Mrs Bennet, and her friends and relatives. But, you have the best of it, my friend. You will be removing to Derbyshire; I am obliged to live within three miles of Longbourn.'

'I must write to Lady Catherine, and also to Georgiana and tell her the good news. I shall meet you outside in an hour; we can then ride to Longbourn together.'

22

Jane received a polite note of congratulations from Caroline, which she showed to her sister. 'I am glad that she has written to me, but I can assure you, Lizzy, I shall not be taken in by her again.'

'I am glad to hear say so. She treated you abominably and although she is to become family it does not mean you have to be bosom bows.'

'I have no need of other friends when I have you. I shall write her a kind letter and that shall be the end of the matter. Charles does not wish to invite her to spend Christmas with us at Netherfield, which is a great relief to me.'

The letter finished, Jane went to join her sister who was examining fashion plates with some enthusiasm. 'Are you looking forward to going to London tomorrow? I could not believe that Papa gave us permission to travel unchaperoned in a carriage with Darcy and Charles.'

'As he will be travelling in the Longbourn carriage with Mama at the same time, he could hardly raise any objections. After all we shall be chaperoning each other.' She tossed aside the magazine. 'These gowns are far too ornate for my taste. I have no intention of wearing a dress smothered in frills and rouleaux just to be considered stylish.' She pointed to the drawing she had discarded so suddenly. 'Look at that, Jane. Would you wish to walk around wearing something that resembles a coal scuttle on your head?'

'It is fortunate that we do not intend to parade around in the *ton* or we should be obliged to look as ridiculous as that.' She yawned. 'It is time we retired. We have to make an early start tomorrow.'

As they assisted each other to disrobe, conversation continued about their double wedding. 'It is going to be most unusual to have two brides walk down the aisle with the same gentleman, don't you think, Lizzy?'

'Unless one of us is prepared to be given away by Uncle Gardiner, or I wait my turn, there is no other way. I told you I would be quite happy to be escorted second but you would have none of it.'

'I should think not; we have always shared everything and it shall be the same on our wedding day.'

Jane was snuggling into her side of the bed when her sister giggled.

'I do hope you are not intending to share my husband as well.'

* * *

'I am not certain you shall enjoy traipsing all over London with Elizabeth and Jane, Darcy. You have never been one for shopping of any sort, but for feminine fallalls?'

'I have absolutely no intention of entering any such emporiums. I would rather have my teeth pulled. What I am going to do is have the Darcy diamonds reset for my future wife, and also escort her to the theatre and the opera in the evenings.'

Charles was somewhat disappointed. He had been looking forward to suffering alongside his friend. 'Then I must endure it alone. I have given my word that I shall help Jane choose materials for her trousseau.'

Darcy chuckled. 'You do realise that you will be accompanied by Mrs Bennet, and be the only man in the warehouse apart from those that are serving?'

'Good grief! In which case I shall cry off and restrict my shopping expeditions to those that I can do with Jane alone. There must be something she would like to add to the furnishings at Netherfield.'

The carriage arrived. 'I am actually looking forward to the journey to Town. It will be amusing travelling with our future wives. I hope this is the first of many such outings. Lizzy and I wish you and Jane to spend time with us at Pemberley.'

'We are all coming to stay with you this weekend, are we not, to meet Georgiana?'

'I was referring to visiting without Mr and Mrs Bennet in tow, Bingley, as well you know.' They were still laughing when they arrived at Longbourn. Not waiting for the steps to be set out, Charles jumped down to greet Jane.

'Did the baggage cart leave first thing with our trunks, my love?'

'It did. It set off several hours ago. It is so kind of you to ask my family to stay at your London house. It will be so much easier to visit the emporiums and warehouses from such a prestigious address. Cheapside is rather far out for such excursions.'

He glanced across and saw that Darcy and Elizabeth were deep in conversation and then he heard the unmistakable tones of Mrs Bennet approaching from inside. 'Come, sweetheart, let us get back into the coach before we are waylaid.' He was amused to see that the other couple also moved with alacrity and they were all safely installed, and the door firmly shut, before his future mother-in-law arrived.

* * *

For Jane the journey to London was a revelation. She saw Mr Darcy in a new light. He was amusing and as full of fun and teasing as Lizzy; between them they filled the miles with entertainment and much hilarity. When the carriage halted outside an imposing three-storey house in the best part of Town, she was almost sorry to have arrived.

Two footmen had the door open and the steps let down before she and Lizzy had time to draw breath. She had no time to be nervous, and resting her hand on her beloved's arm entered what was to be her own house in a few short weeks. She was delighted to see several familiar faces standing in the group of servants waiting to be made known to her.

After the introductions Charles handed her over to Nicholls who escorted her upstairs to the chamber she was to share with her sister during their three-night stay. 'I am so pleased you are to be mistress here and at Netherfield, Miss Bennet, if you will permit me to say so.'

'Thank you, Nicholls. I shall be relying on you to help me in domestic matters when we return from our wedding tour in the middle of December.'

Sarah was waiting to curtsy in the delightful sitting room that led from their chamber. 'Good afternoon, Miss Bennet, Miss Elizabeth. I have everything ready for you.' She pointed out two girls, as like as two peas in a pod, who were standing nervously behind her. 'These are Emma and Jenny and they are to help in any way they can.' She lowered her voice and whispered to Jane, 'I've no idea which is which, miss, but they're good girls and ever so willing. This is a grand house, I can tell you. I've never seen the like before.'

'Thank you, Sarah; have tea brought up directly, please. And we wish to change and refresh ourselves before we go down.'

Jane was surprised that she had been able to take charge so easily. She was more used to letting Lizzy give directions to the staff. This was to be her home, so it was incumbent on her to take on the duties of hostess whilst she was under its roof. It would be Lizzy's turn when they removed to Pemberley at the end of the week.

'This is a splendid house, Jane. Darcy does not have a house in Town; he always stays here with Bingley.'

'I hope that you will continue to do so, my dearest Lizzy. The only thing that is marring my happiness is the knowledge that you will be so far away in Derbyshire. I am going to miss you dreadfully.'

'We shall both be so busy learning how to be wives that we will not have time to be sad. Do not you remember how Lydia said married women are too busy to write letters?'

This sally made her smile and restored her composure. She heard the noise of her parents being escorted along the wide corridor to their own apartments and wished that Mama had rather less to say about everything she saw.

The visit to Pemberley was everything it should be and she thought the Derbyshire countryside quite splendid. Her father made himself at home in the library, and her mother wandered from room to room exclaiming loudly on the fineness of the furniture. She knew exactly why Mr Darcy had told her sister he would not visit Netherfield once he was married.

When they returned to Longbourn, it was to find Charlotte

and Mr Collins had returned from Hunsford for an extended stay. She had barely been back in residence an hour when Charlotte arrived to offer her congratulations to them both.

'Lizzy, Jane, I cannot tell you how pleased I am that you are to be married and to such handsome gentlemen. Lady Catherine is not at all pleased, so Mr Collins has decided it best that we remain away until after the wedding.'

Jane turned to her sister. 'Shall Lady Catherine and her daughter be attending the wedding, Lizzy?'

'They have been invited, but whether they attend is another matter. For my part I shall not be sorry if they do not come. Colonel Fitzwilliam will be there, but I am afraid the church will be filled with Bennet relatives.'

'Do Lydia and her new husband come, Lizzy?'

'Fortunately he is unable to get leave, Charlotte. It would be intolerable for Papa to have them here.'

'I have exciting news to tell you. It is another reason we have come home. Can you guess what it is?'

Jane looked at Charlotte and could see a new bloom to her countenance, a sparkle in her eyes. 'Are you increasing, Charlotte? When is the baby due?'

'Next spring, and we are both so excited. Mama cannot believe she is to be a grandparent, but I should have been disappointed if this was not the case. After all, for what other reason would I have wished to marry Mr Collins?'

'You look radiant. Impending motherhood obviously agrees with you. I am so pleased for you.'

'It is strange to think that this time last year our lives were so different, Lizzy. I had no thought of ever being married and you thoroughly disliked Mr Darcy. But you, Jane, you were already in love with Bingley, were you not?'

'Indeed I was, Charlotte, but it has taken a year for us to find each other again. I can hardly believe that in less than three weeks I shall be Mrs Bingley and Lizzy shall be Mrs Darcy.' She glanced around the pretty sitting room she had shared with her sister these past five years and her eyes filled. 'I shall miss Longbourn, and all the happy times we have had together. Being apart from Lizzy is going to be like leaving an arm behind.'

'Fustian! You will be so busy you shall scarcely have time to write a letter, let alone pine away for Lizzy.' Charlotte looked at Jane in bewilderment as she and her sister dissolved into peals of laughter.

The day for Jane and Elizabeth's nuptials dawned fair and bright. Jane was up first. She had hardly slept all night, knowing this would be the last time she shared a bed with her sister or slept under her father's roof.

She walked across to the curtains and drew them back. The sun was creeping over the horizon, bathing the park in crimson glory. It was a good omen. Her movements caused her sister to stir.

'I am sorry, Lizzy. I did not mean to disturb you so early. I have been awake so long I could not remain in bed another minute. I will be a little sad to leave Longbourn, but miserable to be parted from you.'

Elizabeth was immediately beside her, offering comfort and reassurance. 'Derbyshire is not so very far from Hertfordshire, my dear. You must come and visit often. Pemberley is a vast place; it needs to be filled with friends and family.'

It had already been discussed between them that Elizabeth and her new husband would not visit Netherfield; it would have to be they who went to Pemberley. Mr Darcy found his new relatives difficult to be with, especially Aunt Philips and their mother.

'I am so glad that the Gardiners are here to celebrate our

marriages, Lizzy, and relieved that Lydia and Wickham could not come down from Newcastle. With Georgiana here as well it would have been impossible.' Jane had been deeply shocked when her sister had told her exactly why Mr Darcy held Lydia's husband in such dislike.

'I can hear movement downstairs, Jane. I believe that our wedding day has now officially begun. To think, in a few hours' time I shall be Mrs Darcy and you Mrs Bingley! My only regret is that poor Papa shall be deprived of both his favourite daughters on the same day. Darcy and I have decided to invite him to visit Pemberley whenever he should wish to come. Although he does not like to travel much, I believe he will come to us sometimes, if only to get away from Longbourn.'

Laughing, Jane ran to her sister and they embraced fondly. 'He shall always be welcome at Netherfield, but I expect he will often be accompanied by our mother. I am not sure whether living so close will be an advantage or disadvantage. But I shall not think of that today. I am too happy to consider anything else apart from what will take place at the church this morning.'

Downstairs they were to eat their final breakfast as a family. Even their father was there. Kitty and Mary were almost more excited than Jane was herself. They both had new gowns and bonnets and were looking forward to being the only Bennet girls in residence.

'My dear girls, Lizzy, Jane, are you both absolutely certain that you wish to go ahead with the ceremony this morning? It is not too late to call the whole thing off.'

'My dear Mr Bennet, how can you say such a thing on the morning of their wedding? Of course they do not wish to call it off. They have their bride clothes sewn and the wedding breakfast is being made ready even as we speak. I do not understand why you should wish to have them cancel the ceremony.'

'Mama, of course we do not wish to cancel, do we, Lizzy? We are both eager to become married women, to have own establishments, to marry the men we love.'

Her father answered. 'In which case I shall say no more on the subject. I shall be sad to see you go, but happy that you marry such sensible men. I shall be visiting you both frequently, so be prepared for it.'

'You will be most welcome at Pemberley, Papa, but remember we shall not be there until the spring. We do not return from our trip until the middle of April.'

'Mr Bennet will not be travelling about the countryside, Lizzy, even to visit you and Mr Darcy at Pemberley. He does not like to travel, you know, and certainly not when the roads are bad and the weather inclement. Do not expect to see him before the summer.'

Jane saw her father wink at Lizzy and was astonished at it. She rather thought her mother was going to discover that her husband had developed a decided interest in travel, especially to Derbyshire.

She noticed that Lizzy ate as little as she did, and was glad when Mama declared it was time they go upstairs to get ready. 'I shall be along very shortly to oversee your preparations. I cannot understand why you should have chosen such plain dresses, both of you. I saw fabric that would have done better than the silk that you both selected.'

'It is our wedding day, Mama, and God will bless our union. Neither Lizzy nor I wished to wear anything elaborate. Your ensemble is splendid enough for both of us.'

A strange noise coming from her sister made her glance in that direction and she wished she had not. Now was not the time to succumb to a fit of giggles. 'Shall we go upstairs, Lizzy? Hill said the hot water would be in the bath at this time.'

* * *

When the carriage containing the wedding party arrived outside the church, it was greeted by cheers and applause from the assembled villagers. Jane in her gown of cream silk, her sash of emerald green, her bonnet trimmed to match, looked even more beautiful than usual, if that were possible. Her sister was wearing a matching gown, but her sash was gold and her bonnet ribbons also.

'Dearest Lizzy, if I look half as lovely as you do at this moment, then I shall be happy indeed.'

'Jane, you look twice as beautiful, and it is our husbands who shall be happy. I do not believe there can be two such accomplished and delightful brides anywhere in the country.'

Mr Bennet smiled at Jane. 'Well, my dears, are you ready?' He beamed in pride. 'I must own that today I shall gain two of the best sons-in-law any man could hope to have. I wish I did not have to lose my favourite daughters in order to do so.'

He held out his right arm and Jane placed her hand upon it. Her heart was full. It was the moment she had been dreaming of for so long, but although it was the beginning of her life with the person she loved most in the world, it was the end of her life as Miss Jane Bennet.

Inside the church, Charles turned as the congregation stood. His heart filled and his eyes glistened as he watched the woman he loved more than life itself glide towards him down the aisle. He heard Darcy move to the left of the aisle; but he saw only *his* bride. He scarcely noticed Elizabeth on the left arm of Mr

Bennet. Jane looked so lovely in her wedding finery he could see nothing else.

The ceremony passed in a haze. They repeated their vows in turn and before he knew it he was staring into the eyes of his wife. The congregation broke into a round of spontaneous applause, much to the annoyance of the vicar. As Jane was the eldest she was to leave the church first, her sister to follow behind with Darcy.

'Mrs Bingley, would you care to take my arm?'

Her eyes were sparkling as she gazed up at him. 'I believe that I would, Mr Bingley.'

They paraded down the aisle, nodding and smiling at the assembled guests until they were outside. The bells were ringing, the sun was shining and the villagers were cheering and tossing their caps in the air.

He turned to Jane. He could not help himself, knew it was unseemly, but she was his wife now, and her actions his responsibility. In front of the gawping crowd of spectators he gathered her into his arms, holding her tight to him for the first time. He did not need to tilt her head; she did it for him. He lowered his mouth to cover hers in a kiss of such sweetness he thought his heart would burst with happiness.

His action was greeted by a second roar of delighted appreciation. Reluctantly he loosened his hold, but kept his arm firmly around her waist. As they turned together he saw Darcy not just kiss his bride, but lift her from her feet in order to do so. Oblivious to the third cheer, they continued their embrace until Mrs Bennet emerged from the church.

'Darling Jane, I love you so much. I am going to make you the happiest bride in England.'

Darcy overheard his comment. 'I wager that Lizzy shall be the happiest, if I have anything to say on the matter.'

'We shall all be happy,' Elizabeth said. 'When two couples marry for love how could there be any other outcome?'

'Lizzy, as always, you have said exactly the right thing.'

* * *

Jane and Charles returned after their wedding trip to London eager to settle into their married life at Netherfield. In the flurry of morning calls and invitations, they scarcely had a moment to themselves. Then it was Christmas and it behoved them to hold dinner parties and a dance for Jane's family and their neighbours. Mrs Bennet treated Netherfield as her own.

The sound of carriage wheels on the stones alerted Jane. She took a deep breath and tried not to wish it was anyone other than her mama and her younger sisters.

Charles looked up from his newspaper and frowned. 'If that is Mrs Bennet, Jane, I'm retiring to my library until she has departed.'

'I have no idea who it is, dearest, and you must go wherever you please. I'm sure that no one expects you to be present at a morning call.'

She had sounded more acerbic than she'd intended. He tossed his newspaper aside and stood. 'No doubt I shall see you at dinner, my dear.'

Without a further word he strode from the room. Jane wrung her hands. Things had not been as easy between them since they had returned from their wedding trip. It was so difficult to balance the demands of her family and her obligations to Charles.

The door opened and the butler announced formally. 'Mrs Bennet, Miss Bennet and Miss Kitty to see you, madam.'

'Thank you, Peterson. Kindly ask Nicholls to have refreshments sent to the drawing room directly. There will be no need for a cup for Mr Bingley.'

She braced herself and her mother bustled in all smiles, her happiness writ plainly on her face. 'My dearest girl, I have such news for you. I could not wait another moment to come over and tell you in person.'

'Come in, Mama, Kitty, Mary; I am pleased to see you. What can possibly have happened since you came yesterday?' Her visitors had already dispensed with their outer garments and, as always, took the seats closest to the roaring fire.

'It is Charlotte Collins, my love. She has been brought to bed with a daughter.' Her mother looked pointedly at her own slim shape and pursed her lips in disappointment. 'I imagine she will wish to produce a son next time. I do hope you and Bingley are not going to keep me waiting for grandchildren too long?'

Jane flushed. She had no wish to discuss such a delicate subject with anyone, and especially not with her garrulous mother and her two unmarried sisters.

'I must write at once to Charlotte and give her my congratulations. No doubt Lady Lucas will be going up to visit them as soon as the weather is more clement.' The windows rattled and a swirl of hail hit the glass, making them all jump.

Kitty came to sit next to her. She had come to like her sister a great deal better. Now she was without the pernicious influence of Lydia, the girl was turning into a mature and obliging young lady.

'I am so sorry to be here again, Jane. I tried to dissuade Mama, but you know how it is: she will not budge once she has an idea in her head. I fear she considers this her second home.'

Jane squeezed her sister's hand. 'It is not your fault, my love, but I do think that the frequency of her visits a trifle excessive.' It would not do to discuss the strain it was putting on her relationship. That was no one else's concern.

It was an hour and a half before she was alone again. Charles had made it quite clear he had no wish to speak to her, so she could not go and search him out in the library. She wandered restlessly around the drawing room. The house was so well run by Nicholls and Peterson, and the army of staff they employed, she had few duties to perform.

They had foregone the usual wedding trip, deciding they would prefer to spend their first festive season together. With hindsight it was plain that had been a grave error of judgement on her part. Charles had wished to stay away longer; it was she who had insisted on returning to Netherfield.

Perhaps it was time to consider further travelling in the spring. Jane had never been overseas, and had no wish to do so now. The original plan had been to travel to Scotland and admire the Highlands, then spend several weeks with Lizzy and Darcy at Pemberley before returning. It was too late to write to Lizzy and suggest this. The last time she had had a note from her sister she had been somewhere in Italy; no doubt they had moved on since then.

It had been a mistake to remain here. She and Charles should have followed Lizzy's example and travelled together. It would have been so much easier adjusting to each other's needs away from the constant demands of her family. She would not dwell on what might have been but make an effort to restore harmony between them.

* * *

That evening she took special care with her appearance. Although they dined informally unless they had company, tonight she would make a special effort to show Charles she was unhappy about the constraint coming between them because of her mother's too frequent visits. The more time she spent in *his* company the more she loved him, and she too hoped it would not be long before she was able to tell him she was adding to their family. She glowed at the thought of holding their child in her arms. They had not discussed the matter, but she knew he would be as happy as she to be a parent.

They did not dine in the grand dining room but in the smaller room that was used for breakfast. It seemed ridiculous to be positioned at either end of a vast table with a dozen servants in attendance when they could be sitting side by side with a single footman to wait.

She left her chamber hoping to meet Charles in the spacious corridor. Either he was still dressing or was ahead of her and waiting in the drawing room. She was wearing her newest gown. It was in leaf green silk with emerald green bugle beads around the hem and neckline. Her gloves and slippers were a perfect match. Her hair was piled up in an elaborate arrangement, and her neck enclosed in the fabulous emerald necklace she had been given by her husband as a wedding gift.

She glided across the entrance hall, her eyes alight and a tender smile upon her lips. She froze at the open doors of the drawing room. He had not bothered to change. He was wearing mud-spattered boots and breeches. Charles could not have made it more clear; *she* no longer mattered. If he still loved her he would have made the effort and not treated her with such disrespect.

Not waiting for him to comment she spun; gathering up her skirts she raced up the stairs, tears rolling unchecked down her cheeks. For the first time since they had been married she ran into our own bedchamber, slamming the door behind her and turning the key in the lock.

Her abigail, Martha, rushed from the dressing room and without comment helped her to disrobe. The room was icy, the fire not burning. The bed no doubt would be damp as well.

Jane had no wish to be comfortable; her heart was broken and she would not rest easy ever again. Oh, how she wished her Lizzy were here now to comfort her.

'Madam, please come into the dressing room. There is a fine blaze in there. I'll get the fire lit in this chamber and a warming pan passed through the sheets on your bed.'

Jane allowed herself to be guided into the dressing room. She glanced nervously at the communicating door and was relieved to see the bolt pushed across. She had no wish to speak to Charles tonight. She was too angry, too humiliated, to converse without distress.

* * *

Charles decided he would feel better for a gallop around the estate. The weather was foul; it suited his mood. Good God! How many days of his life was he to be obliged to endure the company of Mrs Bennet? Darcy had warned him about living so close to Jane's family but he had ignored him. His Jane wished to be close to Longbourn, and he wished to please her on every count.

He had never anticipated the wretched woman would arrive with monotonous regularity on the doorstep every single day of the week. It would be bearable if she came but twice and stayed only for a quarter of an hour. He had hinted to Jane that she should get her mother to limit these visits but nothing had come of it. She had told him she had no wish to upset her parents, that her mother had a good heart and meant well and that the novelty of having free access to their home would soon wane.

This had proved erroneous; indeed she had taken to bringing cronies with her. They would wander in and out of every room regardless of his privacy, as if they had every right to be there. He could not call his home his own.

Each day he spent with his beloved his love increased; he would do anything for her apart from allow Mrs Bennet to trample where she would in Netherfield. He was prepared to put a stop to these unwelcome visits unless Jane did something herself. He had no wish to be considered an autocratic husband, but enough was enough.

Charles returned from his excursion with his mind made up. He would discuss the matter at dinner tonight, make sure Jane understood how strongly he felt. He glanced at the tall clock in the entrance hall. Good grief, it was too late to change for dinner. He should never have dallied at Lucas Lodge so long. He smiled. Jane would forgive him his disarray when she saw what he had in his pocket. He had purchased a charming locket she had admired last time they had been to Meryton.

The discussion about Mrs Bennet could wait until they were private in his apartment. He waited impatiently in the drawing room; Jane was normally ready before him. What could be keeping her tonight?

Her light footsteps were approaching. He stopped pacing the carpet. She paused, framed in the doorway, a vision of loveliness in a gown he had not seen before. She looked like a princess. He raised his hand, his eyes filled with love. To his consternation her expression changed. She stared at him as if seeing him for the first time and found him wanting. Turning in a swirl of green silk she vanished from sight. What had he done? Why had she reacted in this extraordinary fashion?

Surely she could not have taken his lack of evening attire to be a deliberate insult? He was about to rush after her when Peterson opened the door to the dining room and announced that dinner was served. They could not both absent themselves. Cook went to so much trouble to prepare them food they both enjoyed. He would put matters right after he had eaten. With luck she would have recovered her composure and they could laugh together about their misunderstanding.

'Peterson, Mrs Bingley is feeling unwell and would like a tray sent up to her. I shall dine as usual.'

The butler snapped his fingers and a waiting footman hastily removed the cutlery put out for Jane. Charles ate what was set in front of him but tasted none of it.

* * *

'Madam, your bedchamber is warm enough. Cook has sent up a tray. I placed it on the table by fire.'

'I do not require anything to eat, thank you, Martha. Kindly have the food removed. I am going to go to bed. I fear I have a megrim coming.'

This was not a fabrication. As she had been huddling in front of the fire in the dressing room the all-too-familiar throb over her right eye, the strange distortion of her vision, heralded the arrival of the dreaded sick headache. Solicitously her maid assisted her to bed, checking there was a suitable receptacle for when she cast up her accounts, and a jug of lemonade on the bedside table. She much preferred to be left alone at these times. Only complete quiet and darkness gave her a modicum of relief.

It was a full forty-eight hours before she was sufficiently recovered to take notice of her surroundings. Jane belatedly recalled this was the first time she had been so afflicted since her marriage; indeed her husband had no inkling that she suffered in this way.

* * *

When Charles was informed that his wife was unwell he thought it a ruse to keep him away from her. This was not like his Jane. Was he seeing a side of her she had kept hidden until now? When, after a miserable day, his beloved wife still did not come to him but remained behind closed doors, his heart was near to breaking. How could things have come to this pass? A man had to be ruler in his own house. He would not discuss the matter of the visits with her but deal with it himself. When she deigned to leave her chambers, Jane would have to accept that Mrs Bennet was no longer welcome at Netherfield.

* * *

Jane was well enough to dress the next day and the first thing she did was look for evidence that Charles had worried about her sickness. She was shocked to see there had been no note, no hothouse flowers; in fact no enquiries of any kind.

Surely he was not unwell himself? It was mid-morning. He must be in the library or the study, but she couldn't find him. Jane did not wish to be estranged from him. She had been foolish in the extreme to run away as she had. It was unlike her to behave in such a missish way.

She was dressed in a simple buttercup yellow morning gown, the high neck and long sleeves exactly right for a chilly day. Its only ornamentation was a pretty pleated bodice. Her head was still too painful to allow for her usual hairstyle; for once it was simply done in a loose arrangement at the base of the neck.

Gathering her cashmere shawl closely around her shoulders against the wind that whistled along the draughty corridors, she hastened downstairs. Peterson was on duty in the vestibule. 'Tell me, where is Mr Bingley?'

'The master is in the library, madam. He asked you to join him there. Shall I have your tea sent there this morning?'

She shook her head. 'No, thank you; I shall eat and breakfast as usual after I have spoken to Mr Bingley.'

She knocked on the door and without waiting for an answer, stepped in. Charles was standing his back to her, staring out over the sodden fields.

'Charles, have you been unwell?'

She saw his shoulders stiffen and his hands clench. He swung round to face her. What was wrong? Why was he looking at her in that strange fashion?

'Please be seated, Jane. There are things we need to discuss.' Why did he sound so cross? It was hardly her fault she had had a headache. It was not like him not to be compassionate. She settled in the chair on the left of the fireplace. With her hands folded neatly on her lap, she waited expectantly. What she had to say could wait until he had spoken. It must be something portentous for him to look so serious.

'I am sorry you chose not to come and see me until now. I would much rather have discussed the matter with you first, but you left me no option. I have been obliged to take matters into my own hands.'

Her eyes widened. She had no idea to what he was referring. 'What matters, Charles? I am afraid I do not understand to what you refer.'

'The matter of your mother appearing on our doorstep every single day since we returned from London last year. I have asked you several times to do something about this and you chose to ignore my wishes. I went to Longbourn and spoke to Mr Bennet. In future Mrs Bennet is not welcome here. Kitty and Mary can come twice a week. If you wish to see your mother, you must go to Longbourn in order to do so.'

Jane could not believe what she was hearing. Charles had banned her mother from visiting? How could he be so cruel? Mama would be devastated. She had lost Lydia and Elizabeth. Visiting Netherfield was her only solace and now that had been taken too.

She stared at him. She could not have known his true character until now. The memory of her unfortunate experience with the hateful Mr Fox returned. Was Charles another such gentleman? Had he been dissembling until this moment?

There was nothing she could do. She was his wife; his word was law. She could not go against his wishes. She raised her head, almost too distressed to speak. 'Very well, sir, it shall be as you command. I would not dream of gainsaying your instructions. Is there any restriction to the number of times *I* may visit Longbourn or is that also to be limited in future?'

He looked disconcerted. He cleared his throat and then ran his finger around his neckcloth as if it had become unaccountably tight. 'You may visit as often as you please, but I would like to know when you are going to be absent, if that is not too much trouble.'

'Of course. If I have your permission, I would like to take the chaise and go right now.' He nodded. 'Thank you; if you'll excuse me, I have not eaten and am still feeling unwell.'

* * *

Charles felt as if he was living in a nightmare. What could have possessed him to behave like such a complete ass? The shock on her face when he had told her pierced his heart. He wished the words unsaid, but it was too late. He had permanently alienated Mrs Bennet, caused his mother-in-law untold distress, and now his darling wife was looking at him as if she did not know him. He did not know himself. He was a nincompoop. He stopped berating himself as he recalled something Jane had said. She hadn't eaten for two days? Her face had been pale, her expression unhappy. He was a brute to have treated his beloved so callously.

He jerked the bell and waited for Peterson to answer the summons. 'Peterson, was no food sent up to Mrs Bingley while she remained in her room?'

The man looked puzzled. 'Madam was too unwell to partake, sir. Mrs Bingley has only just recovered from her megrim this morning.'

Charles collapsed into an armchair, burying his head in his hands. Jane had been unwell and he had not known. He was so taken up with his own concerns she had languished, believing herself ignored. She would never forgive him; no wonder she had gazed at him in that way. He had destroyed their marriage before it had hardly begun.

* * *

Jane tried to compose herself on the journey to Longbourn. It would not do to arrive with her eyes blotchy and red. She had to be strong, accept that she might have made a grave error of judgement and married a man she did not understand.

Her carriage rolled to a halt; she waited for the coachman to climb down and lower the steps. She arrived at the front door where Kitty was waiting to greet her.

'Oh, Jane, you cannot imagine the fuss and botheration that

has been going on here. Our mama is beside herself. Come in. I have never been so glad to see anyone in my life.'

'Kitty, I have been unwell these past two days or I would have come before. Charles should not have said what he did. It was unkind of him.'

Her sister drew into the small anteroom to the right the front door. 'It is not *that* which has upset Mama. She took your husband's dictum with good grace. She would forgive Charles anything; he is by far her favourite son-in-law.'

Jane removed her cloak and bonnet and dropped them absentmindedly across the back of a convenient chair. 'Then what is it that has upset her?'

'It is Papa. When he discovered she had been going every day to visit you he was furious. She is to remain in the house, not venture forth without his permission even to go to Meryton.'

'Oh dear! So she cannot even go to see Aunt Philips?'

Kitty shook her head. 'She's not to go anywhere. He issued this command and then locked himself in his study. The house is in uproar. Mama is suffering from her nerves and refusing to leave her dressing room. I am at my wits' end to know what to do. I had not thought to see such a commotion; she is as distraught as when Lydia ran off with Wickham.'

'And Mary, how is she coping with all this stress?'

'She has risen to the occasion admirably, Jane. You shall not recognise her. I had no idea she could be so kind and loving.' Kitty halted in mid-sentence, staring closely at her sister. 'Jane, you have been crying. Pray tell me at once what is wrong.'

Jane found herself pouring out her heart to her younger sister in the same way she had once told Lizzy. When she finished the sorry tale, Kitty patted her hands.

'I am sure it is no more than a misunderstanding. You are

famous for doing this to each other. Have you spoken to him? Have you asked why he has behaved this way?'

'I cannot do that. He's made it quite clear by his actions these past few days he has changed his mind about me. That he regrets having married; he hates my family and is in a fair way to feeling the same about me.' Jane mopped her eyes. Why was she such a watering pot today?

'Stuff and nonsense! Now, dry your eyes, Jane, and go and see Papa. You must tell him to make his peace with our mother; tell him that you invited her to visit so often. Put things right between them, I beg you.'

Jane felt ashamed. She was allowing her own distress to colour her judgement. This was at the expense of those she loved. 'You are right to chide me, Kitty. I cannot believe the change in you these past few months. You are a good girl, and I love you dearly. I shall go at once to smooth things over between our parents.'

* * *

Charles felt wretched. He had treated his darling Jane abominably and wouldn't blame her if she decided to stay at Longbourn permanently. He did not deserve to have her at his side. How he longed for Darcy. If he were here, he would give him sound advice.

Was that the carriage returning so soon? He hovered in the doorway, then retreated to lurk behind the drawing room door, not wishing Jane to see him there in case she had no wish to speak to him.

A footman opened the door and instead of his wife, Kitty Bennet rushed in. The girl spotted him instantly.

'Charles, Jane is at Longbourn breaking her heart, believing that you have changed towards her. What is it about you two that you cannot put matters right for yourselves?'

He was dumbfounded. When had this young lady become so forthright? 'Kitty, do not stand here berating me; come in to the drawing room and explain what you mean.'

Her words lifted the weight from his chest. The whole thing was a storm in a teacup. They had blown it into something else entirely. He grinned sheepishly at his sister-in-law. 'We owe you a huge debt of gratitude. What should I do? Shall I wait for Jane to return, or ride pell-mell to Longbourn?'

'What you should do, Charles, is buy yourself a property in Derbyshire. Why do not you move to Pemberley? I am sure that Lizzy and Mr Darcy will be delighted to have you take care of their home in their absence. From what I hear that place is big enough to house a dozen families and not be crowded.'

'You have a wise head on young shoulders, Miss Kitty. Return to Longhorn, beg my Jane to return as I have something most important to tell her.'

'I shall do so immediately. You will not stop my mama from visiting, though. She has little else to do.'

'I am sure you have the right of it. I feel a little like King Canute in front of the waves where Mrs Bennet is concerned.'

He walked his sister-in-law to the door, and on impulse he embraced her fondly. 'Would you consider coming with us, when we leave for Pemberley? With Elizabeth and Darcy away on their wedding trip until the summer, Jane would be grateful of the company.'

'I should love to come, Charles, but only if Jane is happy with the arrangement. Now, I must get back. Your horses have been standing long enough.'

* * *

That night he and Jane discussed the future and found they were in complete accord. Harmony was restored, misunderstandings put right, and the move to Derbyshire was to take place as soon as it could be arranged. When Jane was unwell the next morning she understood what had been causing her unusual behaviour. She was increasing.

She and Charles decided to keep the news to themselves. If Mrs Bennet should get wind of it, she would never let them depart for Pemberley. It was only Mr Bennet's promise to bring his wife to visit in the spring that reconciled the poor lady to the loss of the company of her fourth daughter. Mary was finally the only Miss Bennet in residence and her interest in her studies and music was soon to be replaced by occupying the role of oldest daughter.

Kitty and Georgiana Darcy were immediately bosom bows and vowed never to be parted from each other, unless one of them should wish to marry.

ABOUT THE AUTHOR

Fenella J. Miller is the bestselling writer of over eighteen historical sagas. She also has a passion for Regency romantic adventures and has published over fifty to great acclaim. Her father was a Yorkshireman and her mother the daughter of a Rajah. She lives in a small village in Essex with her British Shorthair cat.

Sign up to Fenella J. Miller's mailing list for news, competitions and updates on future books.

Visit Fenella's website: www.fenellajmiller.co.uk

Follow Fenella on social media here:

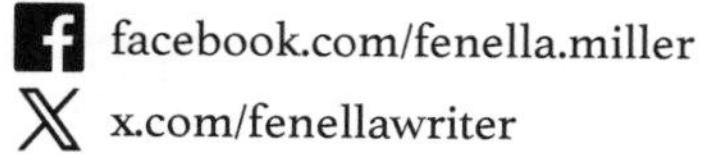

facebook.com/fenella.miller

x.com/fenellawriter

ALSO BY FENELLA J MILLER

Goodwill House Series

The War Girls of Goodwill House

New Recruits at Goodwill House

Duty Calls at Goodwill House

The Land Girls of Goodwill House

A Wartime Reunion at Goodwill House

Wedding Bells at Goodwill House

A Christmas Baby at Goodwill House

The Army Girls Series

Army Girls Reporting For Duty

Army Girls: Heartbreak and Hope

Army Girls: Behind the Guns

Army Girls: Operation Winter Wedding

The Pilot's Girl Series

The Pilot's Girl

A Wedding for the Pilot's Girl

A Dilemma for the Pilot's Girl

A Second Chance for the Pilot's Girl

The Nightingale Family Series

A Pocketful of Pennies

A Capful of Courage

A Basket Full of Babies

A Home Full of Hope

At Pemberley Series

Return to Pemberley

Trouble at Pemberley

Standalone Novels

The Land Girl's Secret

Printed in Great Britain
by Amazon

54569657R00178